SAY YOU WANT me

You don't always get
what you want.

NEW YORK TIMES BESTSELLING AUTHOR
CORINNE MICHAELS

Say You Want Me
Copyright © 2016 Corinne Michaels
All rights reserved.
ISBN: 978-1-682307-54-0

Editor:
Ashley Williams, AW Editing

Proofreading:
Kara Hildebrand
Janice Owen

Interior Design & Formatting:
Christine Borgford, Perfectly Publishable
www.perfectlypublishable.com

Cover Design:
Sarah Hansen, Okay Creations
www.okaycreations.com

Cover photo © Embry Allen Lopez
www.embrylopez.com

SAY YOU
WANT
You don't always get
what you want. *me*

DEDICATION

To the creators of Netflix, I blame you for my unproductive days when I'm on deadline. We should break up, but I can't seem to do it. You're welcome.

"Jump, and you will find out how to unfold your wings as you fall."—Ray Bradbury

chapter
ONE

" **H**OW LONG HAVE YOU BEEN feeling like this, Angie?"
Long enough for me to finally get my butt here.

I hate doctors. Motivating me to finally go to see someone is like getting a bill through Congress. I'm stubborn, but more than that . . . I'm scared. My two cousins battled cancer in their early thirties, and my mom is an ovarian cancer survivor. Each time I have to go for a checkup, I end up convincing myself I'll be next.

It's crazy and irrational, but it's a genuine fear of mine. I remember the hell they all went through.

"I don't know. A few months . . ." I got a crazy cold when I got back from visiting my sister-in-law, Presley, two months ago. Her now fiancé asked me to come when he knew he was going to propose. Even with my deep hatred of flying, I went. I knew it meant a lot to her and my insanely amazing nephews. Although, I never need an excuse to go see them. Cayden and Logan are the closest things I'll ever have to kids. I spoil the crap out of them, and hate that I barely see them now.

But my brother made that my reality when he chose to leave this world two years ago.

"What other symptoms do you have?" the older doctor asks me.

I pull my long blonde ponytail to the side and start to play with it as I run through the laundry list of ailments. He doesn't need to hear about how Presley threatened to kill me herself if I didn't get checked, so I leave it out. It's all minor stuff, but it's affecting the way I live. This week was the worst. I went from vomiting to feeling like I was going to die. I'd had enough.

"Let's do some blood work, get a urine sample, and see what the results bring. In the meantime, I'm going to look you over."

The exam doesn't last long, but since I'm very tender, I spend the few minutes debating whether to kick him as he hems and haws. I hate when doctors do that. Either clue me in or shut up. It's annoying. He finishes looking at everything, and the nurse enters with the vials to collect blood.

Great.

The second most dreaded thing.

"Hi, Angie." The nurse smiles. "I'm Nicole, and I'll be drawing some blood."

I return her smile and nod.

"If I remember correctly, you own For Cup's Cake?" she asks.

"I do." I can't help but grin. I love my cupcake store, which is thriving like crazy lately. One of the local news channels stopped in about six months ago, ran a big story on it, and it changed my world. I've brought in a new partner to help with all the adjustments, and we're talking about opening a second location. Never in a million years did I think that it would be like this.

Presley and I had an idea that we should open the store, thinking that maybe it would give her something to do while Todd worked insane hours as a finance guru. It seemed like fun. And it was. Until Todd's suicide wrecked everything we had built. The store was barely four months old, the company had no money, and Presley lost everything.

I bought her out, even though the business was worth next to nothing, and she left for Tennessee.

"I love it there," Nicole admits. "My dress size doesn't, but everything is so good. And different. How do you stay so thin?"

I snort. "I wish you could see how much I weighed before the store. I've put on a good amount. I can't seem to help myself with the tasting."

"Well, I can't blame you." She focuses on filling the vials.

Huh. I didn't even realize she pricked me.

"Our head baker is amazing. And she doesn't tell me or my partner, Erin, what the next day's flavors will be. It used to drive me insane. Now it's kind of fun. We go into work and she's already redecorated the menu with the flavors of the day."

We chat a little more before Nicole puts the bandage around my arm and leaves.

I grab my phone and text Presley.

Me: I hate the damn doctor.

Presley: Stop being a baby. You probably just need an antibiotic because you refused to go a month ago. Not everything is fixable with Motrin.

Me: Whatever. I just remember this is how Mom started. One minute, she was run down, and the next, it was cancer.

I sigh and fight back the tears. I was fifteen and remember each time she came back from chemotherapy. She was sick, tired, and literally pumped with poison. She had that look in her eyes when she'd glance at me or my brothers. It was a single moment, but it said so much about the reason she kept fighting. Until her fight was over. Then she no longer held the affection I once saw.

I don't want to ever be like her. I don't have anything to fight for.

Presley: No matter what the doctor says, you have me.

Me: In freaking Tennessee!

Presley: I have a spare bedroom.

Me: Over my dead body!

No freaking way am I going to Tennessee. She'd have to drug me to get me to live there. I love Presley, but it's not for me. It's gorgeous and has picturesque landscapes and beautiful homes. But the main reason I won't move there is because there are no Starbucks. The second, which is an equally compelling reason, is named Wyatt Hennington. His Southern drawl, insanely tight ass, and honey colored eyes turn me into a sixteen-year-old schoolgirl. I clearly have no self-control when it comes to him. What my best friend doesn't know is that it wasn't just the one time that I found myself in his bed. No, I'm the idiot who went back for round two, only to have it end awkwardly.

Presley: Bet Wyatt would let you use his bedroom.

I roll my eyes. She's like a damn Yenta trying to marry me off.

Me: No. I'm back with Nate.

Presley: Since when?

Ohh, like this morning when he called and asked me to dinner. Maybe this will get her to stop pushing Wyatt.

Me: It's very recent. You never know, we could hit it off this time.

Presley: Right. The last time worked out sooo well. He's not your type.

Me: He's a good guy. We go out to the same places, and neither of us like eating alone.

Presley: Oh, please. You don't even like him!

It's true. I don't like him enough to ever marry him, and he's god awful in bed, which is why we're not ever going there again. But he's sweet, likes the same restaurants as I do, and we get along. He's a cardiologist at the Children's Hospital and works insane hours. So, we only see each other sporadically.

It works for us.

Presley: And they say romance is dead. Are you sleeping with him?

Me: Nope. I'm trying out this whole celibacy thing.

Presley: That's comical. Looks like Wyatt ruined you, huh?

Me: He wishes! It was good but not great.

I'm so full of shit. It wasn't *just* good. No, it was the absolute, hands down, most unfreakingbelievable sex I'd ever had. The kind that ruined me for all eternity. Where any man who even comes near me won't hold a candle to the things that man did to my body. He played me as if I were his personal instrument. Every touch, every kiss, every swipe of his glorious tongue was done just to please me. I don't know how I managed to walk out of there. He rocked my world and then was gone before I woke.

Not all of us have these epic love stories like Presley does. She fell in love with Zachary Hennington when she was still in the womb, I swear. They were kids, figured out they were each other's lobsters, got engaged before college, and then broke up when Zach got a chance to play pro baseball. He took a contract and left Pres without a backward glance. That was when she met my brother. Todd loved her the minute he laid eyes on her. I threatened to disown him if he thought about it. I was not about to lose my best friend because my brother somehow screwed up. Regardless of my threats, which I thought were very convincing, they ended up married with twins.

Then Todd destroyed everything.

I still haven't forgiven him for committing suicide, and I hate myself for that, but now I have a void in my heart that won't ever be fixed because of what he did. He was my best friend and he took himself away without any answers.

My phone buzzes after a few minutes.

> *Presley: Sorry, I had to help Zach. I love you, Ang. You're going to be fine. I'll be waiting for your call.*

> *Me: Love you more. I'll call with the fated news.*

> *Presley: Dramatic.*

I giggle as I hear a knock on the door.

"All right, Angie. I ran a quick test to check your iron, which is a little low, but easily fixable. Your sugar levels are fine, and we'll send the rest of your blood work out. However, that's not what has you as sick as you've been." He looks up, and I freeze.

Tears form as I know the news he's about to deliver. "You found something in my blood or is there something else?" The muscles in my body clench as I try to smother the fear that's choking me. "Something abnormal?"

The doctor steps forward with a warm smile on his face. "Relax, Angie."

"Please," I plead. "Please just say it!"

"You're pregnant."

My jaw gapes as I try to reconcile the words he spoke.

"What?"

"You're pregnant," he repeats.

No.

No, no, no. Nope. I refuse. I can't be pregnant. I've only had sex with one person in the last six months. Jesus Christ.

I shake my head back and forth trying to unhear the words. "I had my period!" I finally shriek. "Last month! I can't be pregnant. I haven't had sex with anyone in months! The test is confused. You're confused."

If there's anyone in this world that shouldn't be allowed to have kids—it's me. I've killed plants, countless goldfish, my cat ran away, and I have never had that internal clock ticking thing.

The doctor places his hand on my arm. "It's not abnormal to have a period or two. But I checked it twice. You *are* pregnant. Congratulations."

The doctor pats my leg and leaves the room. Oh my God.

I don't even know what to think. I can't be pregnant. I mean, I guess I am, but this is not okay. Not even a little bit.

I'm not supposed to be in my mid-thirties and pregnant. This isn't part of the plan.

> *Presley: Don't forget to call me when you know something.*

I glance at my phone and try to figure out what to say. I guess this would be better in person, plus I need to tell Wyatt. Fuck my life. With shaky fingers, I send out a text.

> *Me: Looks like I'm coming to Bell Buckle. Might want to make up the bed in your spare room.*

chapter TWO

"LADIES AND GENTLEMEN, THE CAPTAIN has turned on the fasten seat belt sign. We are now crossing a zone of turbulence. Please return to your seat and keep your seat belt fastened."

I cinch the belt so hard that I'm positive I'm going to pass out, then I loosen it as I worry it might hurt the baby. I hate flying. I hate being suspended in the air when, clearly, that is not how humans are meant to be. I'm in a tube of death.

Calm down, Angie. You can do this. It's no scarier than finding out you were pregnant forty-eight hours ago.

"You okay, darlin'?" A nice man with a large cowboy hat resting on his knee asks.

I nod because I can't find my voice. My throat is dry and I'm pretty sure my face must resemble Casper's.

"You don't look okay." His drawl becomes deeper with concern. "You ain't gonna pass out on me, are you?"

"No." I give him a tight-lipped smile. "I have a lot on my mind."

Understatement of the year. After leaving the doctor's office yesterday, I took three home pregnancy tests because I truly thought the doctor was wrong. He wasn't. So, I preceded to eat a gallon of Breyers ice cream. This at least explains the other week when I burst into tears while I was watching *Something About Mary*, though. I couldn't figure out what had me so upset, but there I was . . . bawling. No wonder, I'm a hormonal lunatic.

I've never been more freaked out than I am now. I'm not sure how the hell I'm going to do this. Any of it. First, I have to tell Wyatt, which is the point of this trip. Do I blurt it out? Do I get him a hat that reads: Daddy across the front? Maybe I should say, "Hey, partner . . . we're gonna have a kid and we're both almost forty, so get your walker ready for the high school graduation." Not that he talks like that, but whatever. I don't know how he'll react, but the truth of the matter is—we're having a baby, which makes me want to cry.

Then I have to figure out how I'm going to be a single mom. I've never been more grateful for Erin right now. As soon as I told her about the baby, she immediately told me to take a few days off, and handle coming to Tennessee. Maybe it won't be so bad.

"I understand that," the very handsome stranger says. "Are you visiting family?"

"Yes. I'm going to see my sister and my nephews." *And the father of my kid.* "They live in a tiny town somewhere in Tennessee," I explain.

"There's a lot of those." He chuckles. "Are you from Philly or just passin' through?"

"No, I live there. I have for almost twenty years now."

"I spent a week there, interesting place. I've been a Southern boy my whole life. I don't travel much, but my brother got himself a job outside the city, so I helped him move." My heart starts to fall back into rhythm as he tells me his story. "It's definitely nothing like Nashville, that's for sure."

I giggle. "I'm sure it's not. We do have Starbucks, though."

We talk a little more and then the plane lands without incident. Now is when the real shit starts. I'm going to walk off and come face to face with my sister and best friend. I'm going to have to admit what's wrong and why I'm here. It won't be my secret.

It will be the truth.

It all begins now.

"Thanks for keeping me calm," I say to the cute cowboy.

"It's not every day that I get to save a beautiful lady."

When the door to the plane opens, he grabs his bag from the overhead bin, and I realize something.

"You know," I say as he starts to walk off, "you never mentioned your name."

He smiles, extends his hand, and tips his hat. "My name is Wyatt."

Of course it is.

I disembark the plane and head to the baggage area. I need Presley to tell me this is going to be okay, because I'm freaking the fuck out.

Each year that passes, my desire for a family dwindles. The men I've dated look great on paper, but they end up not being what I need. They're selfish, narcissistic, and I've never gotten close to being in a committed relationship. There was the one guy after college, but we dated for six months before I overheard him saying he was screwing someone else, so I dumped him. After that, it was random dates with casual sex.

I've lived all of my thirty-six years content with being the friend who never marries—the eternal bridesmaid and never the bride. It works for me. I like to know I can go where I want, when I want. But now my days of being unhitched to anything are long gone.

All because of one crazy amazing sexfest.

"Ang!" I hear my best friend call out as she rushes toward me. "I'm so sorry I'm late!"

Tears begin to form at the sound of her voice, and the second her arms enclose around me, a sob breaks free. Her touch unleashes the flood of emotions I managed to keep in check through my drive home from the doctor, the mindless packing, and the flight. Now though, I can't stop them.

"Angie? What's wrong?" She pulls back and looks in my eyes.

I see the fear in her own gaze, but it's nothing compared to how I feel right now. There's no easy way to say this, and I know she probably thinks it's something worse than a baby. "I'm . . . I'm . . . I'm just so happy to see you!" There's no good reason why I don't tell her. I just know that I'm not ready.

She lets out a half laugh. "I'm happy to see you too!" Her all-knowing eyes pierce through me as she studies my face. "Are you sure that's all? Not that I don't love seeing you overcome with emotion at being near me, but you look like something's wrong. What did the doctor say?"

"It's not cancer."

Her shoulders slump in relief. "Thank God. I was really worried when you wouldn't say anything other than you needed to visit. Did he say it's anything serious?"

She probably drove Zach crazy since she was clearly upset, but I didn't want to tell her like that. I still don't want to tell her. I want her support, that's why I came, but I don't know if I should tell Wyatt first.

"The doctor said I needed a break. Stress and all that." I wave my hand dismissively.

Her lips purse, and she puts her hand on her hip. "I'm not buying it."

"Whatever. I don't think you're one to give me shit about secrets." I lift my brow. She knows damn well what I mean. Presley has lived most of her life clouded by things she suffered through alone. When my brother killed himself, there were only four people who knew the cause of his death. She struggled so she could keep her boys protected. By doing that, she had no one to help ease her burden—until Zach.

Even then, she wasn't forthcoming about things. The secrets she held damn near destroyed her life.

It's a low blow, but I'm hoping it buys me some time to garner the courage to tell her that her other best friend, and future brother-in-law, knocked me up.

I'm a fucking mess.

Pres grabs my bag in silence.

"I'm sorry," I say, feeling like shit. "I didn't mean that. I'm being a bitch."

"I know. And I'll be the first to remind you that secrets cause damage." She grips my arm and looks at me with concern. "I love you, and I'm worried. I know something is going on. Something that you want to tell me, otherwise, you wouldn't be here. You can sell your stress story to someone who hasn't known you for almost twenty years. Try again."

Damn her. "Give me a few hours."

"How about we grab some Starbucks before we head to Bell Buckle?"

"It's like you know me or something." I smile. This is the best part of our friendship, we know when to let something drop and share a deep affection for coffee.

We grab our drinks. I subtly get decaf, which is pretty much blasphemous, and we start the trip to Bell Buckle. We chat and she tells me all about the wedding plans. It's amazing how much this girl got done in a few months. I shouldn't be surprised, considering she did the same thing with the bakery. It was a concept one day, and then the next thing I knew, we were signing a lease. Presley is smart, hardworking, and has the biggest heart of anyone I know.

When we enter the town limits, my muscles tense. We pass through, and I wonder when I'll see Wyatt. It's going to happen, but I'm so not ready to deal with him.

I have to figure out my plan so when I do see him, I have

answers. Do I want to do this completely on my own? My parents and brother live in Florida (where I will stay far away from), Presley lives here in Tennessee, and the baby's father . . . I have no one in Media other than the people who work for me. Having a baby is hard enough for married couples, but being a single mom with no support system—it will be damn near impossible.

One freaking fantastic night has completely changed my life.

"Angie?" Presley says, pulling my attention away from staring out the window.

"What?"

"I asked if you wanted to go out tonight with Grace and Emily? They'd love to see you."

I sigh as I realize I can't go out drinking. "I don't know. I'm really out of it. And really tired." I'm tired all the time now.

Presley looks at me with confusion clear on her face. "Umm . . . I've known you a long ass time and you've never been one to pass on a night on the town. Are you still sick? You look okay."

The urge to blurt it out claws its way up. Tears start to form as I look out the window to avoid her gaze. Everything is going to change. I'm so beyond screwed. "No. I mean, I'm okay. I'll be fine. I would rather stay home. Maybe tomorrow?" Admitting this tidbit of news is going to change the entire conversation. Presley is a fantastic mother, and I know she'll see this as something great.

Not that I don't love kids, but I never really saw myself as a mom. I'm content with my trendy apartment in downtown Philadelphia, the bakery, and my shitty dating life. It's all that makes me—me.

It hits me then. No one is going to want to date me now.

I'm going to be the single mother that people pity.

I'm going to be alone.

My hand covers my mouth as a tear falls.

"Angie." Presley puts the car in park at the end of her dirt driveway. "Angie, look at me."

I shake my head. "I'm fine. It's fine."

"What did the doctor say?"

Her voice is so full of love and compassion. There's something deep inside me that has a feeling she knows.

I clutch my stomach as I turn to look at her. "I'm pregnant. I'm—"

"Holy shit! You're pregnant?" Presley's hands fly to her mouth.

"Apparently."

I can only imagine the shit rolling around in her head. My chest starts to heave as I think about this absolute mess. I've been in some shit before, but this is a whole new level. I'm going to have something that needs me to survive. There's no way I'll be able to handle this. I can barely handle my own life let alone another living thing. "Oh my God! I can't do this!"

Presley pulls me into her arms as I cry. "It's going to be okay."

"No." I pull back. "It's not. I can't have a baby! I can't even take care of a plant. I'm alone up there. How am I going to do this?"

"You can do it because you're strong and loving. How far along are you?"

My eyes lift to hers, and I almost choke on my next words. "I'm two months."

"That means . . ." I see the wheels turning as she calculates. "Oh! Oh my God! You were here two months ago! For when Zach proposed!"

"Yup." My voice is full of despair.

"Wyatt?"

"Yes. Fucking Wyatt. Why am I so stupid? Why, out of all the goddamn people in the world, does it have to be him? The guy who spent his entire life pining away over you. The damn man who left me in the middle of the night so I could see my way out of his bed? I mean, couldn't it have been some guy in Philly so my entire life didn't implode?"

Her smile brightens, and her eyes shine with tenderness. "I know you're freaking out. I don't blame you, but you're going to be okay. You'll see, this'll be fine. Y'all are going to have a baby! And maybe there's a reason he left you that night . . . which by the way, you never told me about."

That's what she focuses on?

"How? How is this going to be okay?"

"It's not part of your plan, I'll give you that. But Wyatt will be a great dad."

I shake my head. "I don't even know what I'm going to do. Maybe I won't tell him. Maybe I won't keep it or even have it."

She knows me well enough that she doesn't respond. I may not be happy about this, but I know that I'm keeping it. Presley knows that, too. It's just so much. Too many things to think about. Telling Presley was the easy part—it's going to be telling Wyatt that will be difficult. He has a right to know, but it's the last thing I want to say to him. With that will come a barrage of questions and issues. Things I haven't even figured out myself.

"That's your choice, babe. I can tell you that it's not you."

I groan. "I hate you."

"I hate you right back."

"It's your fault this even happened!" I throw my hands in the air.

Presley's eyes widen. "Me?"

"Yeah," I say as I point right at her. "If you hadn't made me come visit, I wouldn't have slept with him. If you hadn't fallen in love with Zach again, I wouldn't be here."

"Well, since we're passing blame. If you hadn't gone to college in Maine and weren't my roommate, I wouldn't have met

SAY YOU WANT *me* 17

Todd. If I hadn't met Todd, I wouldn't have been married and living in Pennsylvania. If all that hadn't happened, I wouldn't be back in Bell Buckle. So, whose fault is it really?"

"I reiterate again that I hate you."

She laughs and shifts the car back to drive. "I love you, too."

We pull up to the house, and the boys are already there waiting for us, jumping and waving. The sadness and dread I felt moments ago dissipates as I rush out of the car. "Cay! Logan!"

"Auntie!"

I pull them into my arms and squeeze. They're such great kids. They've been through hell but still smile. A lot of that is thanks to both Presley and Zach's families, which I guess includes Wyatt.

"My boys! How's school?" I ask, knowing the grumbles will come.

"It's great. Logan has a girlfriend!" Cayden sniggers.

"Oh?"

"I do not!" Logan punches Cayden. I giggle and instantly feel lighter.

"Angie," Zach says with a smile from his spot on the porch. "So glad you're here. Pres needs someone to rein her in on this wedding stuff."

"I don't know if I'll be any help with that." I grin as I walk forward to embrace him.

There are times when I miss my brother more than anything, and this is one of them. I wouldn't be hugging this man right now. I'd be curled up on the couch—not pregnant—with my sister-in-law and brother. We'd have wine and talk about the boys and how I need to stop living like I'm twenty. Todd would grumble about how no one is good enough for me, but in the next breath, he would comment about how I will die alone if I don't find someone halfway decent. It would've ended with us laughing and me falling asleep on the couch. I'd go get donuts in the morning, chat with Todd about the morning news, and then head home. I wish it were him I was hugging.

"You look great." He smiles.

I feel like total shit. "Thanks. The place looks amazing!"

"We're so happy here," Presley says as she wraps her arm around Zach's middle.

The last time I was here, the walls were going up and there was a constant stream of contractors. But this is gorgeous. The house is huge and overlooks the lake on Zach's property. A massive wrap-around porch, adorned with Adirondack chairs, gives them the perfect view. It's brand new, but the way they built it makes it appear as though it is meant to be here. I take it all in and feel happy for my friend. Regardless of what I'm going through, Presley deserves a life filled with everything she could want.

"It's perfect. I—"

"Well, well." It's a voice I'd know anywhere. "If it isn't Big City."

Son of a bitch.

I turn and come face to face with the flashing smile, honey-colored eyes, and brown hair that I've dreamed of. Wyatt Hennington stands before me in a pair of fitted jeans and a black shirt, and he's looking at me with heat in his gaze. Everything inside me clenches, especially my belly. God, he's fucking hot. I fight leaping into his arms and remembering the way he kissed. A shiver runs down my spine as that night flashes back to me. Why does my body react this way to him?

He extends his hand so his fingers run against my cheek, just barely touching me. The skin burns as he trails to my lips. I stand like a statue, staring at him. He shouldn't be able to render me speechless, but he does.

"Why are you here?" I ask with a touch of disappointment.

Wyatt Hennington holds me captive as he closes the small

distance between us.

"You look beautiful, Angel." The way his eyes intensify when he says that makes my heart stutter.

"Why don't we go inside?" Presley saves me, and I let out a sigh of relief.

"Sounds great."

"Come on, Auntie, I'll show you my new room!" Cayden says, turning and running into the house and leaving Logan to trail behind.

Okay, so this isn't what I planned, but then again nothing seems to be going my way. I can handle going inside, eating, and waiting for him to leave. Then, I can freak out. I have a little bit of time that I need to keep this to myself. A plan. I need a plan.

"Well, come on then," Presley says, amusement clear in her voice.

"We'll meet you in there," Wyatt says, and I watch in shock as Presley and Zach go inside, closing the door behind them.

My jaw falls slack. I can't be alone with him. I'm not ready to tell him anything. Although, that's the damn reason I'm here. But not yet.

"I think I should go in . . ." I start to walk.

Wyatt's fingers grip my arm, stopping me. "Talk to me for a second."

I turn, look at his fingers, and back to his eyes. "There's nothing to say."

"How are you, Angel?"

"I'm wonderful. Thanks for asking. I'm going inside now." I start to move away, but he holds tight.

It's a mystery to me how he never married. From everything that Presley says, he's a great man. He's kind, loyal, considerate, clearly he's hot, but he refuses to do any serious commitment. I often wonder how much of it is because of the fact that he was in love with my sister-in-law. He spent his entire life loving her and watching her love his brother.

She and I have spoken at length about it. Her heart broke when he told her all those years ago how he felt. They've been best friends since they were little, and they still are, but she never returned his affections. Wyatt is the man who pushed Zach back into her arms. He loved her so much, he let her go.

"Don't be like that." He rubs his thumb across my wrist.

I can't believe this is happening right now. I thought I'd have a day or two before I saw him. Clearly that isn't the case. I barely mustered the courage to tell Presley, now I have to figure out a way to tell him. Fuck my life.

"I just want to go inside, Wyatt. I really need to talk to Presley." I whine the last part. If I can get away from him, I can get my head on straight. I'm only here for a few days. I figured we would talk for like five minutes before I left, and then I could be on my merry way.

"Well, I think we should talk about the last time you were here." His voice drops an octave lower.

"I don't think there's a point." I pull my hand back.

I bite back the words about how the last time I was here, our "talking" altered the course of our lives.

"I think there is."

"What would you like to talk about, Wyatt?"

"We could skip the talking if you'd prefer. I'm sure Presley and Zach wouldn't mind having their house to themselves." He grabs my wrist again and pulls me close. "And you can try to come on to me again. Only this time, I won't fight you so much."

Bastard.

"I think you're confused." I was not the chaser, he was. "You wanted me the minute you saw me. You watched every time I bent over, you couldn't help yourself, could you?" The heat between us just rose about a hundred degrees. "You wanted me, Wyatt Hennington. You were the one who was too busy trying to charm me. I was here for my friend, and you made it your job to bed me."

Our mouths are mere inches apart. It would be so easy to kiss him. The desire we both have eclipses any anger or frustration sitting below the surface. All that surrounds us is this. I breathe him in. The heat ripples off his body. A body that I know is solid and damn near perfect.

Kiss me, Wyatt.

No. I don't want that. It's the damn hormones.

"You don't even know me," Wyatt says as our noses almost touch. "You have no idea what I was doing."

"I know what you *weren't* doing." I push back. "You weren't being a gentleman."

He smirks. "If I remember correctly, you don't like gentlemen."

"Maybe I like them *after!*"

He's right. I liked him very much not being a gentleman while we were in bed together. What I didn't like was waking up and finding him gone, as if he expected me to show myself out like I was some whore. The thought stops me for second. I don't know . . . maybe I was. I did give it up pretty early. I guess the saying, "Why buy the cow when you get the milk for free," is accurate. But that doesn't mean I'm not pissed.

"You have some nerve." I rip my arm out of his grasp.

"Why the hell are you so mad?"

This man is out of his mind. "You left me! I woke up to find you missing!" I can't even believe this. "I waited for thirty minutes. Then it was clear that you left so I could see myself out. So I did. So much for Southern charm."

"Women. Y'all are the most confusing creatures on the planet." Wyatt gets close again and grabs my waist.

"You're not any better! You chase me for almost two years, telling me how fantastic it was the last time and all the new things you want to do to me, but then you get it and you're gone." His hand stays where it is, even when I try to pull back, so I keep going. "And to top it off, you didn't even bother trying to call or anything after. I mean, nothing." My eyes narrow as I really get pissed. "Don't even act like you couldn't get my phone number, Wyatt Hennington. I just wasn't worth it."

"Honey." He leans in closer.

"Don't call me 'honey'."

"Darlin'." He grins. "I work. Every single day."

And this affects me how? "Whatever that means." I cross my arms and wait for him to finish. I don't know what working for Presley's parents have anything to do with him leaving.

Wyatt ignores my snip and continues, "See, down here, the horses don't give a shit if it's Sunday. They need to eat. And since I work for the Townsend's, I have to make sure the farm is taken care of. I didn't leave you or want you to leave, but I wasn't going to wake you at five in the morning . . . not unless it was for another round."

I didn't even think that maybe he was working. I assumed he was done with me, but I was apparently wrong, which bothers me. I don't know why. Not that it matters, because that's not what I care about anymore anyway.

"What does any of this even mean?" I ask the sky.

Wyatt touches my cheek. "It means I didn't want you to leave, Angie Benson. It means I liked having you next to me. It means the next time you're in my bed with your blonde hair on my pillow, you should stay there. It means I wanted you to stay."

The connection between us is so strong that it terrifies me. I barely know this guy. He lives in Tennessee, and he rides a freaking horse. He's the polar opposite of me in every way. Yet, the desire to kiss him is so great. I remind myself that he doesn't know that because of the night in question, our lives will forever be tied. We created a life, and now both of ours are altered.

"Say something," he urges.

I say the only thing that matters anymore. "I'm pregnant."

chapter THREE

Wyatt

SHE'S WHAT?

"I'm sorry." I shake my head. "You're what?"

"I'm having your baby." Why does it sound like she just had her dog run over?

"You're sure?"

"Yes, I'm sure. It's why I'm freaking here! Congratulations, Dad." She keeps talking, but I can't hear anything.

She's pregnant.

I'm going to have a kid.

I start to go through that night to see how the hell this could happen, but we were smart. Nothing happened that I know of. The condoms were fine. Yeah we went at it quite a bit that night, but I wasn't even drunk.

This is wrong. I'm careful. Very fucking careful. It can't be mine.

"Honey," I say now that I've figured it out. Her eyes dart to mine. "I'm sorry to hear that you're goin' through this." Her lips part as she sucks in a breath. "But it's not my baby. I feel bad and all, but there's no way it's mine."

"Are. You. Fucking. Kidding. Me?" Angie screams each

word. "Not yours?" Her voice grows louder. "I haven't had sex with anyone else! I'm nine weeks. Do the math, genius."

I watch her foot tap as she waits.

"We used a condom."

I can see the steam coming from her ears. "News flash! It didn't work!"

"You're absolutely positive?" I ask again. "I mean, it's a hundred percent."

"Yes, Wyatt. I'm one hundred percent pregnant." She sighs and then adds, "With *your* baby," as if to clarify one more time that I am, in fact, going to be a dad.

"Shit."

It's possible, and I doubt she'd come all the way down here to trick me into something. It's not like she likes me very much or thinks I'm this great guy. If she's nine weeks, that's exactly when she was here last time. It's also safe to assume that my soon to be sister-in-law knows, and she wouldn't lie—not about this.

"That's what I'm saying. So, yeah . . . we're having a baby. You're the father." Her eyes pierce through me. "So, now what?"

"Okay." I start to pace as my mind gets ahold of the idea that it's definitely my kid. "You're pregnant. Right? I mean, it's not ideal, but it's not the end of the world. We'll be fine."

"Fine? How the hell is this fine?" Angie's eyes start to water. "None of this is fine, Wyatt."

My need to fix this kicks in. I'm a man. A man who can fix things. So, that's what I'll do. "I'll tell you how. You'll move here. We'll get married. I'll put an addition on the cabin, and then we'll get things settled. You can always work for my brother. Then, I'll go back in as an owner so we can—"

"Whoa! Hold up there, buddy!" Angie yells. "Are you out of your mind? Married? Move here? No. No way!" She shakes her head and starts to gasp for air.

I rush over and grip her shoulders. "Easy. Breathe." She

takes a few deep breaths as I lead her to the steps. "Sit. You need to calm down."

Angie looks at me, and I see it all. Her fears are clear in those deep blue eyes. I'm taken aback by the fact that I can't stop thinking about how pretty she is. The first time I saw her, I wanted her. It was crazy, since I've always been attracted to brunettes with green eyes. It's no wonder why. But Angie is something else.

Her attitude only makes her more irresistible. We had our one time, and then I knew I had to have her again. When she came back for Zach and Presley's engagement a few months ago, she was more than willing for round two. The sex was explosive, but more than that . . . I was drawn to her like I haven't been with anyone else.

She lit me up and then left me burning. No one can blame me there. She was right when she said I never called, but I haven't heard from her either. I went out to handle the ranch, only to come back and find her gone. Presley told me she took an early flight home, and that was the end of our fling. When Zach let it slip that Angie was coming to town, I figured we needed to air some stuff out, so I showed up. I had no clue the girl was knocked up.

"I'm not marrying you." Her defiance is cute.

"You'll change your mind."

"I'm not moving here either." Angie crosses her arms.

The hell she's not. "We'll work that out."

"I'm not kidding. I'm pregnant, but that doesn't mean—"

"It means everything," I say while grabbing her hand. "It means everything to me. I'm not going to be okay with you raisin' our baby in Pennsylvania. And that means that everything is different."

She sighs and pulls her hand back. "A minute ago you didn't even think it was yours. Now suddenly you want to marry me?"

"I wasn't tryin' to hurt you, Angie. But you show up here

after months without a word, sayin' you're pregnant. I'm not sure what you expect."

She stands and releases a groan before looking back at me. "I expect nothing."

"Well, now you can expect me to be a man and take care of my responsibilities, and that means we'll get married, you'll move, and I'll take care of you."

"You're insane!" She grips the side of her head. "Maybe that's how shit works in Bell Buckle, but not where I'm from. I'm not going to marry you just because I'm pregnant. We're not sixteen and in high school. I don't need someone to 'take care of me'," She does that in air quotes. "The last thing we should do is get married out of obligation. It's not fair to either of us or our kid. I'll be fine on my own."

What the hell is wrong with women? Are they all this thick headed? Or maybe it's just the females I'm around all the damn time. "Let's get one thing straight." I move around so we're face to face. "You're not alone. You're not on your own. We," I move my hand back and forth between us, "are having a baby. You and me. Not you on your own."

"I appreciate that. I really do, but I don't know much about you other than you've been in love with my best friend since you were a kid and that you're really good in bed."

I don't miss the tinge of hurt in her eyes when she says the first part. She's not wrong. "We've known each other for almost two years now. You know more than that about me."

Crap. It really has been that long. We've spent that time bickering, annoying each other, or screwing.

"Right."

"And you know a lot more than the bullshit you spewed." I challenge her. "I spent a lot of my life in love with Presley, but I spent just as much time knowing she wasn't mine to have. You know that I would do just about anything for anyone. You've seen the way I am with Cayden and Logan."

"I know." She finally turns her eyes to mine. "I know you're a good guy, but I don't really know you."

"Just like I don't really know much about you, other than you really like when I did that thing with my teeth—"

She slaps my arm with her free hand. "Shut your face."

"I'm saying we both have a lot to learn about each other. But seein' as we're about to spend the rest of our lives raisin' a kid. I think we should spend the time before that happens—together?" I ask it as a question, but the truth is that I'll be around for this baby.

I'm not letting my child grow up without a daddy. I want to teach him how to hunt, farm, ride a horse, and a lot of manly things. If it's a girl, she'll be a princess, and I'll make sure to teach her what evil little shits boys are. I deserve that chance. I won't let her take our kid up north where I can't be part of his or her life. It ain't fair, and it ain't happening . . . whether she wants it or not.

chapter FOUR

Angie

"I DON'T THINK IT'S SUCH a bad idea to move here," Presley says as she works in the kitchen. Wyatt and Zach left to go handle some work on the ranch, so since we're alone, Pres has taken this opportunity to try to sell me on all the ideas she's concocted in the last few hours.

"Do you know me at all? Do I look like the kind of girl who can wake up on a farm? I don't like livestock. I don't do dirt. I'll die out here because a coyote will eat me! I'm a city girl. I can't handle the lack of shopping, restaurants, and overall—life here."

I've always lived downtown. There's not one thing that I can say I dislike about how I live. I have everything I could want.

"You'd have us," she says while keeping her eyes down.

"*Ohhh* no you don't." I see the game she's playing. Pres didn't want to leave Pennsylvania, but she had no choice. I do. I don't have to live here. I can afford my life fine on my own. Will it suck? Yup. But I can manage. Coming down here would be more of an upheaval than having a baby in Philly. "You can't use this to get what you want."

She looks up as she puts the knife on the counter. "I'm not using anything. Look," her features soften, "you're up there all alone. Your parents are gone. Your brothers are gone. I'm gone. I want to know my niece or nephew. There's so much here that would make it easier for you, Ang. You'd have an entire support system. I think you're being stubborn."

"I am not!" Well, I kind of am. I know she's partially right, but it feels like I'm losing everything. "I can't move here. I can't give up everything because Wyatt lives here and I live there. What about the bakery? What about my *life*, Pres? I feel like I'm screwed either way."

"You have Erin at the bakery. She's more than capable of handling things for a bit. It was the whole damn reason you brought her on," Presley throws back at me. "And as for your life? Babe, it's going to be all about the baby. You'll see. It's the most rewarding job you'll ever have."

I groan. "I'm not ready for all this. I didn't want kids. I mean, I did in theory, but the more years that passed, the more okay I was with not having them. Now I'm having a baby with a guy who lives like four states away. It sucks. It's not ideal at all."

She doesn't get it. I don't expect her to. I don't know what the right thing to do is. All I know is that I'm truly pregnant and that things are going to change drastically after the little nugget gets here.

Presley pauses and then her face brightens. "What if you stayed until the baby came? Or maybe until the wedding and then see how you feel?"

"I need a drink," I grumble. "But I can't have one! I already hate being pregnant."

She chuckles and goes back to cooking. "You have no idea, my friend."

"You can shut up now."

"Whatever you want." Presley grins and busies herself.

We sit in comfortable silence. I give myself a few minutes to calm down and start to make a list of pros and cons. I can't even believe I'm even considering this. I love Bell Buckle—in theory. It's peaceful, full of heritage and beautiful homes. There's so much history that I don't even have to look to find it. It's just not *my* home and I can find plenty of history in Philly. Here, I can't find a quick Chinese food place or grab a cheesesteak from Geno's. I'll have to cook. My coming here also means losing the bakery. It means dropping the one thing that I've really done on my own.

God, this sucks. Already all I can think about is food.

The pros are the people, though. Presley, Cayden, Logan, her family, Zach, Wyatt, and his family. They'll be here to help with the baby, and they've already accepted me into the family. It's a pretty big pro. I won't have that in Philly. The Chinese food guy won't come watch the baby so I can shower. I shudder. That would be gross and creepy. Plus, it doesn't matter if I have all the cheesesteaks in the world, they won't give me a shoulder to cry on. I also can't ignore the fact that when I'm in Philly, I miss Presley and the boys. I would be lying if I didn't wish we were living in the same town again.

"Pres," I whisper. "I'm scared."

When I drag my gaze away from the countertop I was staring at, she's already leaning against the edge watching me. I know that look. I've seen it many times. She's trying to find a way to talk me off the proverbial ledge. "I know you are. I would be, too. This is a lot for you and I can't give you the answers, but I can tell you that you're loved. You would have a lot of people who would help you."

"Where would I even live?"

Her mouth opens and closes before she lets out a heavy sigh. "You know you can live here, right?"

"I couldn't." I shake my head.

She's getting married in six months. The last thing I want to do is disrupt her new life with Zach. There's not a shadow of a doubt that they'd welcome me in. But I have to think of not only them, but myself as well. I would kill her. I love her, but living with her isn't all it's cracked up to be. I like being able to kick off my shoes and eat ice cream from the carton. Presley wants the shoes in a neat row by the door and believes there's a reason for a bowl. We're different. I'm more free spirited. She's more organized.

I need to be on my own.

"Why not?" I give her a look that says everything I thought and she giggles. She knows that if I don't kill her first, she will off me. "Then the only other option is Wyatt."

I sigh. Damn him. "You know he was all alpha stupid with saying we will get married?"

"I'm not surprised. It's not being alpha—it's being Southern."

"Meaning?"

"Meaning he wants to take care of you. He's a good man, Ang. He will always take care of his responsibilities. He was raised that way, and his mama raised him right. He may act like a child most of the time, but he'll do right by you and this baby."

"That's the problem. I don't want to be his charity case. Just because we had sex, it doesn't mean he needs to give up everything. He can still be a father to our child without me having to move here. I would never keep the baby from him."

She nods. "I don't think anyone is disputing that, but do you remember when the boys were little?"

"Yeah?" I don't know where she's going with this.

"A lot happens when they're little. The first smile. The first time they start to crawl or walk. It's a lot of little things that only happen for the first time—once."

I don't disagree with her. "That said, I'm not certain that means I should uproot my life."

"Don't you think it would be nice to have help with an

infant? He'll be a good dad, and he wants to be there."

"I know he'll be a good dad, Pres. I've seen how he is with Cayden and Logan."

I believe that deep down in my soul. Wyatt made it clear that he'll be around for the baby. He wants to be involved, and I'll never begrudge him his own child, but I'm not marrying the man. He's lost his damn mind if he thinks I'm going to because he thinks it's "the right thing to do." Whenever I finally decide to marry someone, which will probably be never, it's going to be for the right reasons.

"It'll work out," Presley says with conviction. "I know it."

"Ugh!" I drop my head in my hands. "Everything is so fucked up!"

"Or maybe everything is finally falling into place."

SINCE I'M NOT REALLY SURE about the rules for pregnancy and coffee, I grab a cup of tea, head out to the wrap-around porch, and plop myself in one of the Adirondack chairs. With everyone still asleep, the house is quiet, and the pre-dawn morning is peaceful. I take a sip of my drink, wince, and make a mental note to ask my doctor about my coffee allowance. There's no telling what kind of awful bitch I'll become if I can't have it, but I don't want to do anything to hurt the baby in the meantime.

I sit, staring out at the rolling hills before me. I hold the cup in my hand as the steam rises, and then I spot the garden figure I gave Presley when she bought the house in Media. Two girls sit on a swing, holding onto each other as if they're all the other one needs. After college, I wanted to be sure she'd always have me close (not that I was ever really far to begin with), but seeing she brought me here to her new life, I can't help the smile.

Presley's life hasn't been easy the last few years thanks to my brother. She had everything. A husband, kids, a new business, and happiness—then she lost it all. It fell apart, no, it imploded. Losing my brother by suicide was awful enough, but then I lost her in my everyday life and it was devastating. But she didn't fall apart.

She didn't quit.

She rose up from the ashes, and while it wasn't an easy road, she did it with grace. I know some think otherwise, but I've known her most of my life. I've seen her weak. I've seen her distraught, and I've seen her be brave for her kids.

That's the one thing that I can honestly say about her, she always puts those boys first. They're her priority, and her choices may not be what I would do, but they come from love. I need to find that part of myself.

I need to be brave in order to take on this new life and be the woman who cares for her child. And who knows? Maybe this will be the best thing to ever happen. I didn't plan this, but I'm still going to be someone's mommy. The baby needs me, and I know once it's here, I'll love the little nugget.

"This isn't going to be easy," I say as I rub my stomach. "I don't know how to do this. So, just a forewarning, I might suck as a mom. I figure you should probably know I don't really have that trait. Your Aunt Presley is the one who does that. I'm probably going to be a mess for a while, but I promise to try really hard to be better." I whisper the words to the tiny child growing inside me.

And I *will* try.

Because that's what moms do.

I rock back and forth in the chair, looking out at the lake. "And so it begins."

"What begins?" A deep voice rumbles, causing me to jump.

My teacup falls forward, clanking against the ground as I let out a loud squeal. "Shit!" I glare as Wyatt stomps up the steps. "Wyatt! You scared the crap out of me."

"I was hoping you were awake," he says as he leans down and grabs the cup. His eyes lock on mine, and I have to remember to breathe. He looks unbelievably attractive in his faded Tennessee hat and dark blue jeans, which cling to his legs and outline his perfect ass. The gray Hennington Horse Farm T-shirt, which is clearly adored and fits him perfectly, allows me to peruse every muscle in his chest. Everything about him causes my mouth to water. He's sexy without even trying. Nothing he's wearing is to impress anyone. He's just impressive. "You okay?" he asks after I still haven't spoken.

"I'm fine. Trying to get my heart to calm." _And my libido to ebb._

He sits on the chair next to mine. "I didn't mean to scare you. I figured you heard my truck."

"I guess I was lost in my thoughts."

"Have you thought about this situation?" His voice has a tinge of hesitancy.

"That's all I've thought about, Wyatt."

His hand lifts and pushes a strand of hair behind my ear. His finger brushes across my cheek and I actually sigh aloud. Like a freaking idiot. Wyatt smiles at the sound and cups my cheek. "Me too. I can't stop thinking about it or what you're going to do. We need to talk. We need to figure this out."

"I'm trying."

Wyatt drops his hand. "Again, it's not just you. It's my baby you're carryin'. I want to help you."

He's right. It is his baby, and I already know what he wants. He's not once asked me what I want. "I won't keep him or her from you. I'm not like that."

"I know." His lips press together. "Tell me what you're thinkin'. Maybe I can help ease your mind."

I wish it were that simple. There's nothing that I'm going to say that will ease his mind. If anything . . . I'm going to lose my own. "What am I thinking? You really want to know?"

He leans back, tossing one ankle across his knee and painting an easy smile on his face. "I'm all ears, honey."

"Okay, you asked for it." I make sure the warning is clear in my tone. "I'm freaking out. We're having a baby, and we're not even together. My choices are: be alone in Philadelphia and raise this kid or move here—neither choice is appealing to me. I feel as if someone has taken away my life and then I feel like a selfish bitch for thinking that way," I ramble the words as fast as I think them. "I hate this. I hate that I'm having a baby with a man who doesn't even like me, let alone love me. This should be a joyful time in my life, and it's not. I feel robbed. I didn't get to pee on a stick and hide it from my husband so I could do some grand gesture to tell him we were having a baby." Tears start to fall as I let it all out, all the while Wyatt holds my hand. "I never really thought much about having a kid, but at least when I did, I figured it would be with my *husband*. Instead, we get this! How is that fair? It's not. I wish this never happened. I wish I never went home with you. I wish I could go back in time and take it all back."

When I say the last word I instantly regret it.

That was mean, and it's not true.

I don't regret being with him. I had every intention of doing it again when I boarded that plane two months ago. And I want this baby. Sure, it's not the way I wanted it to happen, but there's a human being growing inside me, and I'm going to love him or her, I'm already starting to feel better about it. I need a little more time.

Wyatt's face shows nothing. His eyes are soft, and I don't see a hint of judgment in them. "I'm sorry," he says with so much sorrow it breaks my heart. "I know I'm not your first pick, but I can tell you not everything you think is true. And I'm sorry you feel that this has taken your life away from you."

"No." I take his hand in mine. "I'm sorry, I shouldn't have said all that. You don't deserve it. You got robbed, too. We did this together, and I'm being selfish."

He lets out a light chuckle. "You're not selfish. I said close to the same shit to Trent last night. I wanted to be married and have kids with a woman who knew what a catch I am."

I laugh.

"I'm serious." He stands and looks at me with an overly serious expression. "I'm the most eligible bachelor here in Bell Buckle."

"Slim pickings, huh?"

"You're about to be a very hated woman here. You don't know how many girls love me."

"Your humility is truly astounding. I've heard all about your sexual escapades."

He laughs. "You've also been one of those escapades, honey."

I roll my eyes. He's right. I have been. "I want us to at least be good friends. You know, like, *know* who the other person is. For the baby's sake."

Wyatt smiles and extends his hand. "Come for a walk with me."

I place my fingers in his palm and let him pull me to my feet. "Okay."

We start walking, and he hooks my hand into the crook of his arm. It's sweet, and a little part of me thaws. Maybe this isn't what I wanted, but this, right here, is nice. Wyatt doesn't say anything, but I can feel him tense a little. It's as if he's preparing for something and trying to build up the courage.

"I want you to consider moving here while you're pregnant," he says after we break through the trees on a dirt path. "Now, I know what you're feeling. I know you feel like you're losing everything, but what if something happens and you're up there? What if you need help? It would take a long time for me to get there."

He's going to make it damn near impossible for me to say no. "I'm not some damsel in distress."

"No." He stops walking. "You're not. I don't think you've ever been that, but you're the mother of my child. It's my job to care for you, and whether you believe it or not, I do care about you, and I have even before I knew you were pregnant."

I'm speechless. What he said was probably the single most perfect thing to say. "That means a lot to me. Thank you, but what would I do here?"

"Anything you want. We're not backwards here. You don't have to work if you don't want to, and you can take some time to yourself. Hell, write a book. You could open a cupcake place in town. You can do whatever the hell you want. I'm just asking for some time."

The bakery is what keeps tripping me up. I'm sure that Erin could take it over for me. Since we got the manager up to speed, I don't do very much there anyway. I was going to start focusing completely on opening another location.

This is crazy.

There's so much to ruminate. But I can only imagine how he would feel if something happened to me or the baby while I was in Pennsylvania. I don't know if it's enough to make me do this, but it's something to weigh.

I can't even believe I'm considering this.

"What if we find out we hate each other? What if all we were was a night of unbelievable sex? Where do we go from there?"

Wyatt takes my face in his hands. "What if we don't hate each other? Or if we do, what's the worst that can happen? You'll be close to Presley and your nephews. What if you realize that I'm the best man on the planet and you can't live without me?

Don't you think we owe it to ourselves and to the baby to find out? Give this a chance."

"What does that even mean? Us?" I ask.

His hands drop to my shoulders as he holds me in place. All I've ever felt for him was an intense physical attraction. He was a means to a very long dry spell. It was easy to let myself sleep with him since he lived here and I was there. Plus, there were no real emotional ties for either of us. We knew what it was and that worked fine for me.

"Us." Wyatt's word echoes in my head. "A real chance at us. It means we date or something. You'll keep cookin' my kid. I'll take you out and show you I'm not the crap you've heard. I was up all night thinkin' about this. I want you to move here and just see . . ."

I shake my head because he's crazy, but I wonder. "I—" I stop.

I'm confused. The picture he paints is alluring. I know he's a good guy at heart. If he weren't, Presley would never speak so highly of him. The boys adore him and constantly talk about Uncle Wyatt. There's a lot of unknowns.

What if he's right? But what if he's wrong?

"You?" He pushes.

"I-I I don't know!" I blurt out. "This is too much." I push back from him, needing some space to breathe. When he's close like this, it confuses me. I want to say yes even though it's probably the last thing I would ever do. I turn my back to him and look out at the trees, but then I feel his heat as he steps closer to me.

"It's a lot, but I'm trying." His deep voice vibrates through me. "Give me until you have the baby. I at least want to see my first kid born."

He's trying, and I should too.

"I'll give you three months." I spin around to face him. "I can't promise anything more than that, but I'll come here for the next few months, and we'll work through this."

"Three months?" he repeats. Wyatt crosses his arms and stares me down.

"I can't be away for longer than that right now."

"I don't like it," Wyatt admits, dropping his arms to his sides and showing me a hint of sadness. "But it's a start."

"Wyatt," I warn.

He puts his hand up. "Don't say anything, darlin'. We've got three months of talkin' to do. You need to get home and pack. I'll see you soon." He dips his head close. "Real soon."

It's official . . . I've lost my ever-loving mind.

chapter FIVE

~ Three Weeks Later ~

"I MADE SPACE FOR YOUR stuff in the closet," Wyatt says as he unloads my car.

I'm living here.

In his house.

While I carry his baby.

"Thanks," I say, trying to get my head on straight. I agreed to this, but I can't stop myself from feeling as if I had been forced. But it's me who is forcing this to happen.

After I left Bell Buckle with a plan, I became focused. I knew that the goal was to pack a few months' worth of things, get Erin all set up, and find someone to watch my apartment. Presley, who was over the moon about my extended stay in Bell Buckle, recommended letting one of our bakers house-sit since she still lived at home with her parents. She was more than excited, and then I was moving—well visiting for a long period of time—to freaking Tennessee.

Wyatt called me at least once a week, probably to make sure I wasn't backing out, and I did my best to sound hopeful. He told me he'd done some work in the house, and was looking forward to me coming. We spent no more than fifteen minutes on each call, but it felt like we said so much in those short periods. It seemed like he was truly excited, and he kept reiterating how much he wanted to spend this time together, which confused the shit out of me.

"I think that's everything." He puts the suitcase on the bed.

I nod, unable to find my voice. My hormones are a *mess,* and I can't seem to stop myself from spontaneously bursting into tears. I had to pull over on the drive down because it became too much. I'm not necessarily sad. I'm overwhelmed. I'm living with my baby daddy, and I don't have a job. I'm a walking disaster.

My eyes roam the small but cozy bedroom. Everything in Wyatt's house is simple and has purpose. There are no decorations on the walls and there doesn't seem to be anything here that doesn't have a purpose. It's clean but comfortable. The walls in his bedroom are painted a neutral cream color, the bedding is a blue down comforter with a ton of pillows. Seriously, the bed is pretty much completely covered with them. The only thing that stands out is the very large television mounted to the wall.

The rest of his house is the same. He clearly lives as a bachelor. The furniture looks as if it's been around a while, maybe hand-me-downs from family or friends who were getting rid of stuff, yet each piece is cared for. He showed me around when I arrived, and while his house seems small, there's a lot of space.

The room I'm most excited to use is the bathroom. Complete with the most amazing claw foot tub I've ever seen and a shower that could easily fit four people. The shower heads line the walls and there are two huge rainfall spouts up top. It looks heavenly.

I put away the rest of my stuff and turn to see Wyatt leaning against the door. "So," my voice cracks a little, "what's the plan?"

"Well, the plan is to get to know each other." He moves toward me and sits on the bed with a grin.

I laugh. "While living together."

"It's like speed dating," Wyatt muses. "We'll use the time we have and see where it goes."

"Well, we can at least skip the awkward after part. We've already tackled that. Oh, and the whole, 'What happens if we get pregnant?' talk."

Wyatt and I both laugh. He takes my hand and pulls me on the bed next to him. "I'm not sure what exactly we should be doing, but we'll figure it out. We take it one day at a time."

At least he's as lost as I am.

"I think we need rules."

His brow rises. "Rules?"

"Yes. Rules," I say sternly. "I have rules."

"By all means." He swipes his hand out in front of him.

Here we go. I'm pretty sure he's not going to like this, but too freaking bad. "Absolutely no sex with each other or other people. No dating other people, either. No going to sleep angry. No using the baby as a way to get what we want. No snoring. No eating off my plate. Do not ever touch my coffee if you want to keep the use of your hands . . . those are my rules."

The last one is really the most vital. But the rest are important as well.

Wyatt stares at me with a funny look on his face. "No sex? Don't you think that ship has sailed?"

"Well, that ship sank, but it'll be good for us to spend the next few months without complicating things more. So yeah, no sex."

His grin grows wider. "What if you can't handle being around me and jump my bones?"

"Not happening," I retort.

If we're going to try this, we're going to do it right. Sex is what got us in this predicament to begin with, and I'll be damned if we make things worse. I already know that the sexual chemistry between us is off the charts. Now, we need to see if the rest of what we're going for has a chance or if it's just the situation making us question it.

He stands, stretching his arms in the air while rotating back and forth. His shirt lifts, revealing his tanned skin and washboard abs. I gulp, unable to tear my eyes away from him. "I think the next few months are going to be interesting," he muses. Wyatt crosses his arms, lifts his shirt off, and tosses it in the corner. "I'm going to hop in the shower."

My mouth waters at the sight of his chest. Each part of his body is solid, and there's not an ounce of fat on him. He's ridiculous. Who the hell actually looks like this? It's not normal.

I make a fist and glance away. If I stare, I'll want to touch. If I touch, I'll end up naked. That would be bad.

"Have fun." I tuck my hair behind my ear.

"Angie?"

"Huh?" I keep my eyes down, pretending there's something incredibly interesting on the ground in front of me.

"You okay?" His voice is smug, which breaks my staring contest with the floor.

"I'm perfect." My eyes meet his, and I pull all my sass to the forefront. If I can stay angry or determined, I might be okay. "Pregnant, but perfect."

He smirks. "Perfect." He continues to look at me as he unbuttons his jeans. "I wouldn't want you to be uncomfortable."

Jackass.

"Nope."

My stomach drops as his pants fall to the floor.

"Good." Wyatt knows damn well what he's doing.

The bite of my nails pressing into my palm stings. I stand without looking in his direction, and walk out of the room, slamming the door on my way. The bastard chuckles.

This is going to be a long three months.

I head into the living room and plop on the couch. I grab the book I brought with me and start reading this book of horrors about pregnancy. No one talks about this crap. They don't talk about the joys of hemorrhoids and leaking bladders. They talk about the baby and how it felt when it kicked. I'm pretty sure Presley left out her nipples turning colors. Each chapter brings a new horrifying reality of what my body is going to go through.

Why the hell do girls have to go through this shit? Fucking Eve and her inability to stay away from that fruit. I blame her. I blame my sister-in-law for not sharing all this crap. I would've had my uterus removed if I had known I was going to have leakage.

Wyatt exits the bedroom, already dressed in his typical jeans and T-shirt attire, and I slam the book shut and sit stunned.

That really happens to some women while they're in labor?

"What is that?" he asks looking at me with concern.

"This?" I hold the book up. "This is a fucking horror novel. Only it's not fiction. *Nooo*, this is reality." I toss it on the floor.

He bends to grab it, reads the title, and chuckles. "You have your own pregnancy guide in Presley. You don't need to read this."

I rise to my feet so we're toe to toe. "You did this!" I point my finger at his chest.

"I'm pretty sure you were an active participant."

So not the point.

"I'm going to get hemorrhoids! And droopy boobs!" His eyes travel to my chest and stop there. "Eyes up here, dipshit."

"You said boobs." Wyatt shrugs.

I groan, and Wyatt grabs my hips, pulling me close. My breath hitches as our bodies touch. "Stop freaking out. You're beautiful, and you still will be after you have the baby."

I fight the urge to cry. My hands rest on his arms as my head drops to his chest. "It's so freaking much."

"It is," Wyatt acknowledges. "But relax a little, Angel. You're not going to care about droopy boobs and whatever else when you're holdin' our baby."

My heart flutters a little when he says that. I remember how I felt when I held Cayden and Logan, and they weren't even mine. I can only imagine the way I'll feel when I hold my own baby. "Maybe."

He smirks and runs his hand up my back, holding me more securely to him. "You'll see. I'm rarely wrong."

I snort while shaking my head. "You're nuts."

"Maybe, but I have an idea . . . let's grab some food and go out for a bit. It's your first night in Bell Buckle and our first date."

I shake my head and let out a sigh. "A date?"

"Yeah." He pushes me back a little and gives me a smile that makes me want to set my panties on fire. "I'm takin' you out on a date. So, go get yourself ready."

This is the deal. I'm here so we can date and get to know each other. I have to be smart, though. I'm not staying here more than three months, so there's no point in letting my heart get tangled up with his.

I have to guard myself. Because Wyatt is funny, sexy, smart, and it would be easy to fall for him. It was effortless when I allowed myself to sleep with him the first time. Then it was damn near impossible to stay away after that. The truth is . . . I like him. He's a good guy.

Which is a bad thing for me.

I peek at him from beneath my lashes. "You don't have to take me on a date."

Wyatt's finger lifts my chin as he studies my face. "I do. But more than that, I want to."

"Oh," I say as my eyes drift to his lips.

"Angie," he says softly.

"Yeah?"

"What is the rule for kissing?"

I'm not sure what he's asking. Something about rules and lips touching, but when his hands are on me, I go stupid. "Kissing is good."

He doesn't say another word. His lips press against mine and my brain shuts down. My fingers grip his shirt, holding him to me as his arms enclose around me. Kissing him is a fullbody experience. I feel it all the way from my head to my toes. All I want to do is kiss him forever. His tongue glides against mine, and I moan. This is an otherworldly type of kiss. The kind that little girls dream of that makes everything else disappear.

It's everything I remember.

Our tongues move in harmony, and his hands hold me exactly where he wants me. I don't care, though. I wouldn't think of moving away from him when his mouth is on mine. His lips are firm and his tongue demands access to every inch of my mouth. I lose all track of time as he kisses me as if I'm his reason for living. He's in complete control of me right now, and that's not a good thing, but I can't find the wherewithal to stop him.

All too soon, he pulls back. "Kissing is very good. Kissing you is fucking unreal."

I'm a fool. My rules are a joke. Kissing is going to lead very quickly to something else. I have to put a stop to it even though I want to do nothing but kiss him.

"Yeah." I retreat a few steps and try to catch my breath. "Kissing is now one of my rules. No more kissing. Kissing is off limits." I have to punctuate this so he knows I'm serious.

Wyatt's eyes blaze as he stares at me. He steps toward me with purpose. "You think so?" His body moves closer, his voice turns deep, and sultry, and his eyes become soft. "You'll be in my bed every night. You think you can keep your hands and lips to yourself?"

"Yup."

He grins and nods. "If you say so. I love a challenge."

I lean in close to his ear. "I can control myself."

Wyatt lets out a low sound from his chest as he grips my shoulders. I lean back and see the desire in his eyes, but I see the restraint as well. "We'll see about that." He releases me and taps my nose.

chapter
SIX

"I'LL HAVE A JACK AND Coke, and she'll have . . . ." Wyatt trails off.

"A Sprite."

The bartender nods, and we grab seats at the bar. For our first date, he took my pregnant ass to the bar. Because that's completely romantic, and why not rub it in my face a little more that I can't drink?

Smooth. Real smooth.

Last time I was here, I ended up going back to his house and . . . well . . . got quite the souvenir.

I look around as we wait for the bartender to return with our order. The dance floor is packed. Some people are spinning around the outside, and others are line dancing in the middle. Lots of girls stand off to the sides, watching and waiting for a guy to walk past. I laugh as they all get a little straighter and puff their already visible cleavage to be more prominent. I wonder how many of these girls have slept with Wyatt.

After what Presley said, I would guess all of them.

He's known for being a bit of a slut, which never bothered me before. I'm clearly no angel, but I can't deny the touch of jealousy I have now. It's insane, but again, I blame the hormones. I also make a note to change the sheets on his bed and possibly burn the mattress. I can only imagine the shit that's gone down in that house. Hell, I know what we did, and if it's that times some unknown quantity . . .

Eww. Gross.

"You okay?" he asks while wrapping his arm around my shoulder.

"Yup. Just looking around."

His eyes travel my sightline, and he stiffens. It's subtle, but I notice it. "I know you've heard a lot of shit."

"You don't need—"

"I do. I'm going to say this one time." He glances at them and then back to me. "I'll never bullshit you. If you ask me, I'll tell you anything you want to know. I'll tell you this: no one has ever stayed the night in my bed. I've never even brought one of them back to my house. You're the only woman who I've had in my bed. Ever."

My eyes go wide at his admission. I'm stunned. He owes me nothing, but he gave me more in that one admission than he probably realizes. He confirmed what I was worried about but soothed it away in the same breath. He also confused me a bit more. Why me? Why has he never brought a girl to his bed? Why the hell me?

"Angie!" Presley yells, stopping me from asking any one of the questions tumbling through my mind. "You're here!"

"I am." I try to smile but fail. I'm still in shock as Wyatt continues to stare at me.

"Stop looking like that." She chides and pulls me in for a hug. "Your face will freeze."

I'm sure she thinks my lack of enthusiasm is because I'm here, but it's because his words are still penetrating. I tear my gaze away from him and try to process. Does that mean there was more that time than just sex? That's crazy because he doesn't know me. We've only spent a small amount of time together, and most of it was spent screwing.

Could there be something?

I glance back at Wyatt as he heads to the other end of the bar where Zach stands. "Sorry, I'm just . . ."

"Settling?" Pres fills in for me.

"You could say that. I'm definitely not in Philly anymore."

Presley's face says she understands it all too well. "I wish I could say something other than I'm sorry. I know you miss home."

Grace, her best friend from grade school, comes over and hugs me. "We'll grow on you, honey. Plus, we all love babies."

That snaps me out of it. "Does everyone know?" I gasp, raking my eyes around the bar, catching several people trying to be inconspicuous as they watch me.

Presley's lips form a thin line, and she shrugs, letting me know the answer is yes. "There are no secrets in a small town."

Great. Now, I'm not only the new girl, but I'm the new girl that Wyatt knocked up. So much for laying low for the next few months.

Grace takes my hand. "Don't worry about anyone here, honey. They're all jealous. The Hennington boys are all coveted."

"They have the egos to show for it, too." Presley jokes.

"Well, both of you fell for their charms." I cross my arms and wait for them to deny it. Presley is marrying one, and it's no secret that Grace has been in love with Trent Hennington since she was a kid.

"I'm not denying anything, but you're one to talk there, prego." Presley smirks.

Grace's mood seems to drop a little. Now I feel awful. Trent and Grace dated for a while, but he's an ass. Trent won't commit to her, so he strings her along and then breaks things off once he's had his fill. Presley has done her best to get Grace to let him go, but her heart is always with him.

I feel for her, though. Having to see him daily and knowing that he'll always be around. She told me about how she wants to get over him, but she doesn't know how.

"I'm sorry." I touch her arm. "I clearly allowed Wyatt to invade me."

She laughs. "Oh, he invaded you all right. Repeatedly."

"Yup, and I was the winner of door prize number two."

We all giggle until I feel someone's hand on the small of my back. "Ladies." Wyatt tips his head. "I know you want to catch up, but my date and I need to dance."

"Oh, don't let us keep you." Pres grins and looks back at the corner table where Zach is sitting by himself. "Your brother looks like he's bored. I better head over there."

He comes around and pulls me up. "Let's dance."

"Okay."

Wyatt pulls me to the floor, keeping his hand on my back until we're in the middle of the dance floor.

It's no surprise he can dance. Guys do not do what he does in bed if they don't have rhythm. He guides me around with ease. Considering I have no earthly idea how to dance like this, it's amazing what a good leader he is. My feet follow his, almost as if there is no other choice. His smile is permanent, as is mine.

The music changes, but he adjusts to the new beat with no effort. I'm having so much fun. Who knew that I would enjoy this? Wyatt twirls me a little more than he did in the beginning, so I must be catching on.

When the song morphs into a slow one, someone taps my shoulder. "Mind if I cut in?" I turn to see a blonde with way too much eye makeup on. Her clothes are skin tight, and her tits might as well be completely out. I don't even think she has a bra on. She looks at me with disdain in her eyes. "Haven't had a dance yet, Wyatt."

"Sure." I start to step back, but Wyatt tugs me closer.

His eyes stay glued on mine. "No thanks, Charlotte."

"But—"

"No." Wyatt's voice is stern, leaving no room for discussion, and not once does he acknowledge her with a glance.

He slides his hand around my middle and twirls me away from her.

I think that's something to add to my pros list.

"You could've danced with her."

I look back at Charlotte, who's shooting daggers at me with her eyes. It's clear I'm not going to be making any friends from his fan club. Whatever.

He rolls his eyes. "I don't want to. I'm on a date with you, and you're only here for three months. I don't have a lot of time to win you over."

"Win me over?"

Well, this should be good.

"Let me ask you something," he says as he lets out a deep sigh. "Why do you think I was at Zach's house the day you showed up a few weeks ago?"

What the hell does that have to do with him winning me over? "Because you like your brother?"

"Or I heard you were comin' and I wanted to see you?"

That thought never crossed my mind. Not once. I figured it was because he was visiting Zach and Presley. "Why? Why would you want to see me?"

"Because I like you. You're not like the other girls I've been with. You're smart, funny, and you know you're beautiful. So, I heard you were comin', and I drove over to see you." Wyatt doesn't look ashamed or slightly embarrassed. He just says what's on his mind. No bullshit.

It's refreshing, and I don't really know what to do with it. I've never dealt with a guy like him before. Not because the men I know have a hard time saying what's on their mind, it's just they usually keep their thoughts centered on pizza or beer or blow jobs. They're not open with what's actually in their hearts.

Wyatt, though, he tells it all, which makes my heart pound rapidly, my breathing accelerate, and heat pool.

"That's . . ." I struggle for words. "Not what I was expecting."

"Why? Because we've slept together two times, Angel. I don't typically go back for seconds if the first time wasn't something."

"That was sex."

"And it was good."

My cheeks warm, and I giggle. "It was."

And God was it ever. I've never come so hard in my life. Wyatt and I were explosive and so in sync. I think it's why I was so angry to wake up to find him gone. I couldn't understand what I had done wrong or what I misread. When you have mind-blowing sex, you don't expect that kind of morning. I felt something deep inside that night. Something that scared me but gave me something to hope for.

It was strange and so personal. I never said a word to Presley. The fact that I couldn't even make sense of it forced me to keep it to myself. She would never understand that something physical brought out something so emotional in me. Plus, Wyatt is known for his sexcapades. As am I. Trying to tie one of us down is a mistake. It makes me wonder what we're doing now.

"What?" he probes.

"We're very similar." I pause, letting him lead me through a few more turns before continuing, "So much so that it's scary. Neither of us are known for our long-term relationships. Yet, we're about to be in one with raising this baby. Are we doing the right thing by complicating this more?"

Wyatt's hands tighten on my back. "I'm not saying it's *because* of the baby. Well, not entirely. I grew up with the best parents. My daddy loves my mama more than anything in this world. She's literally his world. They gave me and my brothers a great life. We had Christmas mornings, Sunday dinners, and everything kids dream of. He taught us that the mother of your child is the most precious person in the world. I don't know if we're right for each other. I don't know if I'll come out of this thinkin' you're a pain in my ass that I hate, or the girl I want to come home to." His eyes hold mine captive, and I wait for him to keep going. We stand in the middle of the dance floor, lost to each other as other couples move around us. "I do know this, honey. I won't walk away without finding out. I felt something for you when we were together. Maybe, just maybe, this baby will be what wakes us both up. Maybe we're supposed to do that together."

Tears flood my vision, and I cup his face. "Maybe that's the sweetest thing I've ever heard."

"Maybe you're rethinking that kissin' rule?"

I laugh and shake my head. "Maybe."

Maybe I'm rethinking all of it.

"OKAY," I WHISPER TO MYSELF in the mirror. "You can do this. No touching, and you'll be fine."

The night was really fantastic. Wyatt made me feel as if no one else existed. His attention was mine. Most of the time we danced, but he forced me to sit and rest as well.

Zach, Trent, and Wyatt sat at the table next to Grace, Presley, and me, but Wyatt angled himself so we were almost at the same table. It was cute that he wanted to be close but didn't care if I sat with the girls while we were on a date.

We ended up leaving fifteen minutes ago since it was late and I'm exhausted. Now, I'm standing here in this insane bathroom that I want to live in, and freaking the fuck out.

We're going to sleep in the same bed.

Sure, one could argue that we've done this already, but now he's my . . . I don't know . . . boyfriend? We're dating. We're exclusively dating. He also understands no kissing and no sex.

I'm stupid.

Time to pull my big girl panties up and climb into bed with a super hot guy who I happen to know is fabulous between the sheets.

Right.

"You comin' out?" he calls as my hand sits on the doorknob.

Here goes nothing.

I watch as Wyatt's gaze travels the clothes I'm wearing. His eyes liquefy when he sees my tiny shorts and tank top that leave nothing to the imagination. I didn't pick this because I wanted to make it harder on either of us. It's just that this is what I sleep in if I sleep with clothes on. Usually, at some point in the night, I kick all the covers off because I'm roasting, which is why I sleep naked most of the time. I figured that would be bad, so I grabbed the least amount of clothing I had.

It was clearly a bad idea.

He clears his throat. "I'm . . . you're . . ." He closes his eyes and releases a breath. "Maybe you should buy some pants. And a sweatshirt."

I shake my head and lift the covers. "I'll warn you now, I'm a violent sleeper. We didn't sleep much the last time we were in a bed together, but I get really hot and rip off the blankets. I also don't like to be touched. Oh, and according to my ex, I kick and knee people."

"Great." He laughs. "Should I wear a cup?"

"Possibly." I climb in with a big smile. "But considering the fact that you knocked me up, I think it's only fair I get one good knee in."

He rolls to his side so we're facing each other. "You want to hurt me?"

"You're not going to have half the fun that I am during the next six months."

"Tomorrow you're twelve weeks, right?" Wyatt asks.

"Yup. Out of the first trimester."

It's crazy that I've got this tiny person growing inside me. They explained the first twelve weeks were the most crucial. I needed to make sure I took my vitamins and called if there were any issues.

Presley got me the information for the only gynecologist within twenty miles of here. He apparently delivered Wyatt, so I can only imagine how old he is, but I'll find out in two days when I meet him. Wyatt, apparently, loves Dr. Borek. He said he's the best doctor around, and I'll soon see why. This should be fun.

His hand lifts and brushes my hair back. "I know this isn't what either of us planned, but I hope you know that I'll always be there for both of you, even if this doesn't work out."

I lace my fingers with his, putting our clasped hands between us. "I promise I'll never be one of those women who keeps him or her from you. I grew up with two parents, but they weren't like yours. They weren't always bad. When we were really little, my mom was awesome. We baked cookies, did crafts, and she was really happy. My dad worked a lot, but he came home smiling and played dolls with me. Then my mom got cancer and everything changed."

"I'm sorry." Wyatt's eyes are soft and sincere.

"Don't be." I never understood what people were sorry for. It's not as if they gave her cancer and then cut me out of her life. "She made her choice. Instead of seeing that she had a second chance at life and living it to the fullest, she shut us all out. It was like her life could go at any minute, and instead of holding all of us close, she pushed us away."

Wyatt squeezes my hand a little. "Still sucks."

I let out a small laugh. "It does, and she's no better now. When Todd died, she really gave up on me. However, she's clung to my brother Josh, since he's the prodigal son."

"I didn't know you had another brother."

"Josh is . . ." I trail off, trying to think how to explain him. "Difficult."

Wyatt grins. "I have one of those."

I wish that Josh were like Trent. As difficult as he seems to be, it's different. "Not the same. Josh is the biggest snob I've ever met. He made a ton of money in his early twenties and let it get to his head. He's stingy, self-absorbed, and pretentious. He lets everyone know it, too. He's a pompous prick that I feel no need to be around. I can only imagine what he's going to say when he finds out I'm pregnant."

Wyatt's body tenses, and his face grows hard. "It's not his place."

"No." I close my eyes. "But he'll still have an opinion."

One that won't be good. I'm sure we'll end up screaming at each other. He'll call me a whore, or some other awful name, and then inject something about Todd. When Todd died he didn't even come to the funeral. He stayed in Florida in all his perfection. God forbid he be there for me, Presley, or our parents. It was easier for him say how Todd made his choice and that he wasn't going to be inconvenienced because of it. Did I mention he's a prick?

I've never been more disappointed in him than I was in that moment.

"No," Wyatt says with no room for question. "He won't."

It's sweet that he's already slightly protective. He's pretty cute when he's being all macho. "It's fine. I've learned to ignore whatever comes out of his mouth."

"Tell me more about your parents," he urges.

We settle in, and I talk about my mother and going through

her treatments. We talk about the fact that I haven't spoken to her in months and really didn't notice until now. It's sad that she wasn't the first phone call I wanted to make, but I've come to accept the relationship she's capable of having. She may not be the mother I wish I had, but I can't change her. I can't force someone to love me the way I want them to. It doesn't work that way.

Time passes and Wyatt and I keep sharing. Sometimes we talk about our friends, other times our family. My eyes grow tired, and I fight to keep them open.

"Sleep." His other hand comes to my cheek.

"No," I say around a yawn, fighting the exhaustion settling over me.

He shifts forward, kisses my forehead, and lies back down. "Good night, Angie."

"Good night, Wyatt."

His other hand slides down my body, and my eyes jerk open. His brown eyes don't move from mine, and he keeps our fingers intertwined. His hand rests on my stomach. "Good night, baby."

I place my hand over his. "Good night, baby."

We both smile at each other, and his beautiful eyes close.

chapter
SEVEN

THE NEXT TWELVE DAYS GO by seamlessly. The doctor was old, but really sweet. He gave me a lot of things to think about, and some advice on how to handle any symptoms I'll probably have. All in all, Wyatt was right. He is a great doctor, which of course I won't tell him. We told his parents last weekend, which I was nervous about but quickly learned I had no reason to be. I still haven't called my own parents, though.

Wyatt works, comes home, showers, and we have dinner. He's typically asleep before I'm even remotely ready for bed, but that's because he's up at the ass crack of dawn.

Wyatt's given me carte blanche in regards to any decorating I want. I've spent hours online and probably spent way more than I should for a three month stay, but at least I know that when the baby is born, the house is pretty.

I flop in the chair with a huff. I'm freaking tired. Like, all the time. I want to sleep and then sleep some more. Who knew that growing a kid would be so freaking exhausting? Not me. Although, I'm sure the book of crap that no one tells you has that little tidbit.

"Knock, knock," I hear someone say from the doorway.

I stand and see Wyatt's mama pop her head in. "Mrs. Hennington! Come in, please!" I smile, glad to have someone here to keep me from buying anything else.

"Hi there, darlin'! I wanted to come see how you were get-ting along here." She smiles with the warmth of the sun. "Also, I brought you a pie."

She's probably one of the sweetest women in the world, and her Southern charm is infectious. I've met her a few times with Presley before I claimed my door prize, and it's clear where her boys get their good hearts from. Macie Hennington has raised her kids with honor and respect.

"I'm hanging in there."

"You'll love it here, I just know it."

Fat chance in hell. I still have no access to a Caramel Macchiato or the cupcakes. I also miss my store, which means I'm getting crankier by the day. Instead of actually telling her that, I decide to grin. If there's one person I really want to like me—it's her. She's close to her boys, and she's the grandma I want for my baby. The one who will bake cookies, give sewing lessons, and smother grandbabies with love. Unlike my mother, who will teach my child how to ignore people properly.

"Oh, you've already made this house so much better." Mrs. Hennington looks around. "Wyatt's room always looked like one of those dorm rooms with white walls and awful posters." She waves her hand. "But you've done such a beautiful job just put-tin' a woman's touch around here."

"Thank you." I grin.

"I can't wait to see what you two do for a nursery." Her eyes are light with excitement. "I'm sorry, honey. I'm just so happy. I know it's a little unconventional and all, but it'll be my first grandbaby. After I chewed Wyatt's hide over how this could hap-pen, I couldn't stop myself from being . . . happy. I hope you un-derstand."

"I'm glad you're excited." *Someone should be out of our parents.*

"I wasn't sure you would be," I confess.

She laughs and pats my leg. "Sugar, Wyatt's a grown man, and I've warned that boy time and time again about carryin' on with women. But of all the girls I could pick to be givin' me my first grandbaby . . . I'm glad it's you. You're a smart, strong, and beautiful girl with a big heart."

"I don't know what to say."

Mrs. Hennington shrugs. "Just tell me you'll be careful with his heart and take care of that baby inside you." She glances at my belly.

"I will," I promise.

"Good. Now, tell me about what you've been up to." She takes my hand as we catch up.

I fill her in on all my very boring and uneventful days. I've gone by the Townsend's each day, had lunch with Presley or Wyatt if he wasn't busy, hung out with the boys, and then came home before him. It's fun, but I need purpose. I can't handle feeling like I'm useless. I'm not the stay-at-home kind of girl. I'm always busy, and if I have a lull, I find some new project to take on. Idle hands and all that.

She's excited to hear that Erin and I are mapping out a possible new location for the bakery. I don't tell her about how tight our timeframe is or how worried I am about being able to open while we're still relevant. The demand is high right now, and For Cup's Cakes is more than willing to be the supply. But I'm here and can't help Erin much.

I need to do something. Decorating Wyatt's bachelor pad isn't as interesting as it sounds, even though he's demanded that any purchase be paid for by him. I would've thought that spending his money would be fun . . . but it's not.

"What's wrong?" Mrs. Hennington pushes.

I debate not telling her, but the way she's looking at me makes it clear she's worried. "I'm bored. I work really hard back home and being here, sitting around, makes me a little stir crazy."

"Oh, sugar, I understand. I worked for Rhett since we bought the farm. It was one thing being a mother and looking after three boys, but I needed to really have something of my own. When I would go into the office, it was like I was livin' again."

"Exactly." She totally gets me, which is nice to have. Presley thinks I'm insane for feeling like this. She stayed home until the twins were in school, and even after she had her afternoons free, she didn't really work until we opened the bakery. She was content being a wife and mom. I would've chewed my arm off.

She nods in understanding. "Have you gone into town?"

"And be gawked at?"

Her head pulls back. "Don't tell me those girls are bein' mean."

"No, no." I try to laugh it off, but she doesn't look like she believes me. "I just feel like everyone is looking at me."

"You pay them no mind," she commands. She sits quiet, and then her eyes brighten again. "Have you thought about working at the bakery in town? I'm sure they'd love to have you!"

It's a good idea. I can maybe learn a few things, too. My business has only been around a fraction of the time that bakery has, and there is a lot I could learn about how they've managed it. Sometimes it's not about how much money you make that determines success, it's about how you weather the storm. I feel this way about all things. When something is easy, it's not worth as much to me. It's the things I have to fight for that have the most value. On the other hand, I don't plan to stay here long so there's no point.

"I don't know. I would hate to leave them in a bind."

She *tsks* and pats my leg. "You don't even worry about that. I'll call Becca right away. Since Charlotte left, she's been lookin' for someone. Especially with the festival coming up next week. I'm sure havin' you around would be a godsend."

Charlotte. The girl with big boobs and a fake smile. After

Wyatt snubbed her, I was the object of all her hate. She bumped into me once, which didn't go unnoticed by my best friend. Presley marched right over and laid into her. I saw Charlotte's breath hitch as she nodded feverously. I can only imagine what was said, but it didn't stop her from the constant dirty looks and whispers.

"I think I've met Charlotte. She and Wyatt were . . . close."

Mrs. Hennington doesn't miss a thing. Her eyes hone in, and she purses her lips. "I'm sorry about that, darlin'." She shifts a little. "The thing is that all my boys have their appeal, I guess. Zach was the star baseball player, but everyone knew his heart was Presley's. Trent," Macie rolls her eyes, "he's a mess that boy. He had the girls hangin' around, but he was more worried about his friends. Then when he took the role of Sherriff, I lost that battle. But Wyatt? He's always been something special." Her smile is huge as she says it.

"Special?"

She nods. "Wyatt has a very different way of thinkin'. He's kind, loyal, and always puts the needs of others first. I know the stories, believe me, I'm not blind. He might have been sowing his oats, but deep down he was searchin' for someone. All those girls had dreams they were it. Charlotte's no different. She wanted him to look at her, but when you're actin' like a hussy, a man won't respect you. Those women want what you have, and they'll try to hurt you, Angie. Don't let them. Wyatt's the kind of man that once you earn his love, you'll have it forever. He'll never betray you or desert you. It's very special to have someone come into your life like that."

I listen to her speak of him with such adoration. The pride that exudes from each syllable is both unmistakable and familiar. It reminds me of the way Presley talks about him. She speaks about his loyalty and how he'd hurt himself for someone else. How he gave up his own happiness for her. How the only time he ever did something selfish was when Zach took over the Hennington Horse Farm and he left.

Zach was dating this awful twat, Felicia, and she made Wyatt's life hell. Her constant undermining and games were too much for him. He gave Zach the chance to get rid of her, but he didn't. So, Wyatt went to work for Presley's family.

"Wyatt is a good man, Mrs. Hennington. I can see that, and I'm glad that if this had to happen with anyone . . . it's him. The baby is lucky."

I truly mean that. If Wyatt Hennington is half the man they all say he is, our child is going to have one hell of a dad.

Her eyes soften a little more. "You are, too, Angie. I can see already how much he cares for you. Now, tell me about some of the flavors you make up there in the North."

My head spins, and the seed of hope starts to take root. Now we have to see if it grows.

"HEY, BIG CITY." HE COMES in the door with a grin.

"I'm going to come up with a nickname for you."

Something he hates. Maybe Tiny Wanker or something to question his manhood. I know for damn sure he isn't lacking there, but I have to find something super annoying.

"Can't wait to hear it, honey," he says as he slaps my ass.

He's been great about my rules. He doesn't even attempt anything at night, which I was most worried about.

However, each night is growing increasingly harder for me. He now sleeps shirtless for one. It's not only his bare skin that is getting to me, it's also his scent. I close my eyes, and his cologne mixed with the clean smell that's Wyatt overwhelms me. I can remember the way his sweat tasted as I kissed his body the last time when we had sex. I can feel the way his hands roughly touched each inch of my skin. Every time I lie next to him, it takes every ounce of my strength not to maul him. Plus, we wake up the same way each morning—tangled limbs and a very hard erection against me.

I'm going to crack.

And very soon.

"You have a good day?" he asks as he places a soft kiss on my temple. I love that he does that. It's as if he's been doing it forever. Weird that in such a short time we've become so comfortable around each other.

When I look at him, I don't see the guy who knocked me up. I see a man who I could like. I see a man that I want to like me, and I want him to know me the way no one else has cared to do before. I worry that he could hurt me, which is always possible. Wyatt wouldn't be a man I could come back from. I can see in his eyes the way he'll own my heart and soul. If I give them to him, they will be his forever. His mother confirmed that today.

Wyatt crouches in front of me and places his hands on my belly. I don't have a bump. If you didn't know that I was pregnant you wouldn't be able to tell. But we know, and each night Wyatt lets me know that he's thinking of the baby in some small way. Sometimes it's a simple touch, other times it's a glance. Then, the other night, he rolled over and his palm rested there. He was sleeping and probably didn't know he did it, but I do. I laid there, unable to move, feeling every emotion possible. It wasn't as if he hasn't done it before, but this time it was an unconscious, protective gesture. It was as if it was the most natural thing to do. To make sure that me and the baby were safe.

Eventually, I draped my hand over his and fell asleep.

"Baby?" he asks again, and I realize he's calling me that, not the actual baby.

I shake my head. "Oh, I did. I had an eventful day."

A slow grin forms across his lips. "Yeah? I can't wait to hear it. I'm going to hop in the shower. Come in and talk if you want."

He wiggles his brows, and I laugh.

"Persistent."

"Hedging my bets."

Wyatt turns and heads into the bathroom. I listen as the shower turns on and wait a minute. The truth is, I want to talk to him. I enjoy when he comes home and we have a little time to go over his day, because really, my day is boring.

"Wyatt?" I ask from outside the door.

"Come in!"

This is a bad idea. "You better be in the shower," I say as I open the door. Thankfully, or maybe not, he's in, and I walk to the other side of the bathroom so I don't see through the glass. "Your mom came by today."

He opens the door and leans out. I quickly turn my head. "Did she?"

"Yup."

"What did Mama have to say?"

I bet he's worried. I decide to be a little playful. "She told me all about you. All the things to watch for."

The sounds of the water splashing do nothing to calm my imagination. He's in there. Naked. And I'm out here, because I'm stupid. No, not stupid. I'm cautious and being smart.

We'll go with that.

I move over to the sink and hop up.

"Did she now?"

"Worried?"

"Nope. I'm her favorite. She'd never sell me out."

"You could at least play along."

I hear the door open, the flap of the towel, and his throaty chuckle. I gaze at the floor as his feet come into view. God he even has sexy feet. I didn't even know that was a thing, but Wyatt's got them. My eyes drift up, taking in his body as he stands before me wearing only a towel. "I would rather play with something else."

Slowly, he starts to unravel the knot tied at his waist.

My hand flies to my face, ensuring I don't see anything. "Put clothes on!"

"You can look," he offers.

I shake my head. He's so close. All I smell is his clean and musky scent around me. The steam from the shower billows around us, and my hormones kick to double time. "I've already seen you naked. It's nothing to write home about."

He shifts forward and nestles himself between my legs. "I think you're lying, Big City. I think right now you want to look."

My eyes flash open and I glare at him. "I'm looking." My voice is laced with venom. "I see nothing I want to play with." I push him back a little and hop off the sink. It's too hot in here.

"No?" Wyatt steps forward, grips my wrist, and places my fingers against his chest. The heat from the shower and the feel of his skin under my palm sends a current through me. Oh God. I can't breathe. His heart beats beneath my hand as his lips graze my cheek. "Are you cold?" he asks knowing damn well I couldn't be. I curse the goose bumps that are giving me away right now.

"No." The word escapes as a plea. I've been doing good. I've managed to keep my hands off him at night, my lips to myself, and my rules intact.

"Just checking." He shrugs, looking completely unaffected.

Meanwhile, I'm a bundle of pent-up sexual tension.

"Asshole."

"Your rules, honey."

I huff and cross my arms. "Whatever."

"Listen, Mama's been quite busy today. She called and said we're needed at dinner tonight."

"Okay," I say with apprehension.

"She said we better be there." Wyatt kisses the side of my head as he passes.

I don't know why she needs us there, but maybe she has

more pie. "Will your dad be there?"

"No." He cracks his neck. "He's up in Nashville. You'll meet him soon."

"When are we going?"

"As soon as you get yourself ready. You know I should probably meet your parents, Ang. We're kinda bound together."

I let out a deep sigh and head into the bedroom. "I'm putting that off as long as possible."

While he knows about my parents, I didn't get too deep. I'm the youngest and by far the most challenging. I tested her at every turn, until she got sick at least. Then I became her caretaker for the most part. My father worked a lot, my brothers were away at college or too busy when they were home, but I was always there. I sat with her at the hospital while she got her chemo. I held her shoulders as she would get sick, and I shaved my head when she lost her hair.

You would think that would forge an unbreakable bond, but it didn't. As soon as she went into remission, she practically erased all the time we spent together from her mind. It was as if every moment we shared vanished with the cancer. Since then, I've been on my own. I don't want her to ruin this for me.

I know exactly how she'll feel about my being pregnant. And Wyatt. My mother expects a certain type of man. She would not be able to find that value in one who works his ass off on a farm. When Todd brought Presley around, there were some ugly things said about where she grew up. Things that I know my brother did not take kindly to. While Todd and Josh can hold their tongue—I can't. If she were to say one hateful thing about Wyatt, I'd lose my shit. No need to bring her into this now. I need to figure out too many other things first.

I exit the room with a sense of unease. "I'm ready."

Wyatt smiles and puts his arm out. "You look beautiful."

"You're not so bad yourself." I hook my hand around his forearm.

"Told you that I'm a catch."

I roll my eyes and smack his shoulder. "You're also a tool."

We walk the trail that leads to his parents' house. It's not far, and I could use the exercise. The short trip is spent with me telling him all the stuff his mother said. He tells me about the crazy day on the ranch and how he couldn't wait to get home. His smile is open and full of warmth. We laugh about Cayden and Logan's antics today and how Trent and Wyatt are teaching them things to do to Zach. Their newest lesson is the art of toilet papering.

Boys.

We approach the house, and Mrs. Hennington is already standing on the huge wrap around porch. "Hi, Mrs. Hennington." I smile.

"Oh, now. You can call me Macie, dear."

"Macie," Wyatt says from behind me. "I'm starvin'."

"Wyatt Earnest Hennington," she chides. "You will call me Mama, or I'll slap you into next Tuesday. Now, gimme some lovin'." She pats her cheek.

Wyatt wraps his arms around her and kisses her. "Sorry, Mama."

"Don't you let him get away with a thing," she tells me.

I giggle. "I won't."

"I'm serious," she says. "You let these boys get an inch on you, they'll take ten miles. And if that baby inside is a boy, Lord help you, darlin'."

My face pales a little. Macie turns toward the door as I stand a little stunned. I didn't even put any thought into the sex of the baby. I mean, I figured it was a girl because . . . I am one. But a boy? I don't know what to do with a boy by myself. A girl I can teach things to, but boys like dirt and bugs. I'm so not meant to be a mother to boys.

Especially if he's like Wyatt. These boys are *boys*. They hunt, fish, ride horses, and for all I know, they ride bulls too. I'm so screwed.

"She's kidding," Wyatt says against my ear. "My brothers and I were angels."

She laughs and shifts so she's facing us. "More like hellions."

"She also has some kind of super hearing." Wyatt throws his arm over my shoulder and turns to her with a smile. "Don't you?"

Macie smirks back. "When you have kids, you learn what to listen for. And if it's ever quiet . . . you know they're up to no good."

She's amazing. I want to be her. It's obvious that she loves her kids and they love her. Wyatt, Trent, and Zach have all stayed close to her. There's a good reason for that. There's also a reason my brothers and I got the hell away from our mother.

Wyatt and I enter the house, and I'm in awe. This house is straight out of a *Southern Living* magazine. The tapestries on the walls are soft creams with beautiful patterns. The floors are a deep mahogany hardwood. The entryway alone is magnificent and has a staircase on either side that meet in the middle. The foyer is filled with photos of their family. There's a formal living room off to the right that looks untouched and a huge dining room on the left. We move farther and pass a powder room and a study.

We enter into the kitchen, which takes up the entire back of the house, and the smells are overwhelming. It's filled with scents that make me feel at home—a pie baking in the oven with a mix of warm foods. I instantly relax. "Well, if it isn't Wyatt and Angie." An older woman stands from her seat at the table.

"Mrs. Rooney," Wyatt says before turning his gaze toward his mother. "I didn't know you'd be here."

"Of course, sugar." She pats the side of his face. "I wanted to make sure Angie knew how happy we all are." She looks vaguely familiar, but I can't place where I've met her before.

"All?" he asks with alarm in his voice.

"We're all here, honey." Two more women step in from the back porch.

Oh dear God.

Now I remember.

These are the four women who were all sitting around Presley's house and plying me with baked goods when hell broke loose. Presley told me all about the older women from the town. All four of them have been friends since grade school, and they know _everything_. They also make the most amazing cake. I swear, I could've orgasmed from one slice.

"Mrs. Townsend!" I walk over and give her a huge hug.

"Angelina Benson, it is so good to see you again." She returns my embrace. "You look just radiant."

She's another one of those moms I wish I had.

We all gather around the table as Mrs. Hennington, Mrs. Rooney, Mrs. Kannan, and Mrs. Townsend talk about the baby and how they can't wait for the wedding. Wyatt laughs and shakes his head at me whenever I start to correct them. "You need to tell them we're not getting married," I whisper in his ear.

"Trust me. You don't want to do that. It's better to let them go off on their tangent. If you correct them, they'll keep you hostage. Think of it as me savin' you."

I glare at him, and he laughs. "Stop being so damn adorable."

My lips purse.

He leans in and kisses my temple.

All the conversations that were going on around us cease. I glance around and everyone is looking at us with expressions of delight on their faces.

I look at him, waiting for some kind of explanation, but he just watches me. I see something in his eyes then. It's there, but it's guarded. That knowing feeling sits heavy in my gut as I wonder if I imagined it. Could we both be starting to feel something more?

I don't want him to fall in love with me.

I don't want to want him.

I want for us to be friends.

I want to *not* fall in love with him.

But there's a very good chance I'm not going to be able to stop it.

Mrs. Hennington clears her throat, breaking the trance. "Have you considered what we talked about, Angie?"

What we talked about? I scramble through the conversations we've had and finally land on what she's talking about.

The bakery.

"I just don't think it would be right." I shake my head. "I would really feel terrible when I have to go back to Philly."

"I'm sure Becca could use the help," Macie says, handing me a piece of pie. "With being short staffed and all, she's a bit overwhelmed. Even if it's only while you're here."

I want to help. It would be great to have something to do back in the bakery, but I don't know if I should. Why put down roots when I'm not planning to let the tree grow? My mind goes back and forth over the pros and cons and if I were to take her up on her offer it will give Wyatt false hope.

"Oh, I would love some help," Mrs. Kannan says with a smile. "Especially with the festival and the weddings I have comin' up."

"I'm honestly not sure that I would be much help, Mrs. Kannan. By the time I got the lay of the shop, I'd be leaving. It wouldn't be right."

Mrs. Kannan and Mrs. Hennington share a look. I'm not too

sure what they're conveying, but I'm wishing that it's in support to let it drop. "I understand, but I sure hope you change your mind."

Crisis averted.

We talk a little more, and Wyatt sits next to me with a grin. He looks confident, as if everything is going according to plan. It makes me wonder what else he has up his sleeve. So far, the first two weeks have been almost too easy. We've laughed, had tons of dates, had a pretty fantastic kiss, and gotten along great. If things continue at this rate, in a few months, I'm going to have a hard time convincing myself to go back to Philly.

And that would be a bad thing.

chapter
EIGHT

WYATT TAKES MY HAND AS we walk back to our house, and I let him. It feels comfortable, which leaves a very uncomfortable feeling in my chest. It shouldn't be as easy as it is. I've never liked guys who were touchy-feely, and it makes me wonder why with Wyatt I almost crave it.

Is it because he's so sweet? Is it because this is how it's meant to be? I don't know about any of this, and Presley is no help. She just smiles when I explain how I feel. It makes no sense that I actually *like* him as much as I do in such a short amount of time.

We continue down the path, and I admire the set up the Hennington's have. They all live on the same piece of land, but they're not on top of each other. His parents live in what he calls the main house. I call it a freaking mansion. Trent, Wyatt, and Zach all have homes on the property, but Zach's original place is no longer occupied since he and Presley built their own home.

"Hey," I say, stopping dead in my tracks. "Why am I staying with you in your house when Zach's house is empty?"

"Because it's not where you belong." Wyatt stands in front of me, and I remove my hand from his.

That makes no sense. He wants me here, but he could at least let me have my own space. I'm kind of pissed at him . . . and Presley. Neither of them thought about how much I would maybe need some separation. "Why? Why would you do that?"

"Where is this coming from? You never said a word when we were makin' arrangements. So why are you suddenly pissed?"

"I don't know, but I am." Probably because I didn't think of it sooner, which isn't the damn point. "You never gave me a choice. You said I would move here and stay with you. It was decided for me. I still could've gotten to know you while living down the road."

"No," Wyatt says with finality.

"No?"

"No. You were staying with me. It wasn't mentioned because it wasn't an option."

My mouth falls open. "And why not?"

"Because you're pregnant and you gave me limited time. You're exactly where I need you."

Once again, he renders me speechless. Where he *needs* me? What does that even mean? I start to think back to some of the comments he's made and try to decipher any hidden meanings. Wyatt didn't protest after he got over his shock. He went into "man mode" and wanted to fix it all. I chalked it up to him being a good guy and wanting to take care of me, but I wonder if there's more. "So that's all I am?" I ask. "I'm just the girl you got pregnant who needs you to take care of her? This is why you went all commando and tried to tell me we were getting married?" I shoot the questions off in rapid fire.

"No!" He steps forward. "Maybe when you first said that you were pregnant, my mind went there. But shit, Ang. We're not kids, and this isn't something new between us. I don't understand why you won't see that you're not some obligation. I like you. I like bein' around you. I didn't offer Zach's place, because I wanted you close to me. I wanted to see if we were more two years ago, but neither of us were going to move, so I let it go. Why won't you put down your guard?"

Because once upon a time when I believed in fairy tales, I *was* the girl who wanted to be married and have a family. I believed that it would happen, yet it never seemed right. No man seemed worthy of my time. No prince ever showed up, and I learned the hard way that a lot of men would treat me like shit, so I let go of that stupid dream and lived in reality. I built my own damn castle with really high walls. It was a fortress, sturdy enough to ensure I could never be hurt. Now, here Wyatt is with his cannon, finding ways to break my armor. He's finding cracks in the foundation, and I have to stop him.

That girl can't be uncovered.

That girl is stupid.

That girl will get her heart broken because this man only wants her because she's pregnant.

"Because . . ." I trail off. "You're . . . such an . . . Ugh! I don't even know!"

Wyatt steps forward, and I have to lean back to see his eyes. The sun is setting behind me, shining on his face, and the way he looks at me . . . leaves me breathless. It's as if I'm the center of his world. It reminds me of how Zach looks at Presley. "I'm doing what's right. You can call me whatever you want. But you're pregnant with my baby, and that means I'm takin' care of you."

"I'm completely capable of taking care of myself. I've been alone and been perfectly fine."

"It means you belong with me," he carries on as if I haven't spoken. "I'm gettin' pretty tired of explaining this to you. I've made it clear to you that I want to make whatever this is work. You're so hell bent on doin' this on your own that you won't even see anything else. If I gave you space, it would solidify your point that you should stay away. You can do this on your own, I know that. But why would you want to? Why are you so adamant about being alone? Why won't you see that there's a whole lot of people who want to be a part of your life?"

"Because it never stays that way!" I yell and cup my hand over my mouth. A tear falls from my eyes as the truth comes out.

And there it is.

In my heart, I know why. He's the kind of guy I want to want me. He's strong, sexy, caring, and so much more. There are layers to Wyatt, and I want to peel back each one of them. It was why I kept finding ways to be around him when I visited. It was why I practically jumped at the chance to sleep with him. Because Wyatt makes me feel alive. He's excavated the parts of me I've buried under sarcasm and attitude, the girl who wants a man to love her.

But fairy tales don't come true.

People die.

And I'm destined to be forgotten.

Wyatt's thumb brushes the tear away. "You've been through a lot of shit, but you haven't actually dealt with it, have you?"

I shake my head. "No, you don't get it, Wyatt. I'm happy. I'm genuinely happy alone. I like my life, my job, my apartment, and now everything is changing. I've kept things exactly the same because they work that way!" Another tear falls. "I don't want to like you. But you're making it impossible. You're going to realize I'm a giant pain in the ass. I'm stubborn, and I won't give up my life for a man. I can't do it. Because when you do realize I'm not worth the effort—You'll go."

"I'm not leavin' you. I'm not leavin' my kid. You're going to have to get used to that."

"You don't know that. You can't possibly know that."

He pulls me against his chest and holds me there. My fingers grip his shirt, and I hold on. I want to believe that he means it. But I've never had a guy stick it out with me. I'm moody, more so with a kid wreaking havoc on my hormones. There are girls like Presley who have epic loves, then there is me. I'm not the type of girl guys love. I'm the type they fuck and move on from. I've been fine with that. Happy even.

Wyatt lets out a deep sigh. "I'll prove it."

I sure hope so, because I could use a Prince Charming rather than the frogs I've been kissing.

We make it the rest of the way home without anymore outbursts. I mull over everything he said and try to put it into categories.

The reasons why I should keep myself guarded.

There's all the pros of why I think Wyatt is great, which is slowly making the former column damn near obsolete.

My world has pretty much been flipped around, so it's likely I'm a little off my game. Normally by now, I'd have found a hundred reasons why he's the last man on earth I want to be with. It doesn't usually take long. I find things annoying pretty quickly, but that list . . . is tiny.

Sure he is too damn sweet, he doesn't really cook much, and he seems to have issues with leaving the toilet seat up, but that's about it. I genuinely like being around him, and I find ways throughout the day to see him.

We both seem to be lost in our own minds as we muddle around the house. I get changed, he puts some things away, and we both climb into bed.

"Wyatt?"

"Hmm?"

"If I wasn't having the baby, would you still want me?"

His body goes still and then I feel him move quickly. The light turns on, and he stares at me. "Why would you ask me that?"

"There's these things I wonder about," I admit. "It's why I keep holding myself back. One of them is how you feel about Presley, the baby, and then where I fit into all that."

It's an honest question, but I don't know why I'm asking it. I just know if I don't, it's going to eat me alive. Wyatt and I have spent the last two weeks being open, getting to know each other, and talking about almost everything. My feelings are growing stronger with each day that passes, but the worry that my feelings are because of the baby won't go away.

"I don't know what I would feel. I liked you a long time ago, but we had our separate lives, Ang. I do know that we *are* having a baby, and I care about you. I don't think there's a real way to answer that."

I know what he means, but if there were no baby, would we even be having this conversation? The answer is no. The baby is the reason I'm here. The baby is the reason all this is happening. Wyatt and I might have hooked up whenever I came for a visit. Maybe we would've spent a few hot and heavy nights together, but I would've gone back to Philly.

To my life.

He would've stayed here—where he belongs.

"Let me ask you a question," Wyatt says. "Why did you agree to come here?"

"Because you asked."

"No." He sits up. "That's bullshit."

"No, it's the answer."

He releases a sarcastic laugh. "Why did you agree?"

"I told you!" Now, I'm getting frustrated.

"Was it because you wanted to see what this was? Was it because you wanted to know me better? Why, Angie? Why come here? Why would you give up three months of your life?"

The pit in my stomach grows. "Because!" I sit up, anger and confusion flowing through me. Why is he pushing me so hard?

Wyatt doesn't stop. "What was your goal? Why would you change your entire world and come here? Just like you have fears, I got them too. I'm trying to get you to see that I'm not playin' around. I'm giving you all I got, and you're holding back."

"I'm scared."

"I am too, baby. I'm livin' with knowing you're packed up and gone with my kid in a few months. I'm going to make you see that what you're willing to give up is more than what you got back home. I'm doing my damn best to ensure you see who I am. I don't know if we'd be doing this if you weren't pregnant. Hell, I know we wouldn't." He lets out a laugh devoid of all humor. "We're both stubborn assholes, and we'd let that game play on for years. We don't have years. We're running on borrowed time."

"Exactly! Without the baby, there would be no us! This is my whole damn point."

It's what keeps me holding back. Neither of us would move for the other. Not for the kind of feelings we had. Wyatt and I were dynamite in bed, but outside of that, we didn't talk much.

"You still haven't answered me. If you weren't going to give this a real shot, why try?"

I don't have an answer to give him, so I give him what I can and hope he understands the meaning behind the words. "You have no idea what it's like to grow up thinking you're worthless. It kept me from letting anyone in. It's been easier to not get disappointed. I've kept my heart safe. So, when I push you, it's because I'm scared. If I let you in fully, you won't let me go!"

Wyatt lies back down, rolling onto his side, and I mimic the movement so I'm facing him. "You have every intention of going back, don't you?"

"I did."

"And now?"

Now, I'm losing more of my hold. I'm slipping each day.

"I don't know. I don't know anything other than we're having this kid. We're going to be parents, and I don't know how I feel about us."

He smiles. "Okay, I can handle that. I'm going to work harder."

"I'm sure you will."

Each excuse that I had as to why this wouldn't work is fading away.

And here I am, falling for him. Fast. I don't trust myself. I've never been in love, and he's only ever loved Presley. What if this isn't real?

chapter NINE

A NOTHER DAY OF SOAP OPERAS and surfing Facebook. I've been going slightly stir crazy the last week. Wyatt has to be ready to kill me. I'm at the farm every day, trying to fit in a little. Presley has been great, and I've been doing half her work since I'm bored. I've learned a lot about cattle, not that it'll help me when I go back to Pennsylvania, but whatever.

Today has been harder for me. I'm depressed and really homesick. I miss the bakery, my friends (not that I have that many), and the city. I would love to take a walk through Old City, stop at a few stores, and then maybe see if anyone wanted to go to a Phillies game. Instead, I'm sitting here folding laundry and waiting for life to become fun again. Wyatt is normally home by now, but he said he had to stay late and help Cooper. Since Presley's brother is the owner of the Townsend ranch, Wyatt doesn't really get a say.

My phone flashes with a number I don't know. "Hello?" I answer.

"Angie?"

"Yes," I hesitate.

"Oh, thank goodness," the voice rings of relief. "This is Mrs. Kannan, sugar."

"Oh, hi," I say with surprise. "Is everything okay?"

A few seconds of a pause. "Not really." She coughs. "You see—" She breaks into another coughing fit. "I'm terribly sick and I have to get those cupcakes for the festival tomorrow." She starts hacking and wheezing. She clears her throat and comes back on the line. "I can't work and those cupcakes won't make themselves."

I see where this is going.

"I'm not the greatest baker. Presley would really be the better option," I suggest.

Presley spent her time in the bakery part and was the real talent behind the curtain. I did a little, but I mostly worked in front and did bookkeeping stuff.

"I asked her, but she's already baking pies with her mama. I'm desperate." She manages the last word before hacking up a lung.

If I say no, I'd be a total bitch. "Okay, of course," I say quickly. "Yes. I'll help out however I can."

"Thank you so much, sugar." Hmm, she sounds much better. "I mean . . ." She starts to wheeze. "You're saving a dear old lady from great embarrassment. I've had cupcakes at the festival since I can remember, which is a *long* time."

I silently laugh. "I'm glad to help, Mrs. Kannan. Do I need to come by and get the keys?"

"No, no, sugar," she replies instantly. "Wyatt knows how to get in. I don't want you catching whatever I have. Bye now."

She disconnects, and I look at the phone. I've been played. Expertly I might add.

I text Wyatt about the call, and tell him I need him to get me into the bakery to help. Thirty minutes later, he walks through the door with dirt all over his face.

"Hey."

"Thanks for coming home. Presley called explaining I need

to make about a thousand cupcakes by tomorrow."

He grins. "Our festival is an affair."

"Sounds like it."

Wyatt walks into the bedroom and returns a few minutes later in only a towel. "I'll clean up and take you over."

I go to protest, but he shuts the door before I can say anything. I wonder why he didn't ask me about going to the festival. I figure that would be something he'd attend. Maybe he doesn't, though? Weird.

Once he's all clean, we're on our way to the small shop that sits in the middle of the main street, which is freaking adorable. The store fronts have the old version of the flag banners that hang in a half circle. There are big tents lining the street and little fair-looking rides down at the other end. If he doesn't bring me here tomorrow, I'll kill him.

"This is so damn cute," I muse as we walk to the back of the store.

"It's something."

"Were you going to take me to the festival?"

He looks over with the key in the lock. "I figured you'd hate it."

"Why?" I ask with shock. "Why would you think that?"

"I didn't know if draggin' you to a big event in town would earn me any points. I can't tell if I should make you go to things or keep you away from them."

That hurt. I guess I haven't really wanted to become a part of the town. Or really a part of anything solid here. It makes sense why he'd feel that way. Ugh. I hate myself sometimes. "I'm sorry. I really would love to go." I put my hand on his shoulder. "If you'd like to take me."

He grins. "Honey, you're working it now."

"What?"

"You agreed to bake, but you also need to be out front to sell the cupcakes. There's no way these ladies are going to let you slide."

I gasp. "You knew!"

"Of course I knew. I've been getting worked by that group since I was in diapers. They knew you couldn't say no. They found an in and you fell for it hook, line, and sinker."

Son of a bitch. I freaking knew it! Then again, I never would've been able to say no even though she was faking. Presley used to joke about their meddling, but I thought she was being dramatic.

They showed me.

We enter the bakery, and I'm taken back in time. The appliances are all older, well used, and loved. It's beyond clean, but not stark. The entire bakery is filled with deep reds, navy blues, and worn whites. It's Americana décor at its finest. All the pieces are eclectic, but purposeful. There's linens on the five tables in the corner. The glass case in front is filled with different cakes and bakery items. The wall is chalkboard with all the flavors and their prices.

"Well." I turn to Wyatt. "I'm going to be here a while, so if you want, I can call you when I'm done?"

Making a thousand cupcakes is going to take me all night.

"I'm not leavin'. I'm your assistant," he announces.

"No."

"Yup."

"I don't have time to show you what to do, Wyatt," I try to explain. "I need to work quickly."

He chuckles. "Then you better hop to it, Big City."

I start to familiarize myself with the bakery. Not that I really know my way around For Cup's Cake either, but this is crazy. With Wyatt's help, I find all the ingredients and start to arrange them.

God I hope I don't screw this up.

"Okay." I sigh and then consider the most efficient way to do this. This shop has two side-by-side convection ovens. They'll definitely be able to accommodate large batches. "I can do this."

"I never had a doubt," Wyatt encourages. "What do you need me to do?"

He stands at the metal table, waiting for instructions. I dish out some things he can do to help. They are small, tedious tasks, but I really suck at measuring, so I hope to God he's better at it than I am.

I grew up learning how to cook with a little of this and a smidge of that. When Presley introduced me to baking in college, what I made was not all edible.

In fact, most was awful.

After Presley taught me that baking wasn't just a little of this and throw some of that in, I got better . . . or maybe I got used to tasting things that weren't edible.

Wyatt and I work together, laughing as we assemble things. He makes the batter, and I handle the frosting. Before too long, we're sliding trays in and out like a well-oiled machine. We may actually pull this off.

We're on the last batch when Wyatt breaks my concentration away from decorating a row of cupcakes. "I don't think we're supposed to be this messy."

I look around at the kitchen we trashed. "Definitely not! My baker would kill me if she saw this."

I turn around to grab the next batch I need to frost, but Wyatt is suddenly behind me. "Shit!" I yell as I almost drop the tray.

He laughs. "That was close."

Wyatt steps into me, and I'm between his hard body and the cold metal table. "It is close."

"Close isn't always bad." His eyes soften.

No. It definitely isn't.

He takes the tray from my hands and slides it on the table, grabbing one of the frosted cupcakes. I watch the wicked gleam in his eyes as he lifts it between us. "Try it." He puts it to my lips.

I'm not going to lie, it smells amazing in here, and I've wanted to taste them. I don't hesitate before I lean forward a bit and lick the icing. My eyes close, and I can't help but to hum my approval.

Wyatt's hand tightens against my back. "Don't make those noises, baby."

My gaze connects with his heated eyes. When he looks at me like that, I want to forget all the rules. He's insanely sexy. He's looking at me like he wants to be the cupcake, and I sure as hell want him to lick me.

"Why not?" I tilt my head and lick my lips. I'm playing a dangerous game, and he'll win. He hasn't pushed, which is a good thing because I wouldn't be able to resist. Wyatt is fire, and if it's anything like we've had in the past, I'll gladly take the burns.

"I know the rules," he reminds me. "I won't kiss you until you're sure. But a man only has so much patience."

I run my fingers up his chest. "Yeah?"

"You're in my arms, sexy as you've always been, and I want nothing more than to make you feel good."

Oh, for fuck's sake. He's going to make me melt.

Who am I kidding? He already has. I want to play this game. I want him to beat me.

"What if we call a cease fire?" I offer.

The wicked smile that dances across his lips sends a shiver down my spine. This is going to be good. This is going to be really good.

"Would I be allowed to do this?" he asks as his lips press against mine.

"Mmm hmm." My mouth doesn't retreat, but he pulls back.

"What about this?" Wyatt's hand cups my breast, and my head falls back. "Do you like when I touch you like this?"

"Yes," I murmur.

"What about if I do that and this?"

I wait for something else, but nothing comes. I open my eyes and look at him as his other hand tangles in my hair. He guides my face to his, but I'm already there. His mouth touches mine, and then his lips open. His tongue glides against mine, making me lose all sense. He could ask me to strip down and then fuck me on the table and I'd let him.

This isn't a cease fire. This is a surrender.

I'm waving the white flag.

Our tongues dance as his hand kneads my breast. He parts my legs with his knee, and the desire to rub against it is so high I succumb. I start to move, but he pushes me more securely against the table. I'm trapped, but I don't want to be anywhere else.

Next thing I know, he's lifting me up and pushing be backward so I'm sitting on the table. I hear the sounds of bowls clanking to the ground, but I don't care. As long as his lips are on mine, I don't care if the place is burning down.

He moves his hand from my breast and slides it lower. "I need more," I beg. "Please."

"Tonight is about you," he insists. "I want to make you feel good."

His lips are back against mine, kissing me breathless. I don't know why I'm being so crazy about this. We've already done the deed. It's just that I want to do things right if we can. However, that doesn't mean we should keep fighting the attraction we feel. At least that's what I'm telling myself.

"Wyatt." I tangle my hands in his hair as his lips move down my throat.

"That's it, baby. Feel what I'm doing to you," he encourages.

I feel it just fine, thank you very much. Thanks to the

increased blood flow and his ridiculous sexiness, I feel everything in vivid detail. It's been so hard not to beg him each night to touch me . . . I'm really glad I won't have that problem now.

He lifts my shirt over my head and then pulls my bra off.

Our lips connect as we both give and take. His thumb and forefinger roll my nipple back and forth. Then his mouth breaks from mine, and his tongue glides across my neck before he licks around my nipple. "Yes." I pant. "Yes," I say again as he swipes across the pebbled peak.

Wyatt doesn't make me wait. He starts to suck, causing me to writhe on the table. I had no idea that my breasts would be so sensitive, but everything feels heightened.

While continuing to lick, suck, and bite, his hand moves over my center. The pressure against my clit is too much. "Please don't make me beg." My voice is full of need.

"Never," he says. He hooks his thumbs into the waist of my shorts, and I lift just enough for him to pull them down. My ass hits the cold metal, but I'm too hot to care. He pulls them off my legs, and I'm now completely naked while he's completely dressed. I reach for his shirt, but he stops me. "You. This is about you." He cups my cheek. "I've been good, but I won't be able to stop myself if you touch me. I'll want all of you."

"Is that a bad thing?" Right now I want all of him too.

He smirks. "Not tonight, baby." Wyatt kisses me. "Tonight, I want to make you come." As he says the last word, his finger moves against my clit. "I want to watch the heat in your eyes." My lips part, and suddenly it's really hard to breathe. "It's up to you, baby. Do I use my finger or my mouth?"

Oh. Fucking. Hell.

"I want your mouth on mine," I say quickly. I want to be able to kiss him. I love the way he kisses. It's commanding and yet yielding at the same time. He takes as much as he gives. I could kiss him all day and be content in life.

As soon as the words are out of my mouth, he slips in a finger. "Wyatt," I groan as my head falls back. His lips close around my nipple as he fingers me, his thumb pressing around my clit, making small circles. I climb toward my orgasm so fast it's maddening, but he's hitting every spot, completely unrelenting.

Wyatt continues to work me hard. "You're so hot, baby. Do you want me to taste you?" he questions, allowing me to decide. "Or I can just do this?" He takes the icing that is in the bowl and spreads it across my chest.

I watch as he licks it from me, moaning as he moves his face, lapping up every bit of the icing. His fingers pump harder and it becomes too much. The cold from the table, the sound of his pleasure, the way his finger curls, the heat of his tongue, and the smell of sweetness mixed with Wyatt.

My senses are overloaded.

I let go and allow the pleasure to be all I focus on.

"You taste even sweeter now." His tongue slides against my skin. "I could do this all night. Feel your body against mine, listen to the noises you make, smell how fucking hot I make you. You're going to bring me to my knees, baby."

"Yes." My eyes slam shut.

"You like that?" He fills me deep. "You want more?"

"Yes!" I pant.

I want it all. I want him. I want to lose myself with him, but he's holding back.

Wyatt pumps his fingers in and out as he latches on to my breast. He sucks and bites, causing my pleasure to spike higher.

"I'm gonna come!" I yell as he rubs faster against my clit.

"Let it go, Angie. Let me make you feel good."

"Wyatt!" I cry as my orgasm rakes through me. His mouth is on mine, swallowing my sounds. I kiss him with everything I am.

His fingers draw out the last of my orgasm, our kiss turning lazy and slow.

My arms are wrapped around his neck, and we both keep our foreheads against each other. "That was . . ."

He chuckles. "Long overdue?" I smile as he kisses me again. "We should clean up. We need to get some sleep, and you should get dressed before I attempt round two."

I raise my brow, thinking maybe that wouldn't be a bad thing.

Wyatt shakes his head. "Don't worry, Angel. I plan to do that again real soon. As soon as you realize how much you really want me."

Then he does the sexiest thing I've ever seen. He dips his finger in the bowl of icing, and licks it clean. "Mmm." He grins. "Angie and icing. I found my new favorite flavor."

Yeah. I might have just come again.

He helps dress me, which is sweet and somewhat disappointing. I notice the large bulge in his pants and feel bad. "I can help you with that," I offer.

Wyatt looks down, and then his face grows serious. "When we go there again, it's going to be because you have feelings above the fact that we have amazing sex. It's going to be about you and me, and what we're buildin' here. I want you." He kisses me. "I want you more than anything. But not when you're holding back, and not when you're feelin' guilty because I gave you the best orgasm of your life."

"Umm," I laugh. "Little full of yourself?"

"You'll be full of me soon."

"Oh, Jesus."

"You can call me Wyatt."

I bust out laughing. "You need Jesus."

He kisses my nose and pats my ass. "Maybe so, but *we* need to get to work."

We both look around at the spilled batter, no longer usable icing, and mess. "I really hope at least some of this is edible."

"You own a bakery, Ang. I'm sure it's great."

Wyatt walks over to me and hands me a cupcake. "Try it."

"Why don't you try it first?" I bat my eyes.

"Now, that wouldn't be very gentlemanly of me." Wyatt lets his deep Southern drawl seep through. I have to say how much I really love it. It's sexy and so different. Kind of like how most American women would drop their panties for a British or Australian accent. There's something about it that makes me get all stupid.

Wyatt extends the cupcake toward me again.

I have no clue if this is going to be good. I figure he should really take one for the team. Then I glance at his still prominent erection and realize he already has. It's really the least I can do.

I take a bite. "Holy crap!" I exclaim. "This is freaking good! It's actually good!"

"Of course it is."

"No." I push away. "I suck. I'm not the baker by any means. I know it's kind of insane since I own a bakery, but I've always let Presley or the bakers do it. But this . . . this is really good, Wyatt!"

My entire day is made. I did this. I created our signature cupcake and didn't screw up. I don't know if the rest of them are bad, but this one is good so I'm going to pretend they all taste the same.

I start to dance around a little, and he captures me in his arms, hoisting me against his chest. "I'm proud of you. You did something really nice for my mama's friend."

My hands hook around his neck as he holds me a few inches off the floor. "I'm happy to do it. She's so nice, even if she did play me." I throw that last bit in. "I had fun with you tonight."

"I did, too." My heart races as he looks at my lips.

Working with him tonight melted another layer in my anti-Wyatt walls. Well, that and the sexy time. Maybe we really do have something.

Maybe he's so much more.

chapter
TEN

"I DON'T WANT TO GET up." I roll over as Wyatt nudges me.

"Too bad."

Doesn't he realize that I'm exhausted? "Pregnant. Need sleep."

"Either you get up on your own or I'm tossing you in the shower with your clothes on." He wouldn't dare. "Or I can strip you down if you'd prefer."

My eyes pop open so I can glare at him. "I hate you."

He smirks. "I think you like me. A lot more than you care to admit."

I give him more of an evil look, but he slaps the bed and hops up. "How are you so chipper this early?"

Wyatt looks at me as if I said something weird. "Angie, I get up for work before the sun rises every day. This is sleeping in for me."

I glance over at the clock and gasp. "It's freaking five o'clock in the morning?" I yell. "Are you kidding me? When does this festival start?"

"I thought you owned a bakery?"

"I do."

"Well, what time do you go in? Don't you have baker's hours?"

I flop back and put the pillow over my head. "I don't. The bakers do," I mumble into fabric and feathers.

He laughs and pulls the pillow away. "Well, baby. You're the baker today."

Yesterday, I thought the coup to get me to do this was cute and funny. Today in the darkness of the morning, I no longer find it entertaining. Now, I want to hurt someone. But I can suck it up for today. Plus, the festival looked like a lot of fun. I love flea markets and fairs. There's always something to repurpose or a unique craft to find. I can only imagine the types of homemade items that will be there today.

"Coffee first," I say as I swing my legs off the bed.

I was extremely excited to learn that I was allowed to have one cup of coffee a day. I explained to the doctor that I would do my best to limit it. I went from drinking four cups a day to one. I had really bad headaches at first, but they're definitely more manageable now.

"You get in the shower, and then we'll get food and coffee."

I complain, but do as he says.

The shower feels great, and we were too exhausted to care about how dirty we were last night. I have batter under my nails, and the sheets will definitely need to be washed. Lord only knows how much flour Wyatt still had on him when we fell into bed.

Once all the cupcakes were done and we'd made a new batch of icing, we had to clean the shop. I have to say that there was nothing sexier than watching Wyatt on the floor scrubbing the mess we made. He was so sweet, telling me to get off my feet and rest. I tried to fight him, but he made a face that was too cute to disobey. I sat there, ate another cupcake, and discovered it wasn't just the first one that tasted good. Red velvet with cream cheese frosting is my favorite, and the only recipe I remember by heart. Luckily, Mrs. Kannan had planned to make something similar, so she had all the ingredients already.

I get out of the shower and throw on a pair of loose shorts and a tank top. It's going to be hot outside today, and I want to be comfortable. Plus, Wyatt is in a pair of basketball shorts and a plain white shirt, so I doubt I have to dress up.

"Ready?" I say as I grab my sneakers.

"Yup." He walks over, hands me a travel mug, and kisses my forehead. "What was that for?" I ask.

"This means a lot to me. I'm glad you helped out a very sick old lady in need."

I laugh. "You mean faking sick."

He tilts his head to the side. "She'll expect that you believe her. One things those women know how to do is scheme. So, for your benefit, you better play along."

"Noted."

I go to take a sip, needing the caffeine, and I'm shocked. "Wyatt!" I yell, pulling a larger amount from the cup. "This is a Caramel Macchiato!"

Oh my God. He made me my favorite drink. I've been searching through Pinterest to find a good copycat since Presley told me it was completely irrational to drive a few towns over for a drink. How did he find one before I did? Do I care? Nope.

"Pres said that was what you liked. I hope it tastes like you wanted it. Like home."

I close the top of my heaven in a cup and rush toward him. My arms fly around his middle, and he lets out a short laugh before hugging me closer. "Thank you," I say with sincerity. "Thank you for doing this. It's so sweet, and it does taste like home."

It tastes better than that because he made it for me. It's the little things that he does without even knowing it. How he texts me during the day, worries about my feet, touches my belly, and is just . . . perfect. I'm used to men who have to go overboard to prove they're so great. But Wyatt doesn't do that. He's just him. God, I'm in trouble.

We arrive at the bakery, and already the town is alive. Everyone is setting up their tables, running around, and chatting with each other.

"Hey!" Presley comes over with Zach.

"Hey, guys." I smile and give them each a hug.

Presley looks at the cupcake display with a smile. "You ready for today?"

"We are," Wyatt says as he carries another tray of cupcakes down.

"Well, if it isn't, Betty Crocker, or are you Duncan Hines?" Zach takes a crack at Wyatt.

"Like you should talk," Wyatt scoffs. "I've seen you do far more embarrassing shit than make some cupcakes for Presley."

Zach rolls his eyes. "Looks like I'm not the only whipped one here anymore."

"You two will never change," Presley scolds. "You're like infants."

They remind me of what my brothers used to be like before Josh became a dick.

Wyatt throws his arm around me. "It's fine, Pres. I'm used to him crying like a little girl. He's mad because Trent took all his money in poker the other night."

Her face falls. "You didn't tell me you were playin' poker with Trent. You said you had to help your brothers."

Zach flips Wyatt off. "Thanks, asshole." He turns to Presley. "I did help my brothers, darlin'. I helped them take my money."

"They always take your money! It's why you said you weren't going to play anymore."

Oh, shit. He's in trouble. I've seen Presley when she gets like this. I lean against Wyatt with a grin. This is going to be comedic gold.

"Don't be too hard on him, Pres," Wyatt tries to interject. "He did win a hand or two. Plus, Trent did call us over to move some stuff for Mama. It wasn't until after we were done that he sucked both of us into a game. You know us Henningtons can't resist the urge to compete."

"Yeah, Pres." Zach agrees. "It was supposed to be in fun."

She glares at Wyatt and then huffs. "You'll pay in other ways, Cowboy. Many other ways."

"I look forward to it."

"I'm going to be sick," I say while shaking my head.

Presley looks at me, realizes I'm only being metaphorical, and she laughs. "We better be gettin' back to our booth before they send out a search party."

"Have fun!" I say with mock enthusiasm.

Wyatt and I go back to setting up the booth the best we can. I have no idea how Mrs. Kannan typically runs things, so I'm winging it. Of course, Wyatt can't remember either, so he does whatever I ask. It's a flawed system, but it's working for now.

About an hour later, the streets are packed. People come from all over. Everyone is courteous, everyone is nice, and it's . . . surreal. Definitely nothing like back home.

We move around the tent, selling cupcakes as Wyatt flirts with the women, who then buy more cupcakes. It's hilarious to watch them fawn over him, and I have to admit that he's adorable.

"Angie! You're a lifesaver!" Mrs. Kannan rushes over, clearly not under the weather.

"Mrs. Kannan, you look like you're well."

She laughs. "Must've been one of those twelve-hour bugs or something. Funny how quick it cleared up with a little bit of rest.

You really saved the day, dear."

I shake my head with a smile. "I'm happy to help."

"Why don't you let me take over? I'm sure you're just exhausted. I remember all too well when I was pregnant. I could sleep for days!"

"I don't mind." I really don't. It's been really fun. I've met pretty much every member of Bell Buckle and the surrounding towns. They all talk about how excited they are to meet me and throw in a good word for Wyatt.

"I insist." She pushes both mine and Wyatt's backs. "Go on now. You know, Wyatt? Your mama was looking for some help at her booth. I think Trent has had enough."

Wyatt's eyes bug out. "I doubt she would want me there."

"You know?" She taps her lip. "I remember now, she told me that you were *required* down there."

I laugh. Payback. "Wyatt." I touch his arm. "You wouldn't want to not help out your mother when she needs you. It wouldn't be very Southern of you, would it?"

He runs his tongue across his teeth and makes a *tsk* sound. "You think so, huh?"

I shrug. "What would Martha Stewart do?"

"All right, Big City. Let's go help Mama since you're in a giving mood."

We walk through the crowds, and I make him stop every few stands to check out some of the things for sale. There's one booth off to the right that has horseshoes dangling from the front. They have different plaques with names painted on them, a few sewn projects, but I love the horseshoes more than anything. They're all engraved with whatever you want on them. I touch the cool metal over the name engraved on the bottom of the display one. "Can we get one?" I ask Wyatt.

He looks perplexed. "Of course, but for what?"

"Well, I was thinking at the bottom it can say: 'Hennington'.

Then on the side here," I point to the left, "we can put the date of conception, and on the other side, we can have it updated to the baby's birthday?"

The smile he gives me lights up the sky. After spending the last twenty-four hours with him, I want to do something special. He baked cupcakes, gave me a stellar orgasm, made me coffee, and so many other things in a small bit of time. It may be insignificant to some, but to me, it means everything. No one ever thinks of me like that. I've never had a man give up his time or go out of his way just because.

Wyatt does that, though, and he does it without selfish intentions. He gives the parts of himself willingly because he has so much more to offer. He doesn't have to tuck pieces of his heart away like I do. He just is.

"I think it's a great idea. We can hang it over the door of the nursery once we get that together" His lips press against my cheek. "I love it."

"I'm glad it makes you happy."

He gazes at me before looking away. "You being here makes me happy."

"I had a really great time last night. It was fun."

"Me too." He wiggles his eyebrows.

"Not that!" I clarify.

Wyatt chuckles. "I know, baby. I had a really good time with you, too. It was fun working beside you."

"Good. You were a lot of help. I couldn't have done it without you."

I don't remember if I told him that, but he deserves to know it.

We place the order, and we're told they'll mail it to us in a few days.

I wave to Presley and Zach as we pass the Townsend's booth. She mouths: *help me.* I shake my head and keep moving as we enter where more fair games are.

There's a little pool with fishing rods to get the frogs and a stand with jugs you have to throw the ball to knock down. "I hate that game," I say as we pass it.

"Me too." Wyatt laughs. "My stupid brother would always pick it."

"Why the hell would you go against the star baseball player in a throwing game?" I ask. Seems a little stupid to me.

"We would rock, paper, scissors for who could choose. Zach always won, so Trent and I were destined to lose." Wyatt explains.

Presley warned me about the three of them. She explained that as much as they bicker, they're unbelievably close. They take the meaning of brothers very serious. If one calls, they all go. She said it's the way they've always been, and that by dating Wyatt, there's a very clear message that they'll have to deal with all the Henningtons if anyone fucks with me. It sounded like the Southern version of the mafia.

"Wyatt! Angie!" Macie yells with her arms open "There you are!"

"Sorry, Mama."

"Don't be sorry. Trent is tired, and at this point we're starting to lose money." She laughs. "I'm going to have to start paying people to kiss him."

Kiss? I look around, and spot Trent sitting in a booth with lips all over it and a sign that reads: Kisses for a Dollar.

Umm. I'm not really sure how I feel about this.

I grab his arm. "You didn't tell me it was a kissing booth." My voice is low, and I'm sure he hears the undercurrent of irritation.

"Awww, you're jealous."

"I am not."

I don't get jealous. It's not like we're married or even really dating. I mean, we are, but that's not the point. The point is, I don't get jealous. I've never been like that, and I'm not going to start now. I'm just not looking forward to watching girls kiss him when I'm not even supposed to be kissing him. That's all. I'm also a hormonally imbalanced freak with a baby sucking up all my common sense.

"Then why do you care what kind of booth it is?" His brow raises. "I mean, wasn't it *you* who said I should help my mama?"

I grit my teeth. I did say that. "I didn't know it meant you'd be kissing other girls."

He runs the back of his fingers across my cheek. "Does it help if I say I'll be pretending they're all you?"

"No!"

"You two okay?" Macie asks with a glint in her eyes.

Oh, these ladies are good. They've managed to orchestrate all this, and they did it with precision. I would bow to her if I weren't too busy freaking out over whatever is going on in my heart. I know I have to play this cool.

"We're fine, Mrs. Hennington." I smile.

"Good. Wyatt, please go relieve your brother. Angie and I will hang here and girl talk."

"Yes, Mama."

I watch him walk off while I burn holes in the back of his head. I can do this. It's fine. I'll prove to myself after the first kiss that I'm not jealous. Wyatt and I might like each other, and I may think he's all sorts of great, but we're going to part ways at some point. This is just practice for the future.

Macie tries to make idle chitchat with me, but I keep missing what she says. Each time I look over toward the booth, she calls my name. So far it's been two minutes and forty-three seconds, and no one has bought a kiss yet.

"I'm sorry. I'm exhausted."

She nods. "I'm sure. It's hard tryin' to pay attention to me and wait and see who he has to kiss."

"I'm not—" I start to say, but she puts her hand up.

"I give you a lot of credit. If it were Rhett, I would've marched his hide right out of this place. There would be no way he was kissin' anyone else but me. I know you and Wyatt aren't really serious, right? I know you're biding your time and all."

"I don't know what we are," I admit. "I also know you and Mrs. Kannan knew exactly what would happen." My tone is soft and bordering on admiration.

Macie laughs and grabs my hands. "Don't be upset. Sometimes us old ladies need to push you young people a little. I happen to know working beside a man can be very eye opening. I also know—" her eyes shoot to something over my shoulder and widen a bit.

I follow her gaze, and my stomach drops. There's a throng of girls rushing toward the booth, and the front runner is none other than Charlotte.

No, no, no.

His lips are *not* touching hers. Over my dead fucking body.

My feet are on the ground and moving before I realize what's happening. We have rules. Rules that included no other people. Rules that he agreed on. I'm not kissing anyone else while I'm here, neither should he, especially not her. I'm perfectly within my rights to fight this. That's the point I plan to drive home.

"Angie," Macie calls out when I'm halfway to the booth.

I don't respond.

I'm on a mission.

I dig in my back pocket for the cash I put in there and head straight to the front of the line, moving Charlotte out of my way. My hand slams down on the counter as his brown eyes stare into mine. "Here's two hundred dollars." I thrust the cash toward him. "You're not kissing anyone but me."

Wyatt doesn't waste a second. He's on his feet, his hands

grip my face, and he kisses me in front of everyone.

There are catcalls and hollers from various people. His lips are planted on mine, and I don't care that he's staking his claim. I don't care if last night was supposed to be nothing. Right here, he's mine.

Wyatt Hennington's lips are not touching another woman's lips while I'm around.

I turn around and see his mother, Mrs. Kannan, Mrs. Townsend, and Mrs. Rooney all standing there with huge grins and clasped hands. I'm surprised they're not doing some sort of happy dance.

"I knew you liked me, Big City."

I roll my eyes and release a deep breath. "Come on, Rhinestone Cowboy. I bought you for the day."

"You bought me for much longer than that."

chapter
ELEVEN

"TWO DAYS IN A ROW you've woken me before the sun came up." I grumble as I throw on some clothes. I have no idea where he's taking me. He instructed me last night that we were going out for the day. Apparently, when I paid the money for the kissing booth, I got the day after too.

"Come on, darlin'. We're going to be late."

"Late for what?"

"Make sure you use the bathroom!" he calls out.

"Why won't we have a bathroom?"

Wyatt refuses to say anything other than we're going to spend the day together.

I grab my sweatshirt, since I have no idea if it'll be freezing at this crazy time in the morning, throw on my sneakers, and make a note to buy a pair of cute cowboy boots. Since I'm here, I might as well. Plus, they're kind of practical and stylish. Grace has a pair with teal on the side, I definitely need to find those.

"You ready?" he asks, holding the door open.

"Not sure why we have to be up and out of the house when I can still see the moon. I don't know many stores that are open this early," I push. I'm dying to know what he has planned.

"The fish bite the best in the morning." He slaps my ass as he closes the door.

"Fish?" I choke. "Please tell me you're kidding."

Wyatt throws a box in the back of some vehicle now parked outside the house. "Hop in."

It's a mix of a truck with no roof and smaller tires, a golf cart, and some sort of wagon. There's dirt and mud all along the side, which makes me think the boys use it for more outdoorsy stuff, which I definitely don't do.

"Angie." Wyatt waves his hand. "Get in the Gator."

"Wouldn't you rather go see a movie? Or maybe have a day at the spa? Do you have a spa close?" I ask with hope.

He laughs. "Do I look like I go to the spa? Get in. It'll be fun and relaxing, I promise."

I don't like the outdoors so much. But I promised myself I would step outside the box, and Wyatt did bake cupcakes, which was clearly not his thing. When in Rome.

I climb in and search for a seat belt, but there is none. "I can't believe I let you talk me into this. How am I supposed to not fall out?"

"You hold on," he says as if it makes perfect sense.

There's a bar in front of my seat that I guess is what I hold on to? "This is nuts. Is this safe?" It doesn't seem very safe.

"You're safe with me. Always." Wyatt has a huge grin on his face as he starts the Gator. "Don't worry, baby. I'll make you country yet."

"I doubt that."

"We'll see." He heads down the road, and I hold on to the bar for dear life. My hair whips around my face, and I silently curse the fact that I forgot a hair tie. The trail is bumpy, and I feel slightly motion sick. Thankfully, we reach the lake fairly quickly.

Wyatt and I exit the vehicle, and he starts getting the supplies out of the back. He has two blankets, some fishing poles, a tackle box, and what looks like a basket of food. When I offer to carry something, he gives me a sideways look and a smirk.

It's gorgeous out here. There's a lot of trees around it, and beautiful views. Everything looks untouched by man, it's so serene.

"This is really gorgeous, is this the same lake Presley and Zach are on?" I ask, scanning the tree line again for their house.

"No. They're over on the east lake."

I stop and look at him, and I'm sure I look silly with my mouth hanging open and my hair a wind-blown mess. "Wait. How many lakes do you guys have?"

"Five, but we only stock this one so that we can fish when we want. I love fishing at the river, but this is much calmer, and I didn't think you wanted to do fly fishing."

Yeah. No. "I don't know the difference really, but I'm going to assume you're correct."

He laughs. "I'll grab the canoe, you stay put."

I'm sorry, did he say "canoe"? "I can't go in a canoe."

"Well, it's actually a Jon boat. And it's going to be awful hard to fish if you don't get in."

"Can't we just stay on the shore? That way if a bear or some other hungry animal shows up, we can get to the truck thing?" His eyes gleam with humor. It seems I'm entertaining him. I slap his chest. "I'm serious!"

"I bet you are, baby." Wyatt kisses my temple. "I never picked you for being a chicken shit. I figured a tough city girl like you could handle bein' out on a boat. But," he puts his palms out, "I guess you're not up for the challenge."

Well played, my friend. He knows damn well what he did. I have two choices. I can steal the Gator, as he calls it, or I can go out there and show him I'm not a wuss. I've never been fishing. I've never even contemplated wanting to do this.

There's also no way I can back down.

"Fine." I surrender. "Go get the boat."

Wyatt steps forward, grips my elbows and pulls me against

him. "I'll reward you, I promise."

I lean in, letting my lips graze against his. "I plan to make you pay."

"I have no doubt about that."

He lets me go and gets busy. I never realized how intensive fishing is. He's got all kinds of gadgets and different boxes. I'm praying the Jon boat or whatever it's called is bigger than what I'm imagining, because I don't know where all this crap will go.

Wyatt pulls a silver flat boat over. It has two benches on the inside and two oars. I cannot believe I'm entertaining this.

At. All.

He puts the boat half in and waves me over. "Hop in. I'll push us off."

I start to freak out a little. Not because I can't swim, but because I don't have any spare clothes or a bathroom close by. Does he expect me to handle fish? My stomach rolls at the thought, but I refuse to look like a baby, so I get in the boat.

Wyatt gets us out into the water without issue. It's clear he knows what he's doing. Maybe I'll be okay.

"All right," he says, breaking the silence. "Move over on this side, and I'll get us set up."

"Move?" I ask.

"Yes." He nods. "Come sit over here. I'm going to put the blankets out and move this bench so we can sit on the bottom."

"Yeah, it's the moving part that I'm not really all that keen on."

If we move . . . we rock the boat. I will freak out.

"Here," he says, holding his hand out. "Trust me." I close my eyes and count to three. I can do this. My hand touches his, and he slowly helps me over. "See, you did just fine."

I'm so out of my element.

"We're doing a spa next time."

"Whatever you say, baby."

Wyatt arranges the bottom of the boat with blankets, creating a bed-like spot for us. He helps me back down and curls up with me. His arm is around my back, and my head rests on his chest. I close my eyes and listen to the sound of his heart. "You know we could've cuddled at home in bed," I joke.

"But this is more intimate." He kisses the top of my head.

He's right. It is. Even with the chill in the air, I could fall asleep.

There are no sounds other than a few crickets and the faint sound of water lapping against the side of the boat. The only light is from the rising sun, and I know that if I opened my eyes to look, I would still be able to see a few stars. Normally the silence would freak me out, but it's exactly like it should be here. The world moves around us, but right here, it's only Wyatt and me. This is the most tranquil I've ever felt.

I doze off, so comfortable in his arms. The sun is finally overhead, and it wakes me. I lift my head to find him looking at me with a grin. "You feel better?" he asks.

"I feel good."

His eyes grow serious as he stares at me. "I want to always make you feel good. You and that baby are my world, Angie. I know you're scared. I see it, but little by little, I want to help show you that you have nothing to be afraid of."

I'm not afraid, I'm freaking petrified. I don't know how to be the girl he wants. I don't fish or hunt. I don't do dirt or animals. I'm the girl who paints her nails and shops like a pro. This isn't me, and I don't know how long he'll find that cute.

"I think you underestimate how different we are." I rest my chin on my hand.

"Different is sometimes better."

"True." I sigh. "It also can mean we're not right for each other."

Wyatt looks at the sky, rubs his hand on my back, and then

moves my face closer to his. "I think the fact that we can lie in this boat, driftin' on the water together, and not need to fill the silence is all the right we need. You're not like any woman I've ever known. I think, considering all the women I've been with, the fact that I've never wanted more with anyone but you says something. You're right; you're different. You're mine because I want you to be."

I smirk. "So I'm yours?"

His grin grows playful. "You will be again."

"Does that mean that you're mine?"

"I've never been anyone else's."

I think about that. Neither of us have taken the steps to be with anyone on a serious note. We've both kept ourselves without strings. I think that means something. But Wyatt has known love. It may not have been reciprocated, but he's felt it. I haven't.

Instead of pushing and possibly ruining a tender moment, I just nod.

"Enough bein' lazy. Fish need to eat, and we need lunch."

"Umm." I sit up a bit straighter. "I thought you were kidding. The only way I like my fish is rolled around some rice."

Wyatt laughs. "You really have a love for food."

"Shut up. I'm serious! I'm not really a fish person."

"Have you ever fished before?"

"No." I shake my head.

"Well," Wyatt chuckles, "how do you know you don't like it? Plus, if you don't catch anything, you're going to be hungry," he says as he grabs the poles. "I only brought stuff for a good fish fry."

My stomach churns at the thought. I'm not a seafood person, especially not if it's a fish we're going to have to handle. I shudder. "That spa better have a salon attached."

He ignores me and hands me the rod. "The line is ready, bait the hook."

I have no idea what the hell he said. "Can you talk city to me?"

"You gotta put the food on the hook." He hands me the tub full of worms.

I shake my head. "No, no, no. Not happening."

"It's a worm. It doesn't bite."

He opens the top, and I start to gag. Oh, I can't. I put my head over the side of the boat in case this baby helps me a little.

"Hey." He touches my back. "I'll do it, baby. Don't get sick." Wyatt runs his hand up and down as I try to focus on anything but hurling. Because *that* won't be embarrassing at all.

I take a deep breath through my nose and push it out of my mouth.

"Better?" he asks as I sit up.

"I'm okay."

The nausea fades, but I know better then to watch what Wyatt is doing. So. Gross.

Wyatt tosses the line over the edge of the boat and then hands me the rod. "Just hold it out there, and if it gets a tug, start reeling it in."

"Sounds easy enough."

No one tells you that fishing is literally the most boring thing. We sit like this for five minutes, and I'm ready to row my butt to shore. After another ten minutes pass with Wyatt sitting there not doing anything and not talking, I can't stop myself. "So?" I ask, looking at nothing. "What do we do now?"

"We wait."

"For the fish?"

"That's the goal."

Wyatt looks content. I try to follow his lead, but I'm no longer tired thanks to our nap, and I'm going out of my skull. There's nothing to watch. No people doing weird things that I can observe. The trees move. That's about it.

"Wyatt, what happens if no fish . . . get snagged?"

"You mean, bite?"

"Sure." I huff. "Bite. Eat. Hook. Whatever the right word is. What happens then?"

He lies back on the blanket and covers his face with his hat. "Then we wait until one does."

"*All day?*"

"All day, Big City."

I can do this. This is country life according to him. People, who I don't know or understand, enjoy this. I guess it would be relaxing if I could actually relax, so I try. I have to remind myself that he made an effort to bake with me, so I can do the same with fishing.

My leg starts to bounce as I wait for a fish to . . . bite. They should be hungry, right? I don't know what stocking a lake entails, but I'd assume that only the Hennington's come here. I'm also safe to assume that they don't come every day because they work. If that's the case, they should want to eat.

"Here fishy, fishy, fishy," I call quietly.

"Angie?" Wyatt's smirk is visible from under his hat. "What the hell are you doing?"

"I'm calling the fish! Maybe they come like a cat?"

Wyatt bursts out laughing.

I remember the old *Sesame Street* episode that my brother loved. It was Bert and Ernie in the boat. Ernie, of course being the sensible one (that's me in this situation), knew he could get the fish to come into the boat. But Bert (Wyatt) thought he was nuts. But the fish jumped up. It was brilliant.

"Laugh away, babe. I'm telling you . . . it'll work."

He sits up, unable to even attempt to control his hyena-style laughter. "I've been fishin' since I was little, and I have never seen anyone call for a fish."

"It worked for Ernie!" I defend.

"Ernie?"

"Yeah!" I say as if it should be obvious. "From *Sesame Street*. He was always the smarter of the two."

Wyatt's jaw drops as his shoulders bounce. "I've gotta see this." He leans back and crosses his arms over his chest.

"Fine." I perk up and lean over the side of the boat again. "Here fishy, fishy, fishy," I say it again, reenacting the scene as I remember it. He sits there, trying to hold it in. I slap his leg. "Stop! Don't laugh at me," I complain playfully. I look at the line that still doesn't move. "The fish are sleeping. That's all. You came out here too early. They're late risers."

His warm, rich laughter filters the air. "You're probably right."

"I know I am. Fish would love me if they knew me."

Wyatt shifts forward on his knees. His hands cage me in. Slowly he leans forward, careful not to jostle the boat. "You," he says, his eyes melting into a hooded softness, "are the single most beautiful thing in this world. The fish would be lucky to get hooked on your line."

Everything inside me clenches. My breathing becomes slightly faster as his lips inch closer. "Me?" Wyatt nods. "Are you hooked on my line?"

"Yes," he confirms. "You're out here on my boat, on my land, and in my life, makin' me see things for the first time. I've never felt like this before. I've never wanted to be something so much, and yet hope it eludes me a little more."

My hand touches his cheek. "You want me to keep fighting this?"

His eyes close as he rubs his face in my palm. "I love watching your walls crumble. I love watching your reasons diminish. I'm really going to enjoy it when you finally realize just how much you want me." His voice drops, and he looks at me again, serious this time. "Because make no mistake—you'll want me.

I'm makin' damn sure of it."

I don't doubt him for a single second.

I shift in my seat a little bit and try to slow my racing heart. "I think we should make a bet."

He grins. "Name the terms."

"If I catch the first fish, you have to bring the fish home and cook it with your brothers on a different day so I don't have to eat it." He nods. "And if you catch it, I'll do this fish fry thing you speak of."

Wyatt puts his hand out. "Deal."

We shake, and then I start praying to the fish Gods, if there are any, to please let me win. First, it would be funny to watch him lose to a city girl. Second, I really don't like fish. They have those beady eyes and some have teeth . . . no thank you. I would much rather stick with an animal I don't have to look at before I eat it.

I'm weird, but I can't do it.

After another hour of trying to guess what shape the clouds are, which sucks after three minutes, Wyatt closes his eyes. I do spot a penis-shaped cloud, but that's only slightly amusing.

I'm too bored to nap again. I truly have no idea how people find fishing fun. My fish calling doesn't work, and gazing at the horizon is about as fun as trying to count leaves, which I got to one thousand four hundred and twenty-two before I quit.

"I'm bored," I mutter.

"Let yourself relax, baby."

Fat chance of that. "This is me relaxed."

He opens one eye and smirks. "You could always try to call for the fish again."

"Shut up."

Wyatt laughs. "You never know, it could work."

"Don't make me throw you off the boat," I retort.

"You could try." Wyatt takes my hand, pulling me on top of

him. "Or you could kiss me again."

My heart races as I look into his eyes. Now that would be fun. My lips slowly make their way to his, but I freeze when I hear this cranking sound.

Both our eyes snap up, and I see the fishing pole moving and the reel spinning. A fish! I don't know whose line it is, but someone has a fish.

Then it dawns on me it could be his line.

Shit.

"Wyatt!" I slap his chest. "Something is hooked!" I climb on to my knees and go to grab the rod, but I have no idea what to do. It keeps spinning and making that noise. I look over at him with a mix of fear and excitement. "Aren't you going to help?"

Finally, he gets up and puts his hand on the spinning wheel thing, stopping it. "Here, reel him in slow."

Wyatt shifts around so his front is against my back. His hand covers mine as he guides me through catching what I'm praying is not dinner. His warm breath heats my neck, and I melt a little into him. "Like this?" I ask.

He nudges his nose in the crook of my neck. "Mmm hmm."

His lips press against my skin, and I have to focus on not throwing the damn rod off the side of the boat.

"Just keep going?" I ask with a double meaning.

He stops kissing me when he feels something that I clearly didn't notice. "Stop for a second." I do, and the line jerks again. "Okay, pull him in nice and slow."

We do and the reel gets harder and harder to turn. Wyatt starts to pull the rod with his arms wrapped around me.

The fish finally comes out of the water, and I gasp. "Ahh! Hi, fishy!" Wyatt brings him over in the boat. "Put it back!" I yell as the fish flops by our feet and all the blood drains from my face.

"Put it back?" Wyatt asks like I'm crazy.

"Yes!" I start gagging a little again. "I'm going to puke!"

He moves around and does something, but I can't watch. Just seeing it was enough to make my stomach roll. I lean my head back over the side of the boat. I may not have any kind of morning sickness, but clearly I can't handle the idea of fish.

I hear a splash in the water, and I look over. The fish is gone. Thank God. I right myself as Wyatt moves back over to me.

"Clearly fishing isn't your thing," he says while wrapping his arms around my chest.

"I tried."

He kisses the side of my head. "You did. And that was your line."

"It was?" I perk up a little.

Wyatt moves his lips to my shoulders. "I think you've caught more than one fish today."

"Yeah?" I ask, moving my head so we're now face to face. "There were two on that line?" I swear I only saw one.

"No, baby. I think you hooked something else."

Okay, fishing may suck, but fishing with Wyatt is pretty kick ass. And I don't think I'm the only one who didn't catch something.

chapter TWELVE

"AND THEN WHAT?" PRESLEY PRACTICALLY bounces in her seat as I relay what happened the other night at the bakery. "Did you guys . . ." She puts the cup of coffee to her lips, and her eyes bug out.

"No. We didn't." I laugh.

Sometimes I forget how innocent Presley has always been. While I was screaming at parties, dancing on bars, and doing a lot of very unladylike things in bathrooms, Presley was studying. She was never adventurous, but she balanced me. I pulled her out of her small-town world, and she made sure I didn't end up knocked up.

Lot of good that did.

"Because you guys might, what? Get pregnant?" She scoffs, clearly disappointed that we didn't.

"No, my dear friend." I roll my eyes. "It wasn't about that. It was about us and pushing a little more."

"I'm sure it was."

I think about how great he was. I always knew he was a good guy. Presley always spoke about him in the highest regard. Plus, I've seen him with the boys. Men don't spend time with other people's kids if they're douchebags. I didn't know he was this fantastic.

"This is going to sound ridiculous, but . . ." I can't even believe I'm going to ask this. "Why the hell did you not date him?"

Pres snorts and purses her lips. "Wyatt and I have known each other since birth. I don't remember a time in my childhood without him. But even back then, Zach was all I saw. Wyatt was my best friend, but I never looked at him like that. Besides, he didn't show interest in me until his brother and I were together." She laughs. "It was like the kid who didn't get the shiny toy. That was when Wyatt suddenly liked me or whatever. But honestly, I could never see him that way. His friendship meant way too much to me. It's not because there was anything wrong with him. I would've been lucky to love Wyatt. He's the most selfless person I know."

She makes sense. I've never had a man I loved like that or a friend I wouldn't risk screwing. "I understand. I think."

"Let me put it this way." Presley shifts in her seat. "If there were no Zachary, I would've married Wyatt before he could've changed his mind. He's the guy you marry, Ang. He's the guy you build your whole life around. He's the guy you move for."

Her eyes grow serious at the last sentence. I know she's saying that I would be an idiot to walk away from him. She won't say that, though. She knows I need to come to this on my own terms and I can't be forced or feel as if there's no other choice. There's always a choice. I just hope I don't fuck it up.

"I hear you, Pres. I hear what you're saying."

So," she draws out the word. "Tell me where you're going on your date with Wyatt next week."

I wish I knew. He won't say a word. The man likes his surprises.

"No clue."

"Typical, Wyatt. He probably hasn't figure it out yet so he can't tell you." Presley has warned me that where Zach is the romantic type, Wyatt is not. He's never had to be. At the same time, I'm not the romance type of girl. I don't need to be wooed. I need to know I'm not wasting my damn time. "But then again, I figure this date is going to be different. You better throw your stupid rule book out." Pres warns me.

"I'm pretty sure we'll break every damn rule I came here with. Multiple times."

She laughs. "Oh, thank God. Did you really think you guys wouldn't hit it off?"

"I didn't want to think about it. I also didn't want anyone to have any outside input."

Presley's eyes study mine, and I remember how much she knows about me. Presley heard me cry many nights when my mother would let me know how much of a disappointment I was. She watched me fall apart the night she told me that having me was a mistake and probably expedited her becoming sick. My mother has blamed me in some way for every horrible part of her life. I don't know why or what I did other than try to be a good daughter, but she's let me know it wasn't appreciated.

She also knows my mother is capable of many shitty things. Presley was on the receiving end of it once, and my brother put a stop to it. On Presley's wedding day my mother made one hell of a scene about where her seat was placed. She called Presley names, threw a king-size fit, and Todd practically threw her out. My father smoothed it over, but it ended with me trying to fix Presley's makeup after she burst into tears.

"You know that her opinion doesn't matter, right?"

And there you have it. She knows exactly what I worry about. "I do."

"Do you?"

"Yes."

She shifts in her seat. "I've known you for . . . well, ever. I've gotten to see some of your family's interactions. Things that neither Todd nor I ever understood. But there was a reason we stayed in Philly instead of going to Florida like your parents begged us to. We didn't want the kids around your mom's constant criticism or your brother's bullshit. Todd never saw you that way, Ang."

When she talks about Todd like this, I start to ache. "Todd was never like them," I say with emotion dripping from each word. He was so much more."

He was more of a protector than my father was. Todd always made sure that he took the brunt of Josh's crap when all three of us were together. Then he left this world without so much as a goodbye.

And I let him.

It's not like I knew he was in trouble, but I should've. I was his sister, and we were close. I should've known *something* was wrong, but I was oblivious. I hate myself for it.

"No." She takes my hand. "He wasn't. He loved you so much. He saw you as his perfect little sister. You weren't just my reason for wanting to stay in Pennsylvania. You were his, too. You've spent your life pushing people away because of what your mother did. Todd and I were the only people you let in. He cherished that, Ang. He was always worried about you. There were so many nights that he would talk about you needing someone to be there for you. I wish he could see you now."

Presley may hide the pain of Todd's suicide well, and she puts up a really good front. I admire her for that, but there's a lot of hurt that we both carry, but she can't hide it from me. "Todd did a lot of damage to us, though."

She leans back in her chair, looks out the window, and then turns back to me. "Yeah. He really did." Presley and the boys have struggled, but with Zach, her family, and Wyatt . . . they've been okay. "But we have choices, babe. We can sit around and feel sorry for ourselves or we can rise up. I didn't want to lose my house, my job, my business, and my life, but I did. I came here, sucked it up, worked my ass off, and by some grace of God, I found my way back to Zach. It was a gift, and maybe Todd is up there giving you one too."

Tears form in her eyes but she holds them back. I know how much she loved my brother. I also know that since she came back to Bell Buckle, we've barely spoken about him. A few times of course regarding the kids, but not about what she and I went through. I'm not sure why that is, but we skate around the surface.

However, the last thing my brother would ever want is me pregnant with a cowboy from Tennessee's baby. He hated this place. And I'm pretty sure he hated the Hennington family. Well, one of them at least.

The thought of him behind this at all is hilarious. And somewhat gross.

"You think Todd's gift to me is a baby?" I try to hold back the laugh, but it tumbles from my lips.

"No!" She giggles, clearly following where I'm going with this. "I think his gift is for you to no longer be alone."

"The baby?"

She shakes her head and looks at me like I'm being dense. "No, babe. Wyatt."

"Maybe." I shrug. "Although I'm surprised it would come in the form of your soon-to-be brother-in-law."

Presley practically shoots coffee out of her nose as she laughs. "I can't imagine he's happy about that. I have to believe he's doing what he can to make sure we're all taken care of, even though he's not here anymore."

"Do you miss him?"

She places her cup down and draws her bottom lip in. "I miss a lot of things."

I give her a few seconds as she seems to weigh her words.

"I miss the happy times. I miss the way he would look at

me." Presley's eyes move back to mine, and I see the tears there. "He looked at me as if I were the reason he existed. That's not something I'll ever forget. To be loved by him was really all-encompassing. But I'm angry. I'm angry that a man could look at me like that and chose to leave. I'm livid that he took that love from me and left me with a mess. It makes me believe that all I had was a lie—a big, horrible lie. And sometimes the anger is so great that I can't see anything else. It's been two years, and there are nights when I close my eyes and can still see him there motionless as I beg for him to come back to life. I will never forget that either. It's a really hard thing to be tied up in two such conflicting emotions."

For all the things that she's struggled through, I can't imagine what she went through that day. I was there for the after, but I can't possibly fathom finding him.

I just can't.

"I'm glad you have Zach." I genuinely am.

"Zach makes me not so angry anymore. He loves the boys. You should see him coaching baseball with Cayden. It's hysterical. He'll do the things their father decided not to be a part of. But more than that," she takes my hand, "he loves me. And I think you're starting to see that loving someone is a gift. It's not that you're incapable, like your mother, it's that there wasn't anyone worthy of it."

"I don't love Wyatt."

She leans back and grins. "You sure about that?"

"I don't. It's crazy soon. I've been here what? Almost a month?"

"You told me once that Todd fell in love with me the minute he saw me," she retorts.

Damn her and her elephant memory. "I thought he was insane."

"Maybe it's a family trait."

"Bitch." I laugh.

Presley shrugs and goes back to her coffee.

I think about Wyatt and the way he looks at me. How his eyes held mine the other night when I was in the kitchen cooking. I felt it all the way down to my toes. No one has ever looked at me like that.

"Now, what's on the agenda for today?"

"I'm going to help Mrs. Kannan in an hour," I admit.

Since the festival I've been stopping in here and there. She's the sweetest woman with the biggest mouth, and like almost everything else in this town, I'm drawn to her. Yesterday she showed me a lot about wedding cakes. I think it's definitely something we could expand on at the store. While cupcake cakes are something we do, she was showing me ways we could incorporate different tiers with the same concept.

It's amazing to watch her work. But I think the thing I've been most astounded by is her ability to know every single customer. She knows what they like, their favorite cake, and what they last ordered. It's remarkable and something I really admire.

"Don't ever let your guard down, my friend." Presley shakes her head, and I know all too well she's right.

"They truly are master manipulators."

She laughs. "I'm telling you, they could take over the world if they ever got bored with just controlling Bell Buckle. We're just lucky they mostly use their powers for good."

"Yeah." I think about how they've used their powers thus far. If it weren't for them, maybe Wyatt and I wouldn't be going on this date. Or maybe this was inevitable all along.

chapter
THIRTEEN

"I 'M IN TENNESSEE," I TELL my mother as I sit on the bed. I haven't spoken to her since I temporarily moved here. I've avoided her calls long enough. She doesn't really care about me, she just needs to keep up her appearances. However, Presley sent me a text telling me that my mother has been calling her and the boys to check on me.

"That would've been something to tell me, don't you think?" She pauses. "I shouldn't have to find this out by talking to Cayden. Of all the things, Angelina, why didn't you tell me you *moved* there?" I've barely talked to her this last year, but suddenly she's hurt. I have so many spiteful things to say, but I also know she's in pain. No mother should ever have to bury their child. Let alone knowing how that child died.

"I didn't move here. I'm staying here for a few months."

"Semantics," she dismisses.

"Well, I'm really sorry, Ma. It was never because I wanted to hurt you. I honestly didn't think much of it. You got the information from a few preteens. Maybe they're assuming something else? I'm only staying for a few months."

At least that's what I keep deluding myself into believing.

Presley and Wyatt keep making plans for six months out. They're completely ignoring my constant reminders that I have a business to run and a partner who expects me back in about two months from now.

"You never call me anymore," she complains. "Your father and I are still alive, you know?"

"I know, and so am I, Ma. I'm alive. I'm here. But you only call me when it's convenient for you or when you want to berate me. Why would I sign up for that?" I'm over being the reason for everything that went wrong. I've carried the burden because she needed me to. Well, now I need a little freaking support.

My entire life has shifted. Things are changing so fast and I'm barely able to keep afloat. I could really use my mother. Instead, I walk to the kitchen, grab a cupcake, and dig in. At least sugary sweets are always there for me.

She huffs. "I have a lunch date in a few minutes. I wanted to verify that my grandson wasn't lying."

"Nope." I shake my head. She's un-fucking-real. "He's not lying."

"Well, maybe when you finally stop being selfish, you'll think of your family."

Wow that hurt.

"Are you kidding me? I've done nothing but think of you guys. I think you forget a lot, Mother. Why is it so impossible to see that I'm not the woman you think? I own my own business, I bust my ass, I have great friends, and I'm doing pretty good on my own."

Her laughter comes through the line. "Please, dear girl. You're not married. You live in a tiny apartment all alone. You refuse to come to where your brother and parents are because you're too proud or whatever you tell yourself. Every time I turn around I hear about some other silly thing you've done."

"Wow," I say on an exhale. "I never realized you thought so little of me."

"Don't be ridiculous," she says. "I never said that. I don't, however, think you make the best decisions. You're much like your other brother in that way. Not like Joshua."

There you have it. I'm too much like Todd. I have a heart, and I'm not a calculating piece of shit. My brother has been married for fifteen years, has countless mistresses, and I'm pretty sure his wife is fucking the pool boy. Yeah, I should aspire for that life.

"Oh, well you'll love this, I'm pregnant and living with the baby daddy. Thanks for calling, Mom. It's always a pleasure hearing all the ways I continue to disappoint you. Don't bother calling me anymore. Tell Daddy I love him."

I hang up the phone and toss it across the table. She can kiss my ass. Everyone can. My anger rises, and I want to scream.

I look at the photo of Wyatt and his family on the table. They're so happy and loving, then there's my family. A sudden rush of emotion floods forward, and I burst into tears. I want that. I want to be loved by my mother unconditionally.

But I get her. I get the angry, bitter, and hateful woman who beats me down any chance she gets.

My feet are moving, and I'm out the door before I can process. I want to be around people who don't suck the life from me. I really want to see Wyatt. He always makes me feel better, and right now, I need him.

As angry as I am, I'm more than that . . . I'm sad. It feels like each turn I make sends me heading the wrong way on a one-way street. I keep dodging cars and pedestrians, yet I'm going to crash. If I haven't already. My heart is breaking because I'm alone. I know I have Wyatt right now, but that will change. I'll go back to Philadelphia and be a single mom.

It's the way it has to be. I can't sell my company and come play house. I sure as hell refuse to move right now. I'm on my own. I have to be stronger than this. The truth is that I'm not sure that I can be tied down.

The walk there takes minutes since Wyatt showed me the

wooded path between the two fields. I've taken it once before, but I navigate it fairly well this time, only tripping twice along the way.

I rush through the clearing and toward the barn. I can't explain why I'm running, but I need to see him. I need his arms around me.

When I break through the field my breathing halts and all thoughts of going back to Philly fall away.

Wyatt stands by the fence, his back to me, with his shirt off. His cowboy hat sits on his head, but as he turns, I can see the corners of his mouth are lifted. I don't see anything else but him. His jeans sit tight on his ass, and the sweat glistens across his back in the sunlight. I stand back, taking him all in, and realize I'm a fool. I could've had this man every night, but I've been living with my rules. Fuck the rules. He says he wants to wait until I'm sure. Well, I'm sure I want more than this. I know I do. I want to really give him everything and be together. I want Wyatt.

I start to head toward him, then he shifts over, shattering my new resolve.

Charlotte stands in front of him, her hand touching his chest, and I realize I wasn't a fool.

I've been far from it.

He's the playboy.

He's the guy who sleeps around, and I'm the asshole he knocked up. I watch them touch each other casually, neither of them notice my presence. There's no reason I should care, except that I requested that we spend these three months without him dating. I thought I was crystal clear at the festival. I thought I showed him that I'm going to really give him this time to see where we land.

This is one of those moments I know I'm crazy for standing here. I should leave, but I can't turn my eyes away. I want to see what happens so that I can always remember. Protecting my heart will be easy after this.

Her head tilts to the side, and I imagine what she's saying. "Oh, Wyatt. You're so funny. I just love funny guys because I'm so dumb I don't know how to be cute on my own." She laughs. "What is that? You think my boobs are real?" She shakes her head.

"No, Charlotte. I know they're fake, just like your blonde hair, but I don't care," he says in my imaginary conversation.

"Want to touch them?" Her nasally voice suggests as fingers touch his chest. Then, she leans in.

"I would love that. I like boobs." Wyatt's hand grips her hips.

The bile rises, and my chest heaves. He's touching her. She's touching him. I know what's going to happen next, and that will be the end of whatever I thought this is between us. I won't ever be cheated on. I won't ever be second best to anyone. Fuck that. There are too many reasons to be unhappy in this world, a man will never be one of mine. I want strength, love, devotion. I deserve that. I thought that's what he could be.

Don't kiss her, Wyatt. Don't do it. Please don't be that guy.

He leans in a little closer, and I fight my eyes to stay open. I want to look away, though. We've been living together for just over three weeks, and I've been . . . happy. I've had hope.

Her body shifts forward again, and I can't watch anymore.

I turn around to head back so I can pack my shit. I'll stay at Presley's tonight, and then I'm going the fuck home. I get a few feet down the path and hear my name.

"Angie!" Wyatt calls out.

I keep going. These fucking hormones are making me weak. Tears form in my eyes, and my heart breaks a little. I don't know why this bothers me so much, but it does. I wanted to believe that maybe there was something. Maybe I wanted there to be more. I needed him to be the man everyone says he is.

He's clearly not. Or I'm not the girl for him.

"Angie!" he yells again.

This time the stupid tear falls. No. I brush it away. I will not cry.

His fingers grasp my arm, and I yank it back. "Do not touch me!"

"What the hell?"

"Don't even act like you don't have a clue why I'm upset." I huff and step back.

He's either the dumbest man alive or an asshole. Maybe a mix of both.

"Because of Charlotte?" He looks confused. "Nothing happened."

"I know what I saw!" My tears fall freely now. It hurts. I'm so freaking confused right now. One minute I'm guarding myself against him, and the next I'm ready to fall head first over the cliff. My head is a mess. I want to cry and scream and kiss him all at the same time.

"Nothing happened, Angie!" Wyatt tries to convince me. "I swear! Why are you so quick to walk away?"

"I won't be that girl! I won't! I'm too old to deal with some guy who's going to run around behind my back."

"You're being ridiculous. Absolutely nothing happened just now."

"We have different versions of 'nothing'. I saw it with my own eyes! You liar!" I start to turn, but then his arm is around my waist and he hoists me in the air. "Put me down you fucking asshole!" I yell, fighting tooth and nail against the way my body wants to melt against him.

His arm wraps around my legs, and he carries me like I'm a baby.

"Nope." He trudges forward. "You're clearly not going to listen. So I'm going to make sure you can't run away."

I continue to struggle in his arms, but he looks unfazed. I slap against his chest, but he pulls me closer. "Put me down!"

Wyatt stops walking but doesn't release me. He lifts me a little closer so we're nose to nose. "For the third time, nothing happened." His eyes hold mine as he continues. "I wouldn't let anything happen. I saw where she was going, and I pushed her away. When I turned around to walk away from her, I saw you and ran after you."

My stupid, traitorous heart believes him. I can't stop crying. It feels like someone is squeezing my insides. "I hate these hormones," I mutter. Wyatt puts me on the ground but instead of letting me go, his arms snake around my back and he holds me tight. "I hate that I'm being ridiculous and crying right now! I hate that you affect me like this! Why do you make me weak? Why do the damn hormones make me a freaking lunatic?"

"Maybe it's not the hormones." My breath stops. I look in his gorgeous eyes that are swimming with some unnamed emotion, and I see red. Did he really just imply that I'm normally this nuts? Before I can start screaming again, Wyatt continues, "Maybe you like me. Maybe you see that I like you. Maybe it hurt to think that I would be with someone else?" Wyatt probes as his words sear through me, cooling my anger as fast as he ignited it.

He's right. It is all that. He's obliterating my defenses so effortlessly. I came here thinking we'd spend a few months together, and then I would be able to leave with no issues. It's been almost a month and already I'm attached to him, which is freaking insane. It's so soon.

Yet, when my mother tore me down, he was who I sought out. I wanted his arms to hold me. I need his touch to make me feel worth something. All I needed was to find the one person who would be there for me. Wyatt brings bold colors to a world where I was only seeing muted tones.

"You're going to destroy me, Wyatt."

He shakes his head. "I won't."

The war inside me is raging. If I give up the last ounce of

reserve I have, I won't be able to come back from him. He's showing me day after day that I can rely on him, using his damn cannon to break down wall after wall that surrounds my heart. Seeing him with her hurt too much. I can't be someone else's second choice. I don't want to love him and find out it isn't really me he loves.

"Don't break my heart," I beseech. "Please, don't make me fall in love with you if you're going to break it."

"What if I want your heart? What if I told you I had feelings for you months ago, before you were ever pregnant? What if I told you that after you left, I couldn't see anyone but you? What if I told you that you and this baby are all I want? What if everything makes sense now, and I want you to fall in love with me?"

I close my eyes, letting each of his questions disintegrate another piece of my resolve.

I want him.

It's clear now that I had no chance of keeping him out of my heart. It's been weeks. *Weeks.* And he's found a way in.

"There's still so much we don't know about each other."

"We still have time to learn." His eyes hold mine captive.

"I need to know things. I need to know it's really me. Not Presley or the baby. *Me.* The real me."

I don't want to fall in love to find out that it's all a lie.

Wyatt's hands slide up and cup my face. "It is you, Angie."

"I want to believe you."

His face dips, and he rubs his nose against mine. "Believe it. I can't explain it, but there's something about you. You're what I want."

I close my eyes, tip up on my toes, and press my lips against his. This kiss isn't about anyone else. This is about us.

chapter
FOURTEEN

Wyatt

M Y BODY GOES STILL WHEN her lips touch mine. I'll let her lead this one because of her stupid rules. But then her fingers hold the back of my head, and I take over. My lips fuse against hers as I seek entrance into her mouth. I need to kiss her. I need to possess her in the same way she possesses me. I want her to feel that. Feel every emotion that I am.

She's everything I ever prayed for in my arms. I tried to explain to my brother, but he laughed. Zach said it's when you know. The first time he laid eyes on Presley, he knew. With Angie, it's as if my life didn't really make sense until her.

Touching her, holding her, talking to her, just being around her makes my entire day. She's got some kind of hold on me. And it's fucking scary.

I thought I loved Presley.

I thought I knew what it was like to want someone so much that I'd go insane without them. This is completely different.

Not that I don't think I loved Presley, because I did. Now I see it for what it was, though. I loved the idea of what she and Zach had. Presley is my best friend, but Angie . . . she's the girl I breathe for.

I hold her in my arms as my mouth stays secured to her. I want to love her the way I should've when we conceived our baby. I want to show her what it's like to be worshiped, because that's what she deserves. This isn't like the night at the bakery. This isn't a cease fire like she called it . . . this is the final fight.

Her fingers hold my head to hers, and I pull her into my arms, and she wraps her legs around my waist. We kiss as I walk with her until I have her back pressed between my body and the rough bark of the tree. I need the leverage and she doesn't seem to care. It's as if we've both finally given in and neither of us want to waste a second.

I need to stop this. I need to take her home. "Angel." I finally break away.

"Don't stop," she begs as she presses her lips back on mine.

Fine. If she wants to keep going, who am I to deny her? I'll kiss her forever. The taste of her sugar lips are heaven. I remember how sweet everything else tastes, too. It's a flavor I plan to reacquaint myself with very soon.

By sheer determination, I've managed to control myself each night. I've had to jerk off in the bathroom each morning, but I've handled it. Waking up with her body wrapped around mine is torture, but it's not just that. It's the little noises she makes in her sleep. All night long she clutches me and moans and sighs. I almost ripped her clothes off three nights ago, even though I promised I would wait her out. Her voice was so needy. Then she started moving against me, her hand snaking down my body until I stopped her. There was no way I could let her touch me like that and not set her rules on fire. As it is right now, I'm going to implode if I don't have her soon.

Right now all I can do is drink her in. Her body molds to mine, and I think about how many other ways we fit.

I slowly back away from the trunk of the tree, and our lips disconnect. When her legs loosen from my waist, I debate stopping. I like having her clinging to me. I'll like it even better when she's naked again.

"I'm sorry I jumped you." She looks away.

"Don't ever be sorry for that."

Her blue eyes brighten as her smile forms. "So much for our rules."

I chuckle. "I'm hopin' you're throwing all your rules out."

"I think we should renegotiate." It's an offer, but I see the white flag she's waving. "Not all of them need to go."

I plan to take full advantage of this opening. She's stubborn as all hell and for her to concede anything at all is a miracle.

My hand reaches out and pushes the hair back from her face. "Angie," I call her attention. "You thought somethin' happened back there, but it didn't. I won't betray you. I know what it means for you to come here." I pause, making sure she's listening. "But there's a bunch of shit you said that I think we need to clear up."

She nods.

"I'm not in love with Presley. I haven't been for a long time. She's got nothing to do with us." I want her to hear that and hear it good. It's the second time she's brought that up. "I never dated her. I've never done anything with her. She's always been my brother's girl. Not that I didn't love her, because I did, but I loved her enough to let her go. And when I let her go, I let go of anything more than friendship."

"Wyatt." She places her hand on my chest. "I saw it, and I freaked. I'm dealing with a crazy amount of doubts and fears. Presley told me a while ago that you and Char—"

"Damn it," I snap, knowing exactly what she's scared of and what Presley may have said about me. I thought we had already covered this her first night here, but apparently she's still worried about it. "You need to hear what I'm saying and really understand it."

"Okay." She sighs.

I don't care if she doesn't want to listen to it. Not because I want to hurt her, but because she has to know without a shadow of a doubt the truth. The only person who can give her that—is me. Lord only knows what the hell Presley told her or what she's twisted in her own mind. It's better to set the record straight now so this can get put behind us.

No need to rehash the same shit.

"I'm an honest man. I live a simple life, and I've done it without givin' a shit about what anyone thinks. I have never led a girl to think there was more than whatever I was offering. I've never brought them to my house. I've never taken them on dates." I raise my brow to make my point. "I sure as shit have never moved one in. Take that for what you want, but you're different. I think you feel it, too."

She doesn't say anything as she stands with her small hand pressed against the bare skin of my chest, probably feeling my heart rate going out of control. I refuse to tear my eyes from hers. I want her to see the truth behind my words. I'm not hiding anything. It's all out there, and all I can do is hope she feels a little of the same.

"I—" I watch as the storms roll through her gaze. I can see how it scares her. Then I see resolution. "I like you so much more than I should. It's different for me, too. I've been happy being alone. I've had my job, my friends, my brother, and I'm a pretty kickass aunt. There's never been this desire to be a mother or a wife. While my friends were getting married and starting families, I was living the life I wanted. They didn't agree or understand me, but I like dating. I like freedom. I like to take care of myself."

There's nothing that she said that I don't understand. But it's in my nature, my damn DNA, to want to take care of her. And that's going to be a fight. One that I'm willing to go toe to toe against her over, just not today. A woman should be respected and cared for. A man should ensure that it's done. I've watched my father do everything for his family, and I'll do nothing less than that for mine.

I'll give her everything.

Angie continues, "I'm now finding out how to be someone else. Someone who suddenly likes curling up on the couch and watching *Big Brother* with you. That's not me. I don't like cuddling and lunch dates. I like space. But then I like you, and you don't like space. It's confusing, but I know that I want to be near you."

I don't let her say another word. I dip my lips to hers for a brief kiss. If it's any longer I'll rip her clothes off in the middle of a dirt path.

"Let's go home."

That's what I want her to think of this as. I dread the argument about her going home in two months. Then again, I don't plan for that to be an issue. She's going to want to stay here after I show her all the reasons we're right for each other.

chapter FIFTEEN

Angie

THE ONE THING I ENJOY most about dating is the pre-date. There's that nervous energy that fills me every time. I've scrubbed, buffed, moisturized, shaved, and plucked every inch of my body. I want this night to be amazing.

Wyatt should be home in an hour, and I want to be ready for whatever he has planned, which he has refused to even give me hints about. I know he'll need to shower, but I won't have to do it side by side. It seems more date like this way.

I scour through my clothes, unable to find anything that I'm looking for. It seems I didn't put my stuff away as well as I thought.

Or maybe I didn't bring my "date" outfits because I didn't plan on dating anyone.

I grab my phone to see what time he thinks he'll be home and see I have a message.

Wyatt: Go to Presley's house. I'll pick you up there at seven.

Umm, that's weird. Why the hell would I go there? Are we going on a double date?

Me: Why?

Wyatt: Because I said so, woman.

I let that slide for now. But later, after I find out what he has up his sleeve, I'm going to make sure he hears all about him bossing me around. That shit won't fly here.

Me: I'm already dressed. It makes no sense.

Wyatt: Since you must know . . . I want to pick you up. I want to drive to a house, knock on the door, have you take your sweet ass time answering, and take you out. So get your butt to Presley's and wait.

My God.
There's only one response that I can say to him.
My fingers type across the screen.

Me: You trying to get laid tonight?

Wyatt: You've made me wait long enough.

I laugh. He's been patient, but this has been hell on me. I swear, pregnancy messes with every part of you.

Me: Maybe tonight you'll get lucky in more than one way.

I toss my phone in my purse, deciding I don't want to see if he responds. It's so much more fun this way. I grab my sweater and look myself over in the mirror. Instead of wearing a dress, I opted for jeans, since they still fit, and a really cute olive green top. I curled my hair so it hangs down my back in soft waves. I dress it up with a pair of heels and one of my favorite chunky necklaces. Without knowing where we're going, this is the best outfit I could muster.

On the ride over to Presley's, I call Erin and go over the details of the building she found. She emailed me yesterday, but I didn't know what to say. The longer I'm here . . . the less confident I am about my being able to actually leave. Therefore, I've put off making any decisions regarding the expansion.

"Angie, we need to move fast. We can't drag our feet." Erin releases an exasperated sigh. "I have to make an offer."

"I'm not sold." It's not a lie, but I also know it's a pretty phenomenal space. It's almost double what we have now in Media and has an area we could use for some tables, which our store doesn't have now.

Erin doesn't say anything. I wait her out, knowing that she's one who has to think things through. It's one of the reasons I brought her on. She's extremely business savvy and always leads with her mind, never her heart, other than with the men she dates. I can tend to be a little more impulsive.

She clears her throat. "I understand you're going through a life changing event. I'm trying to be really understanding."

"You have been—"

"Right," she interrupts me. "You're my partner, though. I invested a lot of money into this company. We've had some huge opportunities, and I think we have to capitalize on them. Now, I see it can go two ways." This isn't going to be good. "You can give me the control of this project and allow me to do what I feel is right, or we table this whole thing."

Now, I have to be the owner. Yes, we're partners, but I'm the owner and founder. I put the car in park as I arrive at Presley and Zach's. "I'm well aware of the position we're in. However, I told you I needed three months. We agreed, Erin. I'll keep doing what I can from here, but I'm not going to sign off on a location that I've never seen. It's unfair to do this to me when I've been gone just under a month."

"I'm not trying to be unfair," she quickly interjects. "I don't want to blow this chance."

I get that. I don't either, but I'm making concessions left and right in my personal life and her making me choose right now is going to push me over the edge. I'm just getting my footing with Wyatt, things aren't secure and until they are, I need my business to stay the same. "I'm not saying no, Erin. I'm saying that I need the time we agreed upon. I need to be there when we choose a location."

I also need to figure out how deep I am with this man.

"So you want to table the expansion?" Erin's voice raises slightly. "Because if we pass on this space, we're clearly not moving forward."

Is that what I want? Am I really willing to give this up for him? Right now, yes. I am. Even if it doesn't work out, this is the most I've ever felt for someone. My heart races when he touches me, and everything settles when I'm in his arms. The fact that I'm even questioning it says something. I'm not the girl who goes all mushy at some boy. I'm the girl who stands strong behind my independence. I don't *need* a man. But I want Wyatt.

Damn it.

"Two months. I'm asking for two more months."

Erin sighs. "I don't agree with your decision, Ang. I think in a few weeks you'll think differently. Did you get the quarterly P&L report I sent?"

We talk a little more about the profits and loss, and in the end, I think she understands. Erin has made back her investment, so I don't have to worry about that. If I have to, I have the capital to buy her out. I like having her, though, and I hope she'll stay on even though she's mad about delaying things.

I walk into Presley's house and greet everyone.

"The boys are getting ready to go for a horseback ride with Zach. He promised them he'd teach them new tricks so they can finally beat me. They've gotten really good at riding, but haven't had a lot of time to practice between school and sports." Presley explains after I barely get a hello from either of them as they run by. "Zach is upstairs, but the boys are going to saddle up."

"Have they gotten close to beating you?"

"Nope." She grins. "One day they'll learn, and I'll have to up my game."

"Not likely."

Presley grabs her wedding book and flops in the chair. "My brother is teaching them how to rope cattle."

"Zach doesn't do that?" I ask.

"No, we were the rodeo kids. The Hennington's were too busy playing sports." Presley shakes her head. "Cooper and I were really into rodeo stuff. Even though my mother was only okay with my brother performing." She rolls her eyes.

"How is Coop? I haven't seen him."

Her brother is great. He's quiet, tall, and almost always busting his ass somewhere out on the ranch. I've asked why he's not taken, but Presley won't say. However, I'd have to be blind to miss how he looks at Grace and not put two and two together. Grace is one of her best friends, Trent is her soon to be brother-in-law, and Cooper is her brother. Talk about an awkward Christmas.

"He's great. He and Zach are doing a lot more business together, which is good. It allows me to see Zach during the day. Although, I pretty much see him whenever I want anyway."

We both laugh. "Because you two don't spend enough time together, right?" I feel like every time I see her, he's right there too. Not that I mind, but isn't she worried she'll get sick of him?

"I kinda like him. You'll see," she looks up. "When you realize how great a guy is, you want to be around him more. You'll crave his company because it makes you light up. Zach gives me that."

"Not all of us are hopeless romantics. Some girls are happy on their own. We don't dream of getting married and playing house. We dream of taking over the world."

She rolls her eyes and goes back to her book.

The boys rush in the house. "Mom," Logan huffs. "Where's

Zach? I can't find him."

"Must be at the barn," she says even though she said he was upstairs.

"Bye, Auntie!" they call to me in unison.

"Bye, turdlets!" I call back.

"Zach!" she calls. "Boys are waitin' on you. You got about ten minutes!"

"What is he doing?"

"He had a call about one of the horses. Felicia, the awful bitch she was, oversold a few of them. Remember how Zach thought it was best to keep her on for a bit?" she asks.

"Yes, and we both said it was dumb."

She laughs. "I know. He thought maybe she wouldn't be vindictive."

"Did he ever actually speak to Felicia in the entire time he dated her?"

"I can't even—" Presley huffs. "A fucking year he let her stay on! A year!"

I seriously don't understand that. I can only imagine how Presley dealt with it. Having to see that girl every time she turned around. Then again, I can understand business wise how he could think it was a good idea. The whole enemies close theory, but that's a little too close for me.

"That's crazy."

"No shit. Anyway, Zach has been cleaning up that woman's messes nonstop. I know a woman scorned is bad news, but dear God. Now she's threatening a lawsuit."

That girl is a piece of work. It's a good thing she left town, because I'm pretty sure Presley would've beat her ass by now if she hadn't. She stole money, destroyed accounts, and shredded parts of the Hennington reputation.

"He's really great with the boys," I muse, steering the

conversation away from Felicia and the mess she left in her wake. "They really love him."

Zach comes around the corner. "I'm easy to like."

"I beg to differ," I say offhandedly.

His hand slaps against his chest. "You wound me."

I shrug. "You'll live."

He leans in and kisses my temple. "You love me."

"Wrong Hennington," I retort. "I like the better version of you."

"Hey now!" We both laugh, and Presley stands there with a grin.

She walks over, wraps her arms around his torso, and looks up with the gooey expression I've gotten used to seeing on her face. "I got the best Hennington."

"And soon you'll be Mrs. Hennington."

The way they stare at each other is so intense I have to look away. I want a love like that. She may think Todd looked at her a certain way, but I've never seen anything like what they share. It's so beautiful, I could cry.

"Not soon enough." Presley's voice is wistful.

Their wedding is in four and a half months. I'm going to be sporting a really big baby bump by then. "Can you move the wedding up?" I ask, breaking their staring contest.

"Why?" she asks.

"I'm going to be eight months pregnant!"

"And you'll be breathtaking," Wyatt's voice rings out from behind.

My breath hitches as I turn around. He leans against the wall with his arms crossed. He has on a dark pair of jeans, a tight white t-shirt with a teal button up over it. I see every muscle in his abdomen when he shifts to walk toward me. The muscles in my body tense as he moves with purpose.

He stops right in front of me, and I tip my head back. "Aren't you supposed to ring the doorbell and wait for Zach to let you in?"

"I have a key." He grins.

I purse my lips. "That's cheating."

He laughs. "Do you want me to go out and do it again? I can ask my brother to clean his gun to scare me off from getting frisky with you."

Now, it's my turn to burst out laughing. "You're a mess."

"And you're beautiful."

"So are you."

He chuckles. "Well, that's good."

I nod.

Geez, I'm a mess. One word and I forget my big strong bravado.

"You guys are so cute!" Presley claps and breaks me from my stupor.

I turn and glare at her as she laughs.

My eyes return to Wyatt to see he couldn't care less. He only sees me. He doesn't even glance away. Instead, he takes my face in his hands with care, bends down, and gently presses his lips against mine. "Ready, baby?"

"I'm ready."

Right now, I know that I chose right. He's worth giving up the expansion for.

He's worth all the possible heartache.

He's worth it all.

chapter SIXTEEN

"WHERE THE HECK ARE WE going?" I ask as we enter our second hour of driving.

"On our date."

Wyatt has been tight lipped the entire drive about what exactly we're doing. I'm going out of my mind, but it seems like he's enjoying my irritation more than anything.

Pain in the ass.

"I know that. But it seems like you're driving me back to Pennsylvania."

He takes my hand in his and doesn't respond.

Okay, then.

I lay my head back against the seat and watch the scenery change. There are rolling hills in Bell Buckle, but this is more mountains. The trees are dense and the air feels lighter. It's absolutely breathtaking as the sun starts to set, and the pink and orange hues paint the sky, making everything feel warm.

I close my eyes and allow myself to feel the heat encompass me. Wyatt's warm hand holds mine as I relax.

"Wake up, sleepy." His deep voice is low in my ear.

I open my eyes, and it's now dark. The sky is a dark blue with tiny shimmering lights.

Shit.

"Oh my God!" I sit up quickly. "I fell asleep! On our date!"

He gently squeezes my hand. "It was a three-hour drive, babe. You're fine."

"Three hours?"

Now I'm confused.

He climbs out of the truck and helps me down. "We needed to do this right."

"Wyatt?"

I look around and realize we're out in the middle of nowhere. In front of us is an adorable cottage. A little smaller than his house but much more opulent. I turn around and see the mountains shining in the moonlight but there aren't any other lights from other houses that I can see. Off to the left, there's a large opening with chairs off to the side and a barn a little farther in the background.

"Where are we?" I ask.

"This is my family's oasis. A few years ago, my brother's and I bought this property and built the cottage. We figured we could rent it out as a bed and breakfast. Instead, we kept it for ourselves. I wanted to share it with you," he explains.

"I-I don't . . ." His family owns this little slice of heaven? "This is . . ."

"It's something I wanted you to see," he says as he takes my hand. "I want this to be special for us."

"I don't . . . I don't have clothes."

I had a nighttime outfit picked out and everything, but that's back at his house. Not that I think guys typically care, but still, the plan was there. I figured for our first time as a pregnant couple, I would put my sexy nightie on.

"You do. Presley packed you some stuff this afternoon."

"Wyatt!" I stop moving as tears fill my eyes, but he tugs my hand until I start walking again.

He opens the door to the cottage, flips the lights on, and I gasp. The entire space is modern and warm. Cream-colored walls and rugs with beautiful couches sit in the middle. The massive king-size bed with upholstered headboard is on the far side of the sitting area. Each piece makes the space feel luxurious. I step forward touching the back of the chair, completely bewildered.

Then I see a box of cupcakes from my store. I rush over and run my fingers over the black calligraphy print we use for our labels. "My store."

He walks over behind me. "Erin sent them here for me. I know you miss home and the bakery."

"I don't even know what to say."

I look to the left as he sets down a thermos I hadn't realized he was carrying. I touch it and know.

"It's your favorite."

"It's perfect."

He really thought this through.

Between working and dealing with my crazy ass, he planned this.

If there was ever a time I doubted he would win me over, I was blind.

Wyatt steps forward, wraps his arms around my waist, and ducks his head to mine. "I've waited a long time for a girl like you. One that I'd want to do these things for. Someone who I want to come home to. When I asked you to come out here, I didn't know this would be how I'd feel. I figured we'd enjoy each other, see that we're from two different worlds, and move on. But the idea of you leavin' makes me crazy."

My breathing accelerates, and my throat goes dry. He's feeling it all, too. I see it all in his eyes—the hope, the fear. We're both in uncharted water, trying to plot the course and hoping we don't get lost.

"I don't know what to say."

"Say you want me." His eyes hold mine.

I lift my hands, take his face between them, and lock on to his eyes. "I want you."

And I do. I want him right here and right now. I can't make grander promises to him, not yet, maybe not ever. My heart and my head don't add up, but I want him. Maybe it's supposed to be like this, but I wouldn't know. I grapple with the conflicting emotions. The want to have this new life and still keep everything I have in Philadelphia.

I've worked hard. I love my company. I don't want to give it all up.

"For how long?" He seems to read my thoughts.

"We'll have to see." I smile. "Maybe longer than I thought."

He doesn't say anything. He holds me close, and I move my thumb across his stubble. His eyes close as he dips his head toward mine. "I'm really glad you said that," he utters before his lips touch mine.

Everything shifts. His hands wrap around my back as he mashes me against his hard body. I moan against his lips, and our tongues connect as my hands fist into his hair. Gone is the tender couple speaking their truths. All that exists are two passionate people ready to prove it.

And I plan to make it the truth all night long.

I've been hungry for his touch again.

I've been starved to feel the unbridled hunger I know exists between us.

I'm ready to give myself to him and take everything he gives me.

Wyatt backs me up, hooks his hands behind my thighs, and lifts me into his arms. I hold on, staring at him, as he moves toward the bed. His gaze is heated and it warms me everywhere. I'm going to enjoy the burn.

"I plan on breakin' all your rules tonight," he promises.

"I plan to let you."

His confident grin paints his face. "I told you it would happen."

I smile and touch his cheek. "I knew you'd rise to the occasion."

He lets out a deep laugh and lays me on the bed. His body covers mine, but he keeps his weight off me. "A lot more is going to rise."

"I sure hope so."

"I think we've"—he kisses me—"already"—another kiss—"established"—kiss—"that I can handle myself."

He sure can, and I can't wait to enjoy it again.

"Make love to me, Wyatt."

Our eyes stayed glued as he shifts his body to the side and roams a hand down my front. His touch is a whisper against my skin as his lips move with mine in a sensual dance. He pulls the strap of my top and bra lower, exposing my breast before his thumb and forefinger roll my nipple back and forth. I want to arch off the bed in pleasure, but I make myself stay still. Everything feels heightened tonight. I let out a low groan as he does it again.

These pregnancy hormones are going to finally prove to be useful.

If this has me practically panting, I can't wait for the good stuff.

His mouth captures my nipple, and he licks and sucks. "God!" I cry out, sinking my hands into his hair to keep him there.

I need more.

Every inch of me is screaming out for his touch. Wyatt doesn't make me wait. His hand glides across my stomach and his eyes meet mine. "This is how we should've made her."

"Her?" I place my hand over his.

He tilts his head. "I think we'll have a girl."

I haven't thought too much about the sex of the baby since the talk with his mother. I've been too busy trying to wrap my mind around the idea of having a baby at all. But when he says it, I can see it. Wyatt carrying her on his shoulders. Him having his nails painted because she wants him to. He'd be that for her. He'd be the daddy little girls pray for.

"I don't care what we have, I just want the baby to be healthy. I worry a lot."

Wyatt heard all about my family history when we met with Dr. Borek. His face blanched a little when I explained my cousin was diagnosed with cancer in her fourth month. He never said anything, and I never brought it up again, but it's always on my mind.

His thumb brushes against my belly. "I don't worry, Angie. We can't control it. All we can control is what we think. I know our child will be whatever we can handle."

"God." I sigh. "You're everything I never knew to ask for."

I watch the shock roll through his gaze. "You're everything I've waited for."

"No more waiting, Wyatt."

He moves into action. My lips and his become one and our hands roam. I lift, taking my shirt off, and he does the same.

His body is glorious, and it's all mine.

I push him on the bed and straddle him. My hair falls, creating a cocoon around us for only a moment before Wyatt gathers it in his hands so he can guide my movements. He controls the kiss from the bottom, and I love it. My hands rest on his chest, feeling his heartbeat beneath me. I try to lean back, but he keeps me steady, his tongue plunging into my mouth as we take everything the other offers.

When he flips me over, I yelp in surprise. I liked being on top of him, and open my mouth to protest, but he's already on his knees removing his belt buckle. I watch as he slowly undoes the button of his jeans and slides them down. I go to mimic what he's done, but he takes both my wrists in his hands and places them above me. "Let me."

Wyatt removes my jeans and underwear, kissing and nipping at my skin as he reveals it, and then tosses them to the floor next to his pants. He stares at me in awe. My skin feels branded by his gaze. My heart feels full from his words. And my body is about to become his.

"Say it," he commands.

I have no idea what he's asking.

"Say you want me," he says as a request.

I lean on one elbow and touch the side of his face. "I want you."

"Again."

He moves to hover over me.

"I want you."

Wyatt's eyes stay on mine as he moves lower down the bed. "I want to hear you, Angie." He hooks my legs over his shoulders and runs his tongue across my clit. "I remember your sounds. I want to hear them again."

"Yes," I moan.

He does it again, and I damn near buck off the bed. Wyatt gets into a rhythm in no time. I twist and turn as the pleasure climbs. My heels press into his back, whether to pull him closer or tell him to slow down, I don't know. I can't take much more, but I don't want him to stop. With each sound I make, he rewards me with a flick of his tongue against my clit.

I climb and climb.

My fingers twist in his hair as I cry out.

I scream his name and thank God we broke that rule.

He crawls on top of me as I try to catch my breath. "One down, many more to go."

Oh. Fucking. Yes.

He takes my now very sensitive breast in his mouth but keeps the rest of his body away from me. "Wyatt." I beg. "Please."

I need him inside me. Tonight has been so much. Some moments that I will never forget. The fact that he brought me here, took care of me, and said so many perfect things. My own truth lies before us as well. I'm not a mushy person. I've never had these deep emotions with men, but with him, it's all real.

The bindings around my soul are free, and it's invigorating. I've never believed there was freedom in loving someone. I always thought it was like being held captive. I was so wrong. Falling in love with Wyatt is beautiful. It's also scary . . . terrifying even. I've never realized how all-consuming it would feel. He's the only person in this world I've ever felt these feelings for. My heart, my body, and my love will be his. I know that once I tell him what is in my heart, there will be no going back.

He'll bind me to him.

I'll let him.

"Are you sure?" He gives me an out.

"I want you to make love to me. I want you inside me."

He looks at me with a cocky grin. "I'm very much inside you."

I roll my eyes and shake my head. "Well, then get more inside."

"I haven't touched another girl since you left," he says with honesty ringing in his voice. "I'm clean. You're already carryin' my baby."

"I'd say we're good on the no protection."

Relief flashes through his face as he lines up. "I've had to endure weeks of your body curled around mine each night. Your sounds as you sleep have been driving me mad, and baby, I'm going to take my time tonight."

"I'm counting on it."

He fills me inch by glorious inch without taking his eyes

away. He stretches me, allowing me to feel him as he becomes fully seated. My lids flutter shut as the feeling becomes overwhelming. I'm here with Wyatt. Pregnant with his kid. And we're making love.

When I open my eyes again, they're filled with tears.

I try to hold them back, but my emotions spin out of control.

We rock together as I struggle to keep myself in check.

Wyatt doesn't miss a thing. "Don't hold back."

"I just feel so much."

"Let it go," he requests.

And I do. I close my eyes and let the tears leak out. I feel him kiss the moisture away.

Our lips find each other's, and I lose myself there.

"This is how we should've been the first time," Wyatt says as he pushes deeper.

I touch his face. "I think this is exactly how it should've happened."

Wyatt continues to rock languidly. "You feel so damn good."

"Show me," I plead.

And he does. He picks up the pace a little more, and my fingers dig into his back. I start to climb again, but there's no way I can handle another orgasm. Yet, it's building. He watches my face, and my cries start to become louder.

"Wyatt—" I hold on tighter. "I can't."

"You can."

No. My head shakes back and forth as my hips rise to meet his. There's no way I can handle this, but every inch of me is burning hotter and hotter for release. "Oh, God. Oh, God."

He dips his hand between us and pushes against my clit, sending me soaring over the edge. My back arches and it's as if every nerve inside me detonates. He anchors me to this earth.

Wyatt follows me over the edge, calling out my name before

we collapse on the bed. I lie against his chest, listening to his heartbeat. His hand rests in my hair, and I close my eyes. I feel safe, sated, and damn glad I threw out that rule book.

We make love off and on all night long. In between, he holds me or we drift off. The sun starts to peek through the windows before we finally sleep.

I could spend every day of my life like this.

This is heaven. This is where I want to be.

I just need to find the courage to do it.

chapter SEVENTEEN

W E SPEND THE DAY AT his family's vacation farm. I can't get over the picturesque views, each time I turn around, I want to snap a photo. I have to admit, if only to myself, that it's hard not to fall in love with this place.

It's modern, but timeless.

"What's with that grin?" I ask as we sit in the rocking chairs.

"I'm observing you."

"And what do you see?"

Wyatt looks back out at the landscape and then back to me. "I see you fallin' in love with my place. Who'd have thought you'd love the countryside, Big City? It looks good on you."

"Hmm," I muse. "I don't know that it's the countryside, Little Buckaroo."

"What did you call me?" He stands quickly.

I've been mulling over the perfect nickname for him. Since he rides horses, and I know the "little" part will piss him off, this seemed perfect.

"Little Buckaroo."

"There ain't nothing little about me, baby."

Oh, how much I love this nickname already. "I figure it's something we can pass down if it's a boy."

His lips form a hard line, but my face lights up with a huge smile. "Nothing about my boy will be little either."

I shrug. "I would encourage you to wish for a girl."

Wyatt steps closer, drops his hands onto the arms of the rocking chair, and gets in real close. "Honey, if we have a boy and you call him that, we're going to have a problem."

"Honey," I say back, "you've got no say in this. You're my Little Buckaroo, and he will be, too." Great. Now, I'm rhyming.

"You know what?" He pushes off and stands tall. "You're going to find out what happens when you call me that next time."

He stands there, all brooding and sexy in his pair of jeans and a Henley. Wyatt is always sexy, but he's doesn't realize he's the drop your panties kind of guy, which is probably why I did just that. Even right now, when he's trying to be a badass, I only see the sweet guy who I'm falling for.

I shrug. "I'll take my chances. You're not so scary."

His grin grows wicked. "I've been behaving."

"Still not scared, *Tiny* Buckaroo."

"You're going to regret that."

I probably will. He really doesn't like the name, which makes me want to use it more. "Maybe you should take me back to the cottage," I offer. The playfulness disappears as lust fills his eyes. I get up, allowing my breasts to graze his torso as I stand. "That is," I say as I look up from beneath my lashes, "if you want me to apologize."

Wyatt's lips are on mine so fast I don't have time to blink. His arms are around my back with his hands in my hair. I love when he does this. It's possessive and protective at the same time. Our mouths move together as the kiss grows heated. I know exactly where we're going. I can't seem to get enough of him.

I pull back, "I'm ready."

He grins and yanks me against him. "Now, where would the punishment be if I gave in?"

Jerk.

I want sex. That kiss sent tingles where I wanted them. But I'm sensing he knew that.

His look says I'm right. "Turd."

He laughs, kisses me again, and releases me. Wyatt tugs me to his side, and we start to walk. "I have a better idea."

"Oh?"

We keep walking, casually he'll lean in and kiss the top of my head. My arms stay wrapped around his middle, loving how easy this feels, until he leads me into the stables. The horses are in their stalls, looking all pretty and strong. I walk over to the one that is looking over the half gate.

"Hi," I coo to the horse. "You're a big guy, huh?"

Wyatt snorts. "Sure, the horse is big, but you call me little?"

I shake my head. "He's just jealous." I pet the horse's nose. He's really a magnificent horse. He's tall, with a shiny black coat and white speckles on his butt. I glance over at the side of the stall where his name is written. "Aww, you're sweet, Desperado. And you're a handsome boy."

"He's an Appaloosa," Wyatt says, coming next to me. His hand rubs Desperado's neck, and then he pats it. "That's why he has the spots."

"Do you have Appaloosas at the farm?"

I don't know a damn thing about horses. I probably should learn if I'm going to be a part of his life.

"No, we breed mostly Quarter horses or Arabians. My mother had an Arabian when she was growing up, so my father indulges her. But Quarter horses are what most people want around us. They're good for working, riding, rodeos, and just about anything else."

"Oh," I say as if any of that makes a difference. Desperado moves slightly and then rests his head on Wyatt's shoulder, and Wyatt obliges him with a neck rub.

"You wanna go for a ride?"

"Can I? I mean, I'm pregnant."

I don't know the rules on that. I was only really concerned with the coffee thing. The doctor didn't give me a list of restrictions other than the things that were obvious. Since I don't smoke, and already knew wine and I were going on a break, I didn't focus on the other stuff. I remembered no sushi from Presley's pregnancy, and there's no sushi place around here anyway.

"You're safe with me, Ang. We'll walk slow. I'll have the reins."

"Right," I say. "But am I supposed to?"

He steps away from the horse and takes my hand. "I've known plenty of pregnant women who ride early on. Plus, before they had cars, pregnant women had to ride. My guess is you're fine."

"Let me Google."

Wyatt laughs. "Google away."

I grab my phone, searching for the answer. It says as long as I'm past my first trimester, not too big to sit in the saddle, and we take it slow then it's okay to ride. Wyatt is more than experienced with horses, so I'm sure it'll be fine.

"Let's saddle up, Little Buckaroo! I'm ready to ride."

Wyatt grumbles under his breath, and I put my hand over my mouth to stop myself from laughing. He's so cute when I piss him off.

I stand back and watch him work. He tacks up the horse (which he told me is the proper term, not "dressing" him.) I'm on Desperado and Wyatt is on a horse named Ginger Snap. I love that he's riding the horse with the girly sounding name.

"Am I doing this right?" I ask for the tenth time as we start to head back to the stables.

"Yes, baby. You're doing great."

We're literally riding at the slowest pace ever, but I'm trying not to look like a terrified kid on a pony ride. Wyatt leans back in the seat, his hand out in front of him like a Marlboro commercial, and I'm clinging to the horn (again he corrected me after calling it the "Oh Shit! handle").

Once we settle in a little and I've loosened my grip, I turn to him and ask something that has been bothering me for a while now. "Wyatt, why didn't you go back to working at your family's farm after Felicia left?"

He looks over with a sad smile. "I was bought out. When Zach came back, we all had to make a choice. Right there. Right then. My father was sick, and Mama couldn't run it on her own since she had her hands full. Zach returned, and I figured he'd leave once he rehabbed his shoulder, but after a few months, it was clear he wasn't going back. All three of us were fighting constantly. He brought on Felicia to help, he sold off a few horses that I had wanted to buy for myself, and Trent was being a fucking idiot. It was just bad."

I watch him as the emotions play across his face. I can see how there's something underneath his words—a pain that still festers there.

"Anyway," he continues, "Trent was the first to decide he wanted out when he took the Sheriff position. Zach and I bought his share of the company, and we were evenly split with forty-nine percent of the company since Mama kept two percent. The agreement was she'd hold those shares so that we couldn't bully the other one out."

"Makes sense. I'm guessing there's a 'but' in there somewhere."

He nods. "I wanted the control and so did Zach. When he made Felicia his right hand, I lost it." Wyatt turns his gaze to me and sighs. "You see, I've fought with my brothers my whole life, but this was like nothing anyone had ever seen. He said a lot of shit. Things that, no matter how much time has passed, still linger between us."

"I'm sorry. I know how much it hurts when you fight with a sibling."

And I know more than anyone. Joshua is the king of horrible things. Even as a kid, he would find my weaknesses and use them against me. It was his way of demonstrating his superiority.

"Zach and I are fine now. We don't talk about it. But I told my parents I wanted out. I sold all of my shares to Zach, and he took over. I left that day and went to Cooper, who gave me a job."

Wow. "And you're okay with it now?"

He looks off at the horizon. "Not at all. But I'll never ask to buy back my half. It wasn't Felicia as much as it was what my brother wanted to do to my parents' company. It was how he approaches business. I believe that money doesn't override loyalty. I feel like my father's reputation was about how fair and generous he was. Zach wanted to take the company in a direction I was not okay with."

I decide that right now is absolutely not the time to say what I'm thinking. I started my business in a dog-eat-dog economy. You're either the alpha or you get lost in the pack. Presley would be like Wyatt, she'd give free cupcakes to people who came in all the time, which only encouraged them to come back for more free stuff. It was horrible, and I had to stop it. I'm career minded, so I can see that Zach was only making smart business choices.

"Well, I'm glad you guys seem to be okay now."

He nods. "We're both happy. I love working for the Townsends. They're good people, and Cooper pays me well—not that I need it."

My face whips toward him, showing how perplexed I am by that statement. "What?"

We start to approach the stables and Wyatt hops off his horse. He comes around, grabs my hips, and helps me down.

"Zach had to buy me out. I don't need the money. I live well below my means, and I've saved a lot of money."

"I had no idea. I mean, we've never really talked money, but . . ."

"I'm not rolling around in my dollar bills." He laughs. "But I'm set for a very long time."

Wyatt's hands wrap around my middle, and I curl into him. "You should know that I can take care of myself financially as well. My store was very profitable over the last few years, but with Erin buying in, it allowed me a lot of breathing room. I'm saying this because I think you should know that I'm not hard up for cash. I don't ever want you to think that my motives are monetary."

I've seen the horror stories. All I want is for Wyatt to be a good dad to the nugget. It's good to know that he'll never slack on that part of things, but at the same time, I'm fine. I'm not a gold digger, and he needs to be aware of that.

"I think it's good for us to have these talks." His lips inch close to mine. "It makes me realize just how lucky I am right now."

"Yeah?" I ask a little breathlessly as he grows closer. "Why is that?"

"Because," his lips graze mine, "I'm winnin' your heart."

He doesn't give me a chance to respond. His mouth connects with mine, and I hold on tight. We both give and take through this kiss, and his words swim in my head as I lose myself to his touch.

Everything feels so strong when I'm with him. If someone had told me this was how I would feel about him, I would've laughed. Wyatt isn't the man I ever thought I would fall in love with. I always saw myself with a business man. He would work downtown, we'd both come home from work, and go to a swanky restaurant for dinner. We'd go to New York when we wanted to see a show or head to the Outer Banks when we wanted the beach. No kids for a long time, if ever.

Instead, I've fallen for a cowboy who has probably never been to New York, and I already have a baby baking in my belly. Definitely not in my plans.

Yet, I've never felt as secure as I do right this second.

If this is what happens when my plans go to shit, I can live with the consequences.

ON THE WAY BACK TO the cottage, Wyatt tells me we're staying for two more nights, and that he wants me to relax and think of nothing. Even though we're living together, it's so different being here. I can't fully explain it, other than this feels like a romantic getaway.

In Bell Buckle, we're living. Here we're free of mundane day-to-day stuff.

Tonight, we're going out to dinner and from what I can tell, it's definitely more upscale. I look through my bag, hoping to find something I can wear, and see my emerald satin cocktail dress. Presley did a fantastic job packing for me. I only brought two fancier dresses with me to Tennessee, and this is by far my favorite. I pin my hair into a messy updo and do my makeup a little heavier for dramatic flair. This dress calls for a little more of everything.

I finish getting dressed and look myself over. The dress still fits perfectly. The front is a lower-cut top that crosses in the front, and it clings past my hips, ending at the knees. It's extremely formfitting, and the baby bump I've been pretending is not there, is now very prominent.

My hand rests against it as I suck in a deep breath. "You're really in there." My eyes won't move from the spot. "I knew you were, but now I can see that you're really in there." I lean against the bathroom counter and look down at myself. It's a moment. A big one for me. My baby, our baby, is there. Growing all on its own.

I'm going to be a mom.

I knew this, of course, but it's really happening. There's proof of it. It's real.

A tear falls, and I wipe it away. I'm overcome with emotions. These last four and a half months have been trying. I've really run the gamut of highs and lows. From being unsure of whether I could do this to knowing I would find a way. Then being so angry about having to move to now being upset that there is a little over a month left before I have to make a choice. Then there's the feelings about Wyatt. Do I love him? Is it too soon? Has it always been written in the cards but I was too blind to see?

Right now, I can't believe how much love I have for this baby. This tiny little person I've never met has already become the center of my universe.

I was so distraught about it, but now I want it more than anything.

I look through blurry eyes, staring at the reflection in the mirror. "I'm going to have a baby."

Once I get myself under control, I fix my makeup and exit the bathroom.

Wyatt stands in the middle of the room, wearing a pair of black dress pants and a white shirt. His dark hair is styled with little spikes on the top. His eyes roam my body, and a wicked gleam forms in his eyes.

"You're gorgeous."

"Look!" I place my hand over my stomach. "There's a bump!"

His big hand covers mine. I take a deep breath, inhaling his musky cologne as I commit this very moment to memory. Standing in this gorgeous house in Tennessee together with

Wyatt's hand and mine both covering our baby.

Wyatt looks down and then up to me. Pride, love, and happiness fill his face. He moves both his hands to encompass my stomach and then drops to his knees. His lips press against my dress as he kisses my stomach. "I already love you, and I'm pretty sure I'm falling in love with your mama." He looks at me, and I cover my mouth with my hand. "So, you keep doing what you're doing, and I'll make sure I keep working on her."

The tears I had smothered before fill my vision. He rises so we're eye to eye. "Wyatt." I place my hand on his chest.

"I'm going to find a way to keep you here, Angie. If you're going to leave me, you better be ready for the fight of your life." His hands cup my face. "Because I'm not letting you walk away, not without layin' it all out. I won't say anything else. Words are just words, baby. It's the action behind those words that matter."

"Your words aren't just words." He presses his forehead against mine. "Your words are your truth."

"And my heart is yours."

And mine is yours. But I can't say it. The words are stuck in my throat. But they've never felt more true.

chapter
EIGHTEEN

THIS LAST MONTH HAS BEEN amazing. Wyatt and I have settled into being a couple. He works at the ranch, I'm at the bakery three days a week, and we have our nights together. I still fall asleep in his arms after we wear ourselves out with all the sex.

Today, though, I'm in a planning session at the bakery with the old biddies of Bell Buckle.

"Angie can't march in there and grab Presley," Mrs. Townsend says with exasperation.

"Maybe she can fake some kind of labor pains!" Mrs. Rooney says.

Mrs. Townsend's head falls in her hand. "She's not even that far along! How would she have labor pains?"

"Right," Mrs. Rooney agrees. "Moving on."

All I've been doing is sitting quietly and eating cupcakes. I think I've figured out their process, though. One of them throws out an idea, two of them talk about it back and forth, the fourth explains why it's dumb, and then they all move on. It's hilarious and exhausting. All in all, it's not a bad gig.

Of course, I would much rather be spending the day with Wyatt. Yesterday we went back out on that stupid Gator thing as he showed me more of the property. We walked along the creek that's between his and the Townsend's property where we had a picnic, and then he showed me why living in the country is great for fooling around.

We definitely couldn't have had sex like that outside in the city. Well, not without an audience.

I'm enjoying our newfound sex life. According to the book of horrors, I'm only going to get hornier, which is the silver lining to all this. Wyatt doesn't seem to mind, and I've told him to enjoy it while he can.

The only thing I have to do is address the elephant in the room—my leaving. He hasn't brought it up, but then neither have I. I know we need to talk about everything, yet I haven't found a good time. I'm not sure if I should go to Erin first or Wyatt. The last thing I want is to sever my ties to the bakery, only to find out that he doesn't want more with me.

So, I let it linger.

But today is our twenty-week ultrasound. We'll get to see the nugget and hopefully find out what the sex is.

I'm hoping after we get through that and Presley's bridal shower next week, we can iron out our future, because the idea of leaving him . . . cripples me.

I glance at the ladies sitting around and decide to interject. "Why don't I tell her I need her to run an errand with me?" I offer up, and they all laugh.

Another idea gets thrown out and dismissed right away.

Back to the cupcakes it is.

"I know!" Mrs. Hennington grows excited. "Why don't we have Angie call Presley, tell her she has to go across town to do something, and that she needs her help?"

I swear I said that.

They all look at each other as if she just spoke gospel. "Oh! That's a great idea, Macie!"

Really? I glance over at Mrs. Kannan. "Yes! So smart, and

Presley will never expect it."

"Umm," I say with bewilderment. "I just said that, and you shot me down."

"Not the point," Mrs. Townsend says. "Can you go over there and take care of this? It's important that she has no idea what's going on. We've been plannin' this event for a long time."

I've learned that Wyatt wasn't exaggerating when he said it was best to humor them. Presley isn't a fool. She asked me last weekend to make sure she has her hair done and is dressed nice when she gets ambushed.

Still, I know I can't tell them that. "It'll be no problem. I'll make sure Presley is completely in the dark."

"Wonderful!" Macie yells. "Now, let's talk about the balloons . . ."

Being the maid of honor in a wedding typically means you have to plan stuff, not here. Not with these ladies. It means I sit back, eat glorious food, and pretend my opinion is at all wanted. It's cute they invite me, but really, I'm just here for the food.

Another half hour passes, and we're all set.

I say goodbye to everyone, but Macie hangs back.

"How are you feelin', sugar?" she asks as she loops her arm in mine. "Any sickness or cramping?"

"Nope." I smile. "This has really been a wonderful pregnancy. I'm so glad I didn't have morning sickness at all. The only thing I'm having now is heartburn whenever I eat sweets. But no cramping like the book said, and I feel really good."

"That's wonderful. I had great pregnancies with the first two boys. Wyatt, though . . ." She gives me a serious look. "He about killed me." *Who says something like that to a pregnant girl?* "Today is the ultrasound?" she asks, completely missing the look of shock on my face.

"Yeah, I'm meeting him back home in an hour and then we head over."

She pulls her shoulders up with excitement radiating off her. "So exciting!"

"I can't wait."

The last time that I got to see the baby was so early that I wasn't even sure it was human. It looked like E.T.'s little brother holding a balloon.

"Have you thought at all about staying a little longer?" She tries her best to look innocent, but it's not an offhanded question.

"I have," I say and leave it there.

"You're going to leave me in the dark, huh?"

I smile and nod. "I think Wyatt and I need to talk first. I hope you understand."

Macie pats my arm. "Of course I do, honey. You don't have to explain yourself to me. I want you to know that if you need anything . . ." she pauses. "I mean anything at all, you call me. And maybe after you find out whether my grandbaby is a girl or a boy you'll let me go shoppin'?"

Shopping. Umm, yeah. "I would love that!"

We stop in front of the car, and she pulls me into her arms. "You have no idea how special you are, baby girl. No idea." Her hands hold my shoulders as her green eyes study mine. "You're a wonderful woman for comin' here. I know it wasn't easy. I know you struggled, but I see how that boy looks at you. I see how you look at him, too. Lovin' someone isn't a choice when you find someone worth lovin'. I believe that there are some things outside of our control that force us into situations."

"Like having a baby?" I ask with a smile.

"Exactly," Macie confirms. "But you and Wyatt are real. You were faced with an impossible situation, darlin'. I want you to know that I love you as if you were my own daughter. I know you already have a Mama," she presses her hand to my cheek, "but you've got me if you ever need a fill-in."

My heart swells, and I can't stop the flurry of emotion that floods forward. Everything inside me cracks wide open. I burst out in a sob and wrap my arms around her.

My mother has never said anything remotely like that. She's never told me how special I am, not that I can remember at least. She left me when she no longer could care. Not physically, but in every way that mattered. I haven't spoken to her in two months. This should be one of those times a girl has her mother.

I weep for the mother I don't have.

I weep for the broken girl inside me who so desperately needs this.

And I cry tears of happiness that I have someone like Macie Hennington in my life.

This is another thing Wyatt unknowingly gave me.

"Don't cry, honey. I didn't mean to make you cry." She rubs my back, and I release her.

"I'm sorry." I step back and rub my eyes. "It's these damn hormones. I swear, they make me a freaking lunatic."

She half smiles and rubs my arm. "Wyatt's told me a little and then Presley told me a whole lot more about your mama. I'm real sorry. I love my boys more than anything, even when they drive me nuts. You're not without people who love you, Angie. You've got a whole town full of Mama's who will come to your side. Especially if we get to love on that baby, okay?"

I nod. "Thank you."

"No thanks needed, honey. It's what family does." Nothing I could say right now would adequately describe what I feel. She seems to sense that and handles it for me. "I really better be on my way. Rhett wants me to make his favorite meal, and I haven't done a thing yet. You go on and find out what you're havin'! Then call me." She winks.

"You got it."

She rushes off, and I head home, which is comical since we live on the same land. The entire time she rides behind me, I replay the words she spoke and how she just held me and let me cry on her shoulder. She is warm and loving—the kind of woman you love instantly. I decide right then that I want to be more like Mrs. Hennington than my own mother.

She veers off toward the main house, and I head to our place. Huh. *Our* place. I really like the way that sounds.

When I pull into the driveway, Wyatt is there waiting. "Hi, baby!"

I jump out of my car and rush toward him. "Hi, honey!"

He gives me a long, wet kiss before releasing me. "How was your day?" Wyatt asks.

"Good. Yours?"

"Better now."

I smile and he leads me toward the truck. Once we get settled and are on our way, I fill him in on my day. He laughs, rolls his eyes randomly, and comments here and there.

"Oh!" I exclaim.

"What?"

"Mrs. Kannan is putting in a cappuccino machine!" I grow excited again. "She said that she'd been thinking about putting one in, and she heard I know a lot about them. She made me promise to show her how to use it when it gets here."

He nods, but his eyes stay focused on the road. "That's great."

I figured he'd comment a little. I mean, he knows my deep love for coffee. This is about as close to a Starbucks as I'm going to get, and I was trying to open the conversation a little. "Wyatt?"

"Hmm?" he doesn't even glance my way.

"Did you hear me?" I ask with a little bite to my voice.

"I did. You love coffee. It's great. I'm happy you'll have the comforts of home while you're still here."

What the fuck?

I lean back in my seat and try to figure out what the hell

crawled up his ass. I don't think I said anything wrong. If anything, I was trying to get him to ask more questions so we could talk about me staying for a bit longer. My mind was truly made up weeks ago, but the last few days solidified it. I'm not ready to leave him. I'm not saying I'm ready to get married or anything . . . just maybe give this parenting thing a real shot together.

Then it clicks. Today is the first time he's going to get to see nugget—he's probably just nervous.

We get to the office where I'll have the ultrasound. He doesn't really say much, but he doesn't miss a beat as he helps me out of the car, opens the office door, and makes sure I sit.

"Did I do something?" I ask, unable to ignore it anymore.

"No, why?"

Am I losing my mind? "You're being distant. I talked about the cappuccino machine, and then it was like *boom!*" I clap my hands together. "Wyatt disappeared."

"I'm sorry, Ang. I've got a lot on my mind."

"Okay . . . like what? We talk about everything. I don't understand why you're pulling away from me right now."

"Angelina Benson." My name is called by a pretty nurse by the door.

I guess this conversation is tabled.

We get up, and he places his hand on the small of my back. I'm half tempted to swat it away, but I'm a little nervous suddenly. She leads us into a room with the ultrasound machine, gives me some quick instructions, and leaves.

I hop on the table and fear starts to invade my mind. I worry my hands, and Wyatt walks over. "What's wrong?"

"Now you want to talk?"

He sighs and takes my hands in his so I can't fidget. "Why are you worrying yourself?"

I pull my hands back. "Oh, you can have your feelings, but I can't have mine?"

"I said nothing's wrong."

Right. He really should be more convincing. "Well, nothing is wrong with me either."

I'm being petulant, but he's being an ass.

He shakes his head. "Women."

I'll give him 'women'. "Asshole."

Thankfully, the technician enters. She introduces herself and gets me set up.

"This is a little cold," she warns as she squirts the goo on my belly. "Do you guys want to know the sex of the baby if I can see it?"

"Yes!" I answer before he can say a word.

Wyatt chuckles. "We'd like it if you can. I think she's going out of her mind not bein' able to shop."

I roll my eyes and look over. With a few clicks on the machine we start to see actual human body parts. "Oh my God! Wyatt! Look!" I wave my hand, calling him closer. His fingers lace with mine as we both watch the screen.

Then, the most amazing thing happens. Our tiny little baby shows on the screen. The sounds of my and the baby's heartbeats echo in the room as we stare at the life we've created.

"That's our baby?" he asks.

The technician smiles and nods. "This here is the heart," she says and points to the image on the screen. "Four chambers. All look healthy."

"It sounds so fast," I say in awe.

"Is it supposed to be that fast?" Wyatt questions.

"It's a very healthy heartbeat, Mr. Hennington. A baby's heart beats at a much higher rate than an adult."

He nods.

I look back to the screen and she continues on. It's so cool and so real. This is nothing like the ultrasound pictures Presley had with the boys. Now the photos look so detailed since it's 3D.

I can literally see the baby's body. She shows us two legs, two arms, and all the organs look good. We can see its little face and all of the features are formed. It's a real freaking baby.

"Okay, now let's see if the baby will cooperate and show us the goods." She smiles as she clicks and twists the wand over my belly.

I can't believe this is our baby. I know I was excited before, but this is beyond my dreams.

"There we go." She smiles.

Wyatt and I both look at the screen closer as she types: It's a girl!

chapter
NINETEEN

"I SWEAR TO GOD, ANGIE," Presley warns. "If you don't tell me what the sex of that baby is tonight . . . I'm not responsible for what'll happen."

I laugh. I've made them all wait for the last three and a half weeks. I don't know why I wouldn't tell them, I just wasn't ready to share, which of course drove everyone nuts. Added bonus.

"I've been patient, sugar, but I'm dyin' here. You wouldn't want to let an old lady die before knowing what her grandbaby is gonna be, do you?" Macie lays on the guilt.

Wyatt glances at me and grins. "Fine," I huff. "I guess we can tell you."

Both of their eyes shift between us and then we yell, "It's a girl!"

"I knew it!" Presley hurries forward and hugs me tight. "You totally needed a girl."

"I agree!" I laugh. "Think of all the pretty stuff we're going to get!"

Mrs. Hennington pulls me into her arms and then Wyatt's dad follows. "I'm so glad you're going to give this family a girl! I don't think I could've listened to Macie grumble for another ten years about the boy things."

He's such a sweet guy. He doesn't say much, but when he

does, it's important. I was really nervous around him the first few times, but then I realized he's a big teddy bear. Wyatt explained that he enjoys the quiet and doesn't feel the need to fill the world with noise.

Everyone laughs and talks about how happy they are. It's the first time all of us have truly celebrated anything with the pregnancy.

Wyatt glances at me every now and then, still in his funk. We haven't talked about whatever is bothering him, and he doesn't offer anything up.

I thought we'd crossed some threshold, but it seems we haven't. Instead, I feel like we've regressed.

We sit around the table for dinner. The boys are excited to get a girl for a cousin. They offer various suggestions for names, which is ridiculously entertaining. Wyatt grumbles about boys and what they think about girls while I laugh.

"You should name her Belle," Logan sniggers.

"I like that name!" I say.

"Because we all *live* in Bell Buckle." He laughs at his own joke.

"Well, cross that one off," Wyatt huffs. "Not that it matters if Belle is in the name."

I glance over at Presley, who gives me a look. It seems I'm not the only one picking up on his mood. "What does that mean?" I ask.

"Nothing." Wyatt looks over and shakes his head. "It means nothing, I'm sorry."

"Okay." I lean in close, drop my voice to a whisper, and place my hand over his. "I feel like something is bothering you."

"What about Gertrude?" Cayden offers.

"No." I shake my head. My grandma's name is Gertrude, and while I love her dearly, it's not a name I'm giving my daughter.

The boys continue with some of the most horrible names possible. I try to picture what she'll look like. Hopefully she has blonde hair, like me. We all know blondes have more fun, and get away with more. I hope she has Wyatt's light brown eyes and his nose. He has a great nose. No matter what, I'm sure she'll be beautiful. I have faith in that.

"What about Faith?" I say as it hits me.

"Faith?" Wyatt repeats. "You like that name?"

I smile and nod. "Faith Hennington."

He puts his fork down and leans back. "I like it." Then he grabs my hand and squeezes. "I like it a lot."

I start to wonder if I'm imagining all of this. His hot and cold mood swings are giving me whiplash, but right now he seems like he's okay. Maybe it's something at work? Maybe he's nervous about the baby? Or is it because he thinks I'm still planning to leave? I still haven't talked to him about it because I want to talk to Erin first. It could take a good amount of time for me to get things in order, and I need to know my life is set before I start making any promises. I doubt he would be this upset about that, though. I've been pretty clear with my actions that he's won me over.

Hell, maybe it's just his man-period.

"Well." I shrug. "We can put it on the short list."

We finish dinner and all sit out on the porch, listening to the rain. Zach and Wyatt argue about some football game and then move on to the problem Zach is having with some buyer up north. Presley and I sit quietly, drinking wine and apple juice respectively.

"I keep feeling these weird bubbles in my stomach," I tell Presley when it tingles for the third time in a few minutes.

She smiles and leans forward. "That's the baby moving, Ang."

"What?" I gasp. "I mean, wouldn't it be like a kick or something?"

She giggles. "Not at first. Not until you're further along, but that tingling, moving feeling that's almost like gas?" I nod, letting her know I'm following. "It's the baby."

"Holy crap!" I rest my hand on my stomach with a grin. "She's become so real to me." I whisper and then worry at my bottom lip. "Pres, what do you think is going on with Wyatt?" My eyes move toward him. "He's being weird. It's making me question things."

I get hung up on this a lot in my mind. With never really loving someone, do I even know what love feels like? I love people, obviously, but loving a man is totally different. It's things that I never experienced before. He's the first thought I have in the morning. I wonder if he brought his lunch or if he's thinking of me, which then usually leads to me stopping by and seeing him on my way to the bakery.

He does the sweetest little things too. The other day he ordered a Keurig and every different flavor of Starbucks cups he could find. I'm waiting for him to hire a barista at this point. Then, he kissed my nose and told me I didn't need a Starbucks, I had it here.

And then he went back to being moody.

"I noticed . . ." she trails off.

"Maybe he doesn't feel the same way about me."

She shakes her head. "No. I know that boy, and I see it in his eyes."

I thought I did, too. "Well, the way he's been this last couple of weeks is not love. He's barely able to tolerate being around me."

"Love can be so many things." She shakes her head. "It can be beautiful, exciting, full of so much hope, even freeing, but it's also scary as fuck. You give yourself to a person in a lot of ways.

But you need to talk to him."

Until the ultrasound, I thought we were there. Now, it feels like we're pulling away more than we're coming together.

"I'm not the one with my head up my ass."

"Uh huh." She laughs.

"What does that mean?"

"It means we have to go forward, babe. Make him listen to you. If you do nothing else, don't let him slip away from you. All we have is right now and, apparently, two idiot men that we love," I laugh as I look at Zach and Wyatt. They're freaking sword fighting with Cayden and Logan. However, they're fighting each other while the two boys watch.

"I've never been more grateful for having a girl."

She laughs. "Yeah, I get the dumbass who skipped the awful baby part and is now teaching them all the joys of being country boys, which means more laundry and dirt in my house."

"Would you change it?" I ask.

"Not one single thing."

I nod. Me either. Even with Wyatt being funky . . . I wouldn't change anything.

"I'M SO TIRED," I GRUMBLE to Wyatt as we drive home in my car. It's almost midnight, cold, and wet. We hung out with Presley and Zach, played some cards, and I ate my weight in cake.

Presley always has cake. Really good cake.

"We'll be home soon. I need to check on the new foal at the ranch," Wyatt explains.

Cooper called him and asked if we could stop by. I wish he would've said no, but he's Wyatt, which means he helps everyone. The Townsend ranch isn't far from us, but I'm so exhausted that I just want to get home.

"I can't believe how freaking cold it is." I pull my sweater tighter around me.

Wyatt cranks the heat in the car, and I shiver.

"I'll get you to bed soon."

"Promises, promises," I joke. "If you don't start putting out again, I'm going to find someone else."

"You wish." He grins.

Back to warm we go. Men are weird. "Worried much?"

Wyatt's eyes shift back to mine. "Not at all. I give multiples."

"Oh, please!" I laugh. "I've had better."

"I heard you and Presley talking." He clues me in. Wyatt's voice shifts to try to mimic mine. "Oh, Presley. You don't even know. Wyatt is so good in bed, I about died. He's the best I've ever had."

My eyes roll so hard I'm surprised they're still in my head. "Idiot."

I lean back, look out at the road, and try not to smile. He's so stupid, but I know that I love him. I need to tell him and then get him to work through this.

"So you really like the name Faith?" Wyatt asks.

"Yup."

"What about Isabelle? We could call her Belle," he suggests.

I shrug. "The boys will still call her Belle and make fun of it."

"Then I'll make sure Zach and I mess with them until they stop."

While that sounds fun, I'd rather not give her any chances of being picked on. I went to school hearing all kinds of fun crap about my name. Angelina doesn't sound like a name that's easy to twist into a joke, but boys will find anything.

"I'd rather not have them start off already making fun of their cousin."

He nods. "Crickett?"

"Like a bug?"

Wyatt chuckles. "Okay, I like the name Emma."

Hmm. I like that. It's really popular, and Emma Hennington sounds pretty. Maybe I can keep it as a middle name. I still can't seem to get my head to stop thinking of Faith, it's as if it has been her name for as long as I've known about her.

"What was your comment about before?" I ask.

"What comment?"

He's playing dumb, which he sucks at. "The one about Belle."

"Just that what does it matter if Belle is her name?"

"Well, we live in Bell Buckle." I shrug.

"No." He looks over. "I live in Bell Buckle."

Okay? I don't know where he's going with that, considering I was hoping *we* were going to live here. Maybe I really did misread everything.

"What the hell does that—" My words catch in my throat, and then I'm screaming, "Wyatt! Look out!"

"Shit!" He screams as he sees it too.

A massive buck is rushing from the woods and straight to the car. It's going to hit my door.

"Fuck!" He yells.

Wyatt slams on the brakes, and his hand shoots out in front of me. I'm already flying forward.

My seat belt stops me, but the pain is instant across my lap.

I scream, trying to cover my stomach as everything slows to a crawl around me.

The deer drops his antlers, and I brace for impact, turning my body toward Wyatt. I know it's not going to matter. We're sliding toward the side of the road and straight toward the woods.

Wyatt tries to correct the wheel, but we skid over the wet ground. There's no way to stop this.

The deer slams into my door, and the sound of metal and glass breaking fills the air.

Pain shoots through my arm as we continue to spin.

Another loud *bang* cuts through the chaos, but I can't focus on anything but the pain that's blooming in every part of me.

"Angie!" I hear his voice, but agony erupts from every inch of my right side as I'm slammed against the door, wrenched left, and then thrown forward against the dash in some twisted dance where someone else is pulling my strings.

My body violently shifts to the left before being thrust forward and against the dash.

My mouth fills with the metallic taste of blood and warmth trickles down my face.

The airbag deploys, and it hits me so hard that whatever air is left in my lungs is pushed out.

I can't breathe.

It hurts so much.

Then everything is still and dark.

I try to move my body, but it doesn't cooperate. I feel the blood sliding down my head and the way my lungs struggle to work.

I hear my name over and over, but I can't open my eyes. I'm going to die here.

I know it.

chapter
TWENTY

Wyatt

"NO!" I SCREAM AS I watch her eyes shut. "Angie! Stay awake!" I scream, trying to get to her. She doesn't move or acknowledge me at all.

I push my airbag out of my face and do the same to hers. I reach behind my back, grab my knife, cut my seat belt, and try to get the door open.

It's completely mangled shut.

"Angie!" I push her head up. "Angie, baby, wake up." She doesn't move. I check for a pulse, it's there, but it's weak. I shift a little, and the car jolts.

We're face down in a ditch.

Fuck!

My hands shift around her body, trying to see if I feel anything. When I pull them back, my fingers are covered in blood. "I have to get us out," I say to her, but she's unconscious, and I'm panicking. "I'll fix this. Just hang on, Angie. Hang on. Please don't leave me," I beg her.

I hold pressure to her head as I try to figure out what to do. Using my other hand, I try to open her door, but it's worse than mine. The deer slammed into her side, and the impact must have buckled the metal.

The phone sits on the top of the dash. How it got there, I have no idea, but I grab it and hold the speed dial button. My fingers shake, but I need to get someone here.

"Someone better be dead or dying," Trent's voice croaks.

"I need help!" I yell into the receiver. "I'm in a ditch on the road between our house and the Townsend ranch. Angie's unconscious, and you need to fucking get here now! Get help! The car is fucking mangled, Trent!" My voice cracks as the panic rises. I have to get her out of this.

"I'm on my way!" Trent yells back. "We'll be there in a minute, Wyatt. Just stay calm."

My brother slips into Sheriff mode. I know he will get help, but there's no calm here. The woman I love and my child are slipping away. I need to get her out of this car and to a doctor. I rip my shirt off, no longer feeling any cold, and tie it around her head, trying to keep pressure on the cuts hiding under her hair.

"God, I'm so sorry, baby." I want to pull her into my arms, but I don't. Even through my panic I know that the best thing I can do is keep her still. I count the seconds as I keep moving my hands around. "I'm so sorry I've been a dick. Just hang on. Please hang on, Angie!"

I'm such an asshole. I should've told her how I feel. Now, she might never know.

No. I can't let myself go down that road. She'll be okay, and I can fix this.

I'll tell her. I'll tie her to the bed and make her stay. I won't let her leave me.

I love her.

Headlights and the rotating red and blues of Trent's cruiser cut through the darkness, tires screech against the ground, and then doors are being slammed shut.

"Wyatt!"

"Down here!" I holler back.

"Shit!" I hear Trent yell. "We're coming! Dad, go on that side," he instructs.

"Oh my God!" Mama's voice yells.

There's a lot of movement as my brother comes to my side. "How is she?"

I relay everything I know, and he nods. "We need to move her, Wyatt. There's gas leaking, and we can't wait. I have a brace in my car. Hang tight."

He rushes to his car and then returns. It feels like hours are passing. Her blonde hair is now matted with blood, and she still won't open her eyes.

"Get her. Get her now!"

"We can hurt her more if we're not careful, brother."

Trent decides the best way to get her out is the already shattered windshield. He knocks out what's left of the glass as I shield Angie as best as I can. More noise filters through the once silent woods as more people arrive.

Presley's voice cuts through. "Angie! No!"

I focus on doing what I can, but there are more lights and more people yelling as Trent, Zach, my dad, and the EMT guys all move to the front of the car. "All right, Wyatt," Trent's commanding tone grabs my attention. "I need to know if you're injured anywhere."

"Just my shoulder. I'm fine," I bite out, watching more of Angie's blood soak into the fabric of my shit.

"Good. I need you to cut her seat belt, and then Zach and I are going to help maneuver her. I need you to stay as calm as you can, okay?"

Anger fills my body. "Stop talking! She needs help!"

I don't know how long it's been. It could be minutes. It could be hours. But we're wasting time. Every second she spends in here is a second I could lose her.

"Calm, Wyatt," Zach says holding my eyes. "We need to move her carefully so we don't cause any damage."

I close my eyes and take a deep breath. "I'm ready."

"Okay, cut the belt." Trent's steady voice commands.

I do as he says, and she slouches forward in my arms. I hold her, trying to leverage myself against the dash. My brothers are on each side of the car, both of their arms extended to take her. We coordinate our movements, careful not to jostle her too much or let her body touch the glass. When she's out, they quickly move her to the EMTs.

My father helps me out, and then I'm by her side.

She's lifted onto the gurney, where Thom and Beau, two guys I've known my whole damn life, start to work on her. They attach wires and start running, yelling things back and forth to each other.

"Get in the ambulance," Trent says. "He needs to be checked too!"

I hop in on autopilot. She's fading away. I can feel it.

"In bound fifteen minutes, thirty-six-year-old female, unconscious from a head injury. Possible internal injuries and pregnant." Thom says into his radio before turning to look at me. "How many weeks?" he asks.

I just look at her as Beau inserts an IV. I watch as he continues to try to talk to her, but she doesn't move. She lies there, blood all over her clothes, glass in her beautiful hair, and cuts all over her body.

"Wyatt!" Thom yells. "How many weeks pregnant is she?"

My eyes don't move from hers. "She's twenty-four weeks."

Twenty-four weeks I've had her.

Please God don't let me lose her.

chapter
TWENTY-ONE

M Y MIND CAN'T STOP SPINNING. I've never felt as desperate as I do now. I'll do anything for her to be okay, but it's out of my hands.

The ambulance ride was agony. I sat there as she had tubes, needles, and monitors beeping every one of her vital signs. They asked questions that I think I answered. She laid there.

Not moving.

And each second that passed, a piece of me died. I should've turned the wheel the other way. I should've left ten minutes later. I should have told her I love her. I should've done so many fucking things. But I failed.

We make it to the hospital, and I hold her hand until they tell me I can't go any farther. The moment when my skin lost contact with hers, I felt like I was going to collapse. I don't know if she'll be okay or when I can see her.

Zach, Presley, Trent, Mama, Daddy, and I all sit in the waiting room. I recount the details of the accident as best as I can. Presley and my mama have a constant stream of tears. Zach and Trent offer me silent support. Each of them grasp my shoulder, tell me it wasn't my fault, but I just keep talking. I tell them about how the deer sent the car into a spin, how the roads were the perfect storm, and how I couldn't get the car to correct. I know what to do when a vehicle is fishtailing or spinning, but it was as if it made it worse.

"There was nothing you could do," Trent tries to reassure me again. "None of us could've prevented the deer, Wyatt."

"If something happens to her . . ."

Zach grips my arm. "She's in the best care possible."

They took Angie into immediate emergency surgery, explaining the baby was in distress and they found signs of internal bleeding. I tried to ask questions, but they said they needed to get in there and would be out as soon as they could.

There's nothing I can do right now but pray.

So I do.

I hold my mama's hand and try to stay strong.

Each time I close my eyes, I see her smiling face. How happy she was when we were talking about names. Just three hours ago, she was sitting on the porch swing, rubbing her stomach with her face filled with life.

I feel like I'm dying inside.

I've failed her and our daughter.

Seconds turn to minutes which fade to hours. Time passes, and I feel as if I'm petrifying.

Each time the door opens, my heart stops.

Each time they talk to another family, my heart breaks.

"I can't sit here!" I stand, needing to move. "I can't wait for them to tell me." I'm shattering. I can feel it. A pained sound rips from my throat, and Trent embraces me. "I can't wait for her to die!"

"Don't think like that. You have to be strong. You have to have faith, brother."

Faith.

Presley releases a sob at that word, knowing damn well that's what Angie wants to name our little girl.

"I need her to be okay. I have to talk to her."

Trent grips my shoulders. "I know. The doctors are working on her. No news is good news, Wyatt. It means she's fighting."

I look at him with blurry vision. "I can't lose her like this." If I say it enough, maybe the world will understand—maybe I can will it to be true.

"They'll do everything they can," my oldest brother says with conviction.

"It was my fault. I was driving that fucking car. I wanted to take the truck, but she said she hated climbing in and out of it. So, I let her convince me to take her car! Now, look where we are! Now look. I should've taken the truck when I saw it was raining. I should've done something!"

"This isn't your fault." My father comes toward us. "I know you're a man and that you want to own this, but this is *not* your fault. And no matter what happens, you can't be thinkin' that way. Understand?"

I know he means well. But if it were him behind the wheel of that car and my mother was fighting for her life and the life of their unborn baby, he'd be feeling the same. That woman is who I love. That baby is my child. I know I've never met her, but I want her more than anything. I want for Angie and Faith to be in my arms—safe—and know how much I care.

I love them.

I will do anything to protect them. If I could be on that table, I would trade places in an instant. Instead, I'm out here, walking around. It should be me—not her.

Before I can answer, the doors swing open. Two doctors in blue scrubs, with sweaty faces and specks of blood on them, walk through.

My body tenses, Presley and my mother flank me. Their hands grab mine as we wait for them to speak. I'm typically the calm in the storm, but right now, my emotions are the outer walls of the funnel. I'm trying not to get swept away.

"Angelina Benson's family?" The doctor on the right says as they walk closer.

"How is she?" I ask.

He sighs. "She's sustained a lot of injuries. The most critical was her spleen. Luckily, we identified it quickly and were able to get the bleeding under control. She has a fractured wrist and multiple contusions along her right side from where the car crushed inward, plus a fractured rib and her nose was broken, most likely from the impact with the airbag. But we're most concerned about the concussion. The CT shows some organ swelling, which we're keeping an eye on."

"The baby?" My voice shakes. "Is our baby okay?"

The doctors look at each other and shift their weight. "Unfortunately . . ."

I stop hearing his words as my heart shatters.

I've lost my daughter.

I fall to my knees as the world as I know it dies. I've lost one. I've lost them both.

"We delivered the baby by Cesarean. We tried, but the placenta ruptured in the accident. The baby didn't make it."

My mother wails, but my father holds her together.

I'm numb. My tears fall down my face as Presley wraps her arms around me. "I'm so sorry, Wyatt."

"She—" I choke as I look up at her. "Did she . . . the baby? Suffer?"

The older doctor shakes her head. "No, the baby never drew a breath. We did our best, but we were unable to do anything."

I nod.

"I'm very sorry for your loss," the female doctor says.

Loss is too easy of a word. I didn't lose her . . . she was taken from me. Taken from her parents before she even got to see us. She didn't know she was wanted. She didn't know our faces or the depths of the love we already had for her.

She didn't know. I didn't lose my daughter.

She was ripped from my life.

"Can I see her?" The words are out of my mouth before I realize it.

The woman gives me a sad smile. "Of course."

"Wyatt?" Presley grabs my arm. "Do you . . . I mean . . . we can . . ." She stumbles over her words.

I shake my head. "I need to do this alone."

Another tear falls from my eyes, and I wipe it away. I have to be strong. I pull myself to my feet and turn away from my family. I hear my mama's cries, but I need to see my little girl just this once.

We enter a small room with a rocking chair in the corner. The doctor leads me there and talks a little, but I honestly don't know what she says. I can't focus on anything other than the pain in my heart.

Then I think about Angie. I can't lose her too. I won't survive it.

A few minutes later, a nurse and another doctor enter. "Mr. Hennington," she says softly. "We can give you some time, but I want to make sure you understand." I try to focus. "Your daughter is very small. She was only a little over one pound. We'll be outside if you need anything, okay?"

"Do you know anything more about Angie?"

"She's out of surgery and in recovery. We don't know when she'll wake up, but I'll come find you as soon as she's stable enough for visitors."

"Thank you." I wipe another tear.

"Of course." She squeezes my hand.

The nurse wheels in one of those plastic basin things where my daughter lies. They've wrapped the baby in a blanket and hand her to me.

The minute she's in my arms, I lose it. Tears fall, and I shake with sobs. "I'm so sorry, Faith."

I know she's tiny and fragile, but I want to hold her close. I want to pump life into her. The grief is overwhelming. I'm her Dad. I *was* her Dad. This shouldn't be how I held her for the first time. It should've been a happy moment that was filled with smiles and tears of joy.

Not tears of sadness.

"I'm so sorry." I cry harder. She's beautiful, even now. How could she not be? "I love you so much. Your mama does, too. I should've—" My lungs ache as I try to speak. "I should've protected you." I rock back and forth with an angel in my arms. "I should've saved you, baby girl. This shouldn't be how we met."

I take her in. I study every line and angle on her tiny little body. She fits in the palm of my hand. My little girl. Gone to heaven.

While my other angel fights for her life.

I've failed them both.

chapter
TWENTY-TWO

Angie

THERE'S PRESSURE ON MY HANDS and a steady beeping behind me. The first thing that comes to my mind is pain. I'm in so much pain. My entire body feels sore and achy. But that's nothing compared to my head. It's throbbing, and I can feel the blood pounding against my skull.

Then I remember.

The deer.

The tumbling.

The unbelievable pain as my head slammed against the glass, the dash, the airbag.

Wyatt calling my name as the fog crept over me.

The fear.

Then the blackness.

"Wyatt," I croak while trying to move my hand. Agony sears through my veins from the smallest movement. "Wyatt?" I try again, not sure if any sound is coming out.

I hear someone move. "Angie?" A sigh. "Baby—" Wyatt's voice cracks, and I try to open my eyes to find him.

Our baby. I feel hollow and confused. I don't know what's going on. Fear fills the emptiness, and I need to know what happened. Am I okay? Is the baby okay? Is Wyatt okay?

My eyelids won't move, so I use every ounce of strength I have to push them open. The light blinds me, but I hold them steady. "The baby?"

He moves to the side and presses a button. "Relax, okay? Are you in pain?"

I glance at my stomach, which is flat. "Where is she?"

My eyes close as the panic and pain become too much. I try to curl into myself, ball up and block out whatever truth he's going to give me. Before I can muscle through the pain in my body, his hand is on my shoulder. "Please, don't hurt yourself."

I force myself to look at him again. "Is she okay?"

His brown eyes fill with tears, and his lips tremble for a second before they mash together. "I . . ." A tear falls. "They tried."

Oh, God. My breathing accelerates as the monitor beeps louder, faster. I can't breathe. He has to be lying. She can't be gone.

"No!" My heart ceases to exist, that beeping is a lie. "No!" I cry again as Wyatt takes my hand. The pounding in my head intensifies. "She can't . . ." I hiccup.

"They tried so hard, Ang. They did everything they could," he explains.

"She was so strong." Tears fall. They come down like rain as the realization that I lost my baby settles deep inside me. I'm alive, he's alive, and she's not.

"Baby." He takes my face in his hands. "I'm sorry, Angie. I'm so sorry. I begged them to save her. I begged God to take me and let you keep her. I would've done anything."

My chest heaves as sobs rake through me. I don't care about the pain. I want to revel in it because it's real. My little girl is gone from my body. I was supposed to keep her safe. I kept her alive. Now she's gone. "No! Please," I beg.

Wyatt wraps his arm around me, holding me as I fall apart.

"Shhh." He tries to calm me.

"Angie." I hear Presley's voice. Wyatt loosens his hold as my best friend walks over to my other side. "I don't know what to say other than I love you so much."

"She never had a chance." My voice is full of anguish. "It's too much, Pres."

"I know." She wipes the tear from my cheek. "It's not fair."

I look over at Wyatt, the strong man who looks like he's falling apart. His hair is disheveled; his usual scruff is almost a full beard. There are cuts on his face that look like they're healing. "How long?" I choke on the words.

Wyatt's lip quivers and a tear falls down his face. He glances over at Presley.

She squeezes my hand. "It's been four days." She sniffs. "Four days, and you underwent surgery. You ruptured your spleen, which is why they had to remove the baby. You fought so hard for her, honey." Presley's tears fall rapidly. "She just couldn't hold on."

My tears don't stop falling. I lost my brother two years ago, and I thought there was nothing that could rival that pain, until now. That was a gentle kiss across the skin compared to this knife slicing through my chest. There's nothing to fully express how completely empty I feel.

I look out the window, wanting to slip back into the darkness. When I was there, I still had her. I had everything.

Now, I have nothing.

"Angie?" Wyatt says, but I can't look at him.

The nurse walks in. "Hi, honey." She's careful not to sound too happy. Her eyes take in the scene of people around me crying. "I'm going to check you over and then give you something for the pain, okay?"

"Whatever," I reply.

I don't have any strength for any emotions right now. I'm

broken. Once again, someone I love has been stolen from me. I've been robbed of the family I thought I would have.

She looks at my vitals, types something into a small computer, and then injects something into my IV. "That should help with the headache." Her hand gently squeezes my arm. "Your family has been at your bedside the entire time. You should get your rest, honey. The doctor will be in soon since you're awake now."

Presley's red-rimmed eyes lock on mine. "I know you're hurting. You both are." She looks at Wyatt. "I just . . ." She stumbles for words. "Know that if you need me, for anything, I'm here."

I close my eyes. "She's gone."

"She is. She's gone and it's not fair. It's awful and cruel, but you're here, Wyatt's here, and you both need to lean on each other. You need to grieve and know that you have people around you who will do whatever you need."

A pained sound escapes my mouth. "Give me back my daughter. Bring her back! That's what I need. I need you to give me back my child!"

Wyatt releases my other hand and walks toward the door. His back is to me, but I can see his shoulders shake. I watch him fall apart. His hand braces on the window sill, and he wipes his face with the other. He doesn't let me see him, but I know he's trying to keep it together.

Presley chokes on her sob. "I can't do that. I wish I could."

"That's what I thought," I look away. "I want to go to sleep."

She kisses my forehead. "Okay, babe. Rest if you can. We'll talk more later. I love you."

I draw in a shaky breath. "I know."

Presley turns, goes to Wyatt, and grips his arm. She says something too low for me to hear, and he nods. Her eyes glance back at me one last time before she slips out the door.

Wyatt heads toward me with a pained look in his eyes.

After a few minutes of silence, I whisper, "Why? Why did this happen to us?"

"I'm sorry."

I close my eyes as everything starts to sink in. "Did you see her?"

"We don't have to talk about this now." His voice is so hesitant, so sad, but I don't care.

"I need to know! I-I need!" I start to get hysterical. I was out for days while they've all processed this. I just found out I lost my baby. I need to know what happened. Was she hurt? Could I have done something? As I start to move to sit up, a stabbing sensation hits my side. I suck in a breath and close my eyes.

"Okay." He pushes my hair back. "Okay, please just try to stay calm."

I nod and slowly relax myself. "I need to know, Wyatt."

"I held her." He tells me. "I held her in my palm and cried over her." I close my eyes and choke back the tears, but they slip past my eyelashes and fall down my cheek anyway. "She's beautiful and tiny. I told her about how much I love her. I told her how much you do, too."

"I can't." I stop him. "I can't. I thought I could."

His body slumps a little, and he leans against the side of the bed. "Okay." Resignation settles between us. "We don't have to do this now. When you've rested, we'll go from there."

There's nowhere to go—not unless he's able to bring back what is gone, which he can't. No one can. We're going to have to find a way to be childless parents and get through our days. I'll have to look at my stomach every day for the rest of my life and know she's gone.

"HONEY." MRS. HENNINGTON HAS BEEN talking at me for

what feels like an hour. I say "talking at" because I haven't really been responding. I can't. How can I talk when I'm dead inside? "We have to make arrangements."

I don't want to do any of this. "Please," I beseech her. "Just pick whatever." I want her to go away.

Presley shares a look with her, and Wyatt stares out the window. This morning, the chaplain came to talk to us about the loss of a child and how important it was to grieve. As if I didn't know enough about that. He urged us to name her, spend some time with her, and allow ourselves to let go.

Then the doctor explained that there were no policies regarding infants, and we just needed to let our wants be known.

After they left, Wyatt spoke as I sat here crying and listened, wishing I could soothe his pain. He was in agony, but I was so deep in my own, I didn't know what to say. I held his hand as he spoke of our baby and all she means to him. He told me how scared he was that I wouldn't come out of it. That he would lose me too. His pain was palpable as he expressed his guilt and remorse.

It wasn't his fault, but I couldn't get the words out. Not because I don't believe them, but because I'm struggling to breathe.

I want them to leave me the fuck alone. That's what I want. Everyone.

"Pick whatever you think is best. I really don't care." I try for a calm tone, but judging by the way their eyes widen, I failed.

"Did you decide if you want to see her?" Presley brings it up again. "We don't want to do anything until you've made up your mind, Ang. We can't undo it after that."

I don't know if my heart can handle it.

But I have to decide if I want to see the baby I couldn't protect.

"No." I turn my head away and touch my stomach. "Not yet."

Wyatt's hand touches my shoulder. "We appreciate your help," he says to them. "Why don't we let Angie rest, and I'll let you know if she changes her mind about a funeral."

They bid their goodbyes and let me have my space.

A few minutes pass without either of us saying a word. I'm struggling with a myriad of things. I'm in physical pain for one, but my heart is broken . . . completely and utterly shredded.

When I sleep, I dream of her.

When I'm awake, I cry for her.

Everyone offers sympathy and support, but there's nothing anyone can do to fill the hole in my heart.

"I'm not trying to push," Wyatt says, breaking the silence.

"I know."

"If you want me to be with you when you see her, I will. I'll do anything you need, Angie. Anything."

He's trying. Hell, we both are. There's no hiding how difficult this is for him. His tear-streaked face, puffy eyes, and constant worry is evident. I know he's swimming in the same sea of grief as me. Both of us barely treading water. Both ready to be taken under.

I've gone back and forth on what I should do, but I think I know. "I want to see her."

He nods. "Do you want me here with you?"

This will hurt him again. I know it'll kill him. But I need him by my side.

"I don't want to ask you to do it," I say with a shaky voice. "I know it's selfish, but I don't think I can do it alone."

Wyatt rushes forward, wrapping me in his arms. I don't care that I'm physically in pain from his touch. I want him to never let me go. Right now, I can breathe just a little bit. "You don't have to do this alone."

I allow myself this comfort. I cling to him, to us, and to the ache that binds us together.

After we both collect ourselves, Wyatt calls for the nurse. She explains the process to me and lets me know what I can expect. There's no way to truly prepare, I don't think. How does a person ever ready themselves to say goodbye to their child?

No, I never held her and never heard her cry. I didn't get to tie her shoes on her first day of school, but I loved her.

I named her in my heart.

I carried her in my belly.

And I gave her everything I could.

Now I have to say goodbye to her.

chapter
TWENTY-THREE

"WE'LL SEE YOU BACK AT the house?" Mrs. Henning-ton asks.

"I really just want to go to bed." I sit on the grass, picking the blades around me and wishing I could float away in the wind.

It would be so easy to drift, letting the breeze take me where it wants to go. Instead, I'm sinking deeper into the ground.

Wyatt, his parents, Presley, Zach, and Trent all stand around, looking unsure of what to do. Today we buried our daughter. This was the last thing we needed to do. The hospital explained that in doing this, we'd start to heal.

They're full of shit.

It's been eleven days since the accident, and it's not getting any easier to accept what's going on.

I've sat and cried, waded through unbelievable anger, and I'm slipping into numbness. Wyatt tries. Lord knows he wants to fix this, but there's nothing he can do.

We buried Faith Emma Hennington under a big oak tree on the Hennington farm. She overlooks a beautiful hill with a small pond. It's peaceful here, and I find some tiny amount of solace that she's surrounded by beauty.

"Okay, sugar. I'll stop by tomorrow with some food." She crouches next to me. "I love her, too." My eyes snap up. "There is nothing in this world like a mother's love. Not a single man can ever understand the depths of that. I know you're in pain. I've never lost a child, but just imagining it—"

Macie Hennington is the most caring woman I've ever known. Everyone here today is feeling some level of sadness. They fought to get me out of that car, they cried when they found out we'd lost Faith, and they've been at the hospital day in and day out.

This little family is struggling right now.

"I never imagined it would hurt this much," I admit.

She cups my chin. "The minute you accepted that you were going to carry that baby was the minute she owned your heart. You grieve, Angie. You feel what you need to feel, but let us be here." Macie kisses my cheek and wipes her own tear.

Presley curls up next to me as the three brothers stand in a circle off to the side. After a while, I lie on her lap, and her fingers brush my hair back. We don't have to say a word. That's the beauty of true friendship. She continues to run her fingers through my hair, allowing me the quiet. Tears fall, simply because I don't know how to stop them.

They explained my hormones would go through the same rapid changes they would if I had delivered at full-term. Apparently, a body doesn't know the difference between bringing home a baby and having to bury one. I sway from one extreme to another, but mostly I stay in the bleakness.

"We've lost a lot the past few years," she speaks softly.

"I'd like it to stop."

"You don't know your own strength until you're forced to face it."

I tilt my head to look at her. "I'm doing the best I can."

Presley shakes her head quickly. "You're doing great, babe. Listen, I don't want you to freak out, so I'm telling you now."

I roll on my back and wait for it. Presley's lips turn down, and she sighs. "Zach and I decided to put the wedding off another two months."

"No!" I wince. "Please not because of this."

"It's not. I promise," she reassures. "We have a lot going on with the horse farm and with being sued by Felicia for wrongful termination. It's better if Zach and I don't actually marry before that's cleared. So, after speaking to the lawyers, we decided to push it back two months."

"Are you sure?" I ask.

"Yes. We already live together, and he's my husband in every way other than on paper."

I close my eyes and smother the tears. It feels as if everything is falling apart. I really hope the accident isn't the reason. I knew Felicia was going after Zach, but I figured she'd drop it after his team of lawyers threatened to countersue.

My mind drifts back to the hell we all endured when my brother killed himself. It was like that one single event tripped a wire, and we all got hit with shrapnel.

"Do you think we're going to struggle like we did with Todd?"

"I hope not." Presley returns to playing with my hair. "Do you remember when I was sitting around the house after he died?"

She was a ghost. Presley would answer if she was asked a question, but she'd completely lost herself. It was as if she'd died along side of him. "Yes."

"Don't let the pain over run you. I can only say this to you because you're my sister, my best friend, and I love you. I've been right where you are. I've felt the pain so deep I wanted to let it consume me. I did let it." Her eyes hold mine. "You made it stop. You forced me to dig deep and breathe again. Don't get lost, Ang. Don't let it eat y'all alive. You lived, don't let her death be in vain."

Presley stands, brushes the grass off her legs, and then helps me up as well. I know what she's telling me is coming from a place of love, but I've never felt like this. "How? How do I move on from this?"

Losing Todd was completely different. He was an adult, and it was his choice. This wasn't. This was a terrible accident that altered the future I thought I would have.

"By living. By loving someone. By forgiving yourself, Wyatt, and anyone else you blame. For understanding that the time you did have was precious. Look at what you've learned. Look at what you've found." Her eyes move toward the guys.

She doesn't get it. Wyatt may have been falling in love with me, but he truly loved the baby. She's gone now. I have no idea what any of this means for us, and honestly, I don't have the wherewithal to care. I was supposed to be leaving here in a week anyway. Clearly, I can't drive with a broken wrist and staples in my stomach, so I've had to postpone it.

"Now that there's no baby between us, I don't know if there even is an us," I say, feeling a new wave of sadness. "Is this what you felt like when Todd died? Just empty and as if you'd lost everything?"

Presley's eyes shine with unshed tears. "I did lose everything. I lost my husband, my business, my home, my best friend, and the life I built. I faced every single fear I'd ever had. I was stupid, in pain, and miserable." She glances at the guys and then back to me. "When I got here, Wyatt was who was there for me. I didn't know Zach was in Bell Buckle, but Wyatt was on my farm. He kept showing up, making me leave the house, forcing me to find my footing back in a place I didn't want to be." She smiles and it's both warm and sad at the same time. "Then, as if he knew I was ready before even I did, he pushed me into Zach's arms."

"He was distant and cold before the accident." I remind her. "He could've realized he wasn't reciprocating what I was feeling."

It was what held me back from saying anything to him. He was being closed off and almost angry. He wouldn't talk or do any of the things I'd come to love about being around Wyatt.

She looks out at the horizon. "Guys are weird. Country boys are a whole new level. Wyatt has never had a real relationship, neither have you."

"I had Nate."

She snorts. "You had a guy who was a friend. Someone you didn't even glance at when you left for here. You didn't love him. It's not even close to this relationship."

"The only reason I came here was because I was pregnant. That's it, Pres. I have my business back in Philly that I have to think about. Without having the baby anymore . . ." My chest aches. "I don't know if he even wants to try."

Presley shakes her head. "You accuse me of being dense."

"We'll figure it out." My eyes drift to him. "Maybe not today or this week, but when we can think clearly . . . maybe then we'll see where we stand."

∞

"HI, SUGAR." MRS. KANNAN SAYS as I let her in.

"I was wondering when you were coming," I push the screen door open for her. "I guess you drew the short straw for today's visit?" I give a mangled smile.

"No way! I wanted to see you, darlin'. I've missed you. Plus, I made a casserole and thought you were the perfect person for it."

I chuckle. "Oh boy."

We walk into the kitchen where there are about ten casseroles and a half dozen pies lined on the counter. That doesn't count the ones filling the fridge.

"It seems I'm behind the town," she muses. "Well, mine is better."

"I'm sure it's perfect."

Mrs. Kannan makes herself comfortable at the table. I grab two plates, forks, and the pie that I was eying. I'm intending to eat all of my emotions today. Luckily, I'm in no shortage of baked goods or feelings.

She looks into the living room and back to me. "Is Wyatt here?"

It's been three days since we buried Faith. Three days of Wyatt being barely able to look at me and refusing to say more than a word or two. Sure, he sits on the couch with me, but he's careful not to be too close. Then, once the awkwardness is thick enough to cut, he'll head out to the ranch and stay there until I'm asleep.

He's shattered, and I don't know how to heal him.

"He's working," I explain and shove some pie into my mouth.

Mrs. Kannan nods. "How are y'all holding up?"

I give her the very brief version of how everything is fine. I'm sure she's not fooled, neither are Presley or Mrs. Hennington, but I don't want to analyze it. He's grieving. I'm grieving. There's no right or wrong way to handle this situation. He seems to need more time alone, and I'm doing my best to respect that.

I'm the opposite, though.

I need people.

I haven't been alone for more than a half hour. When Presley see's Wyatt's truck leave, she rushes over. If she can't be here, someone else shows up out of nowhere. It's foreign to me that I'm craving people. I've been independent my whole life, but right now being alone leaves me with nothing to do but think. My mind wanders down paths that it doesn't need to seek. I get caught up in the "what ifs" and "could've beens".

"I know that it gets better with time. It did with my brother." I play with the fork as I think through how I feel right now. "I know it takes a while before you get back into your groove, but everything feels unsettling."

Mrs. Kannan takes my hand in hers. "Of course it does, honey. You were preparin' for a life that isn't going to be anymore. I know it's a lot to handle, but you're doing it. You're healing in a lot of ways right now. It'll get better. You and Wyatt love each other, and you'll work it out."

"Do we?" I ask. "I mean do we really? I would've never been in Bell Buckle if it weren't for the baby. He would've lived his life just fine."

Her brown eyes widen. "Don't think like that. I know you're confused, but don't you doubt what the two of you share. I saw it with my own eyes." Her hand slaps against the table. "I've been around that boy since he was an infant. I've never in all my years seen him look at a girl the way he looks at you. It's not a test of love when things are good. It's how you handle things when times are bad."

If that's the case . . . we're failing. Things can't be much worse for us right now, and he's withdrawing. "He won't talk to me."

"Then you make him talk."

I've been putting off the talk about where we, as a couple, go from here. Part of me is afraid of what words will be spoken. If he doesn't return my love, can I withstand another devastation? I don't think I can. Between the healing my body is doing, the hormones that are wreaking havoc on my system, and Wyatt's mood . . . I can't.

I would rather suffer in silence than be deafened by the truth.

chapter
TWENTY-FOUR

I WAKE WITH A GASP. Sweat trickles down my skin, my breathing is accelerated, and my heart is pounding. I hate this dream. I look over to the other side of the bed, and once again, Wyatt's side is empty. It's the fifth night in a row I've had this terrifying dream. The car tumbling, the pain of hitting my head, the haunting sound of the monitors beeping, listening to them telling me I've lost my baby. Then, I find that my nightmare is my reality.

My feet hit the cold floor, and I go in search of Wyatt. He's lying on the couch with the television on.

I stand here for a few minutes, but he doesn't notice my presence. He doesn't look like the same man from only a few short weeks ago. Wyatt was always smiling, full of joy and warmth. Now he's cold and distant, not in a way that was even before the accident though. He was still him, just with something on his mind.

This is a man drowning in grief. I have to pull him out.

I know this. I have to find a way to get him to meet me half-way so we can get past this awful phase. I've been here before. I know what it looks like and where it can lead. I won't let the man I love get lost in the abyss.

I pull my sweater around myself a little tighter and brace for a conversation we need to have.

I can't live like this anymore. I *need* my Wyatt back.

"Hey," I rasp. My throat still dry from sleep.

"Did I wake you?" he asks, sitting straight up.

I shake my head. "No. I had another dream."

He doesn't say anything as he presses his lips together. I move around the side of the couch, wanting to sit with him. We haven't really spoken at all the last four days. He's been at the ranch or his brother's houses. When he gets home, he's not really here. I'm lonely and sad.

"The accident?" Wyatt guesses.

"Yeah." I curl up on the opposite end of the couch with what feels like an ocean between us. Three weeks ago, I would've practically been in his lap. "I woke up looking for you, but you were gone again."

Wyatt leans his head back against the couch. "I started watching this movie. I didn't even realize how late it was," he explains.

When I look at the screen, there's no movie playing. It's an infomercial about skincare.

"Have you slept at all? It's been a few nights of this."

The dark circles under his eyes tell me he hasn't. "I can't."

I shift closer, hoping maybe my touch will thaw him a little, but he moves farther away. "You can talk to me, Wyatt."

"I'm fine."

Right.

"It might help?" I continue to urge. "We both lost, Faith. We're both in this together. It might help you to talk to me."

When I say her name, his eyes cut to me. The look he gives tells me we're still in the anger stage.

Awesome.

I start putting my steel walls up. I know this is going to be ugly, but I can't let it continue on like this. He's not the only one living in this purgatory of sorrow. I cry every day—mostly in the shower so he won't hear me if he's home. I wake up every morning with my hand on my belly. I'm hurting too, but I've been here before, and it's not a place I want to visit again. We have to move forward in some way or another.

He lets out a short breath through his nose. "What do you want me to say? I'm not sleeping. It's not like you should care anyway."

Okay. "Why aren't you sleeping?"

"Why do you think?" His tone is clearly disturbed. "Go back to bed, Angie."

Breathe, Angie. Do not play into this. It's anger and part of the process. Remember that.

"No. We're going to talk. I think you should tell me why you're not sleeping. I can't know what's going on in your head when you won't talk to me."

His light brown eyes study my face. I won't crack or back down. I need him to talk to me. If he doesn't, this will never be resolved. So I hold strong. I glare right back at him, hoping to instigate an actual conversation.

"You wanna know?" he taunts.

"Yes."

He laughs. "All right, darlin'. I'll tell you why I can't sleep. Because when I close my fucking eyes, I see you dying in front of me. I remember what it felt like to find out that our little girl died. Then, I see your face when I told you Faith was gone. I see every goddamn minute and every goddamn tear you've shed. I can't be around you, because each time, it's all there again. I don't want to sleep, because it's a horror movie that won't stop playin'. Is that what you want to know? I can't look at you, Angie!"

That hurts more than I care to admit. I know I'm supposed to be levelheaded, but I slip.

"So this is my fault?" I stand with my arms wrapped around

my stomach. "I'm causing you this pain?" Tears rush forward as his words cut me deep.

He's on his feet in a second. "No!" he bellows. "It's my fault! I was driving that car. I didn't get you out fast enough to save her. I didn't see the deer. None of this is your fault! But God! I can't look at you and not see it all! Don't you see? Don't you see this is killing me?"

I hold back every tear that wants to escape. He's finally talking, and I'm going to keep him going as long as I can. I know he's struggling with guilt. I can feel it in the air. I wont let him sink. I'm trying to cling to him, and he's got his arm out so far I can't touch him.

"It was an accident! A horrible, horrible accident! One that took so much from us!" I can't stop the tears now. "It wasn't your fault! It wasn't anyone's fault!" Wyatt starts to walk away, but I rush after him. "Don't walk away, Wyatt. Don't do this, don't walk away from me."

He stops moving at my pleas. "I need to get out of here."

"No!" I yell. "No more hiding. This isn't you! This isn't the man I've spent the last three months with. It was an *accident*."

He scoffs. "You can't believe that. I see it in your eyes. I see how you look at me now."

My hand covers my mouth. He's nuts. "I don't blame you! Not one time have I ever said losing Faith was your fault. Not once have I even thought it. It was a deer! A deer ran into our car on the cold, wet road. It wasn't your fault!" I walk toward him, but he steps back. "You can't even let me touch you." The words aren't an accusation, they're the truth. "You haven't hugged me, kissed me, slept next to me, or anything since the burial."

His eyes fill with tears. "I can't."

"Oh," I say with pain layered on that one syllable. He can't touch me? Me? I need his touch. I've fallen for him, and now he can't bear to be around me. Everything is wrong. This isn't how it's meant to be.

It's my worst fear come to fruition. I believe that at some point, Wyatt Hennington fell in love with me. I felt it every time he looked at me. But now he looks at me with something else. It's not love and affection. He's not hot and cold, he's just . . . frozen.

"I'll be back later," Wyatt says as he turns away. "I have to check on the horses."

I don't think that's true, but I'm too shocked to protest. I've pushed him too far. He grabs his sweatshirt and keys. Before he walks out the door, I finally reply. "I'll be here."

He pauses as he's halfway out the door. "For now," he says and then the door shuts.

The air is forced from my lungs, tears fall, and I lose it.

I'm not sure how much a heart can withstand before it gives out completely.

"HEY, ANGIE," GRACE SAYS WITH surprise. "I didn't think I'd see you already."

I couldn't sit in that house another minute. Wyatt was gone, and I don't have a car, so when Trent came by to check in on me, I talked him into driving me here. Of course, he very indiscreetly made a phone call when I was demanding he take me to the bakery. The conversation lasted a few minutes with Trent whisper-yelling as I got ready. I couldn't hear what he said, but Wyatt either didn't care or didn't argue with his brother. Seems he's being a dick to everyone.

Trent tried to convince me to stay home, but I demanded he take me or I was calling his mama.

Here I stand.

"Yeah," I say flippantly. "I was bored. I'd rather be here than staring at the same four walls."

Grace nods. "I understand that. I can't imagine sittin' around all day. I'd go out of my mind," she laughs. "How are you feelin'?"

"Still a little sore. I go to the doctor tomorrow for my post-op check-up. Otherwise, I'm breathing."

"Wanna sit for a bit? I've been dreamin' of these cupcakes for the last few days and would love to not have to eat alone."

"Sure." I smile and come around the counter.

"Presley tells me you haven't decided if you're headin' back to Pennsylvania," she says then sips her coffee.

"Presley has a big mouth." I roll my eyes.

"Sorry, I guess I was just hopin' that maybe you were going to stay."

Grace is sweet, and I genuinely like her. She brought more food than anyone else over the last few weeks. She said when she's emotional, she cooks. It was heartwarming to see a town reach out to us. Even though the loss was by far more of Wyatt's and my own.

"You didn't overstep. Things are . . ." I struggle to finish my thought.

"Wyatt isn't handling things well, is he?" Grace takes a guess.

"No."

She sighs and folds her hands. "I was afraid of that."

"Why?"

Grace leans back in the chair and worries her lip. "We've all been close our whole lives. You don't grow up in a town like this and not know everyone. Wyatt has always been the strongest of the Hennington boys. Zach and Trent have always relied on him in ways that many don't see. Sure, Trent is supposed to be the law, and Zach was the star athlete with the girl of his dreams." She waves her hand as if those two points don't really mean much. "But Wyatt has been their rock. He stood back, watched them do what they do, and supported everyone. He's the fixer. He's the man who pushes them through all the messes they make. Now though, he can't fix this. He can't give you back what you lost, what he feels like he caused."

"He's not worried about fixing me." I look away. "He's too busy breaking me apart."

Grace rests her arms on the table and takes my hand in hers. "I can see that. I don't think he knows how to deal with that. You know what I mean?"

I do know what she's saying. But I don't know what to do about it. "Can we talk about something else? Please?"

"I'm sorry," she says quickly.

"Nothing to apologize for, Grace. I need a break from my life. Tell me, how are you and Trent?"

"Trent." Grace shakes her head and looks away. "I have spent my entire life waiting for the man to love me. It's hard when you love someone like I love Trent. He's hurt me so many times, but I can't walk away from him. Even now."

"What's changed?"

"Cooper."

I know that I have big issues in my own life, but for this minute . . . it feels good to talk about something else. I'm not worrying about all the shit rattling around in my own head, I can maybe help someone else.

"Do you like him that way?" I ask. The last thing I would want is Presley's brother to get caught up in a love triangle.

Grace nods. "I really do. I never saw him that way. He was always my best friend's brother." She sighs. "Now though, I can't stop thinkin' about him. He keeps asking me out, but I can't find a way to say yes."

"Can I offer my advice?"

Her hand grips mine. "Please, I've been going crazy not havin' anyone to talk to. I can't talk to Presley about this, it's her brother and then a Hennington. Emily, who you met once, is too busy bein' a big country music singer . . . I could use a friend."

I place my hand over hers. "If you think that Trent Hennington isn't going to change his ways, then you follow your heart. Cooper is a good man. I don't think he'd risk his friendship, family, and his heart if he wasn't serious about you. A man fights for the woman he loves."

And that right there is the problem I'm having. Wyatt isn't fighting.

He's letting me go.

He's watching me drift away out to sea.

I'm losing him every day that passes, and it's destroying me.

chapter
TWENTY-FIVE

" **E**VERYTHING IS HEALING NICELY, ANGIE. I'd like you to take it easy for another week or so. No heavy lifting, and then we'll start physical therapy for your wrist in about two weeks when we remove the cast," the doctor explains. "Do you have any questions?"

I go over my list of things to ask, especially about travel. It's been four weeks since the accident. All the bruises are gone and cuts are healed. Other than the wound still very deep inside my soul, I'm doing well.

I have to go back to Philadelphia sometime in the next week, Erin has been nothing but supportive while I've been healing, but it's not fair to leave her on her own much longer. Presley offered to road trip with me and the boys. They've been begging to visit some of their friends, and I could use the company. Plus, she misses the bakery, so it's something I have been thinking about.

I glance to the empty plastic chair that Wyatt should be sitting in but isn't. He decided not to come in with me. Again, another show of his new attitude. Each little thing adds a new tear to my already annihilated heart. I don't understand this at all. Maybe it's my lack of relationships that has me so inept in dealing with this. Maybe it's the fact that he's never endured loss and I seem to be a pro at it.

It doesn't change the fact that it's breaking me apart.

Dr. Borek and I exit toward the waiting room. When Wyatt spots him, he stands and heads our way. "Everything okay?" Concern filters through.

"Angie is doing great," he assures him. "How are you handling things, son?"

"I'm doing fine. Getting back to work was good for me."

I want to laugh. He's not doing fine.

The doctor nods. "Good. If you notice you're not yourself, we can get you in to see someone." Wyatt's eyes cut to me, and he mashes his teeth together.

Great. Now he thinks I said something.

"Thanks for the offer, I'm really okay."

I mentally roll my eyes and sigh. "Thanks again, Dr. Borek," I cut in. "I really appreciate everything."

"You be safe on your trip."

Wyatt flinches. "Trip?"

Well, if he were to ever actually talk to me, he would know. But he doesn't. He avoids me at all costs. He's home when I go to the bakery. He's at work when I'm home. And if by some chance he's around me, he does his best to be busy.

"Yes, I'm going to Philly to meet with Erin."

He shakes his head while releasing an inaudible laugh. "Of course you are."

Dr. Borek shifts his weight. "I'll let you two talk. Be sure to make an appointment in a few weeks. I want to check your wrist before you start PT."

Wyatt turns on his heels and walks away.

We get in the truck, and he wastes no time getting on the road. He drives the twenty minutes back to the house in silence. The thickness in the air between us is stifling. I have a feeling we're not going to come out of the fight that's brewing unscathed.

I didn't keep the trip from him for any reason other than he avoids me at all costs. I can't tell him something when he refuses to acknowledge me.

We pull in the driveway, and he shuts the car off. Neither of us moves.

After a few minutes, Wyatt turns to me. "I don't know how to do this anymore."

I look over and sigh. "I don't either."

"Were you plannin' to tell me about you going back?"

"Were you planning to speak to me?" I throw the ball back in his court.

"We talk."

"The hell we do." I cross my arms and swallow my tears. "We don't talk. You don't come home, you don't call me in the middle of the day anymore, and you haven't slept beside me in weeks. I bet you can't even remember the last time you kissed me. I figured you'd be happy I was leaving for a bit."

"I told you I can't right now," he huffs.

"And I've understood that. I know that you're handling this the only way you know how, but you're pushing me out the door. I thought maybe if I go back to Philly for a while, I can give you the space we both need."

"Then what?" His voice shifts. "Then you just come back?"

I'm going to lose it. I'm done being understanding and patient. I'm tired of feeling like I've done something wrong and have to walk on eggshells. Maybe what we felt for each other really was because of the baby. If so, better to figure this out now. Will it hurt to leave him? Yup. But the Wyatt I fell in love with died alongside our baby.

"I don't know, Wyatt. Do I have a reason to come back?"

He slams his hand on the wheel. "So we're going to go around in riddles?"

"This right here," I say, pointing between the two of us.

"This was something special. I fell in love with you. I want to stay and be a family. I love you!"

His head shakes back and forth. "No. No you don't."

"Yes I do! I love you! All I want is for you to stop fighting me now. You told me that night you were falling in love with me. I wanted to say it so bad, but I didn't know if I was crazy. Don't tell me I don't love you!"

It's not right. We were doing so well. We were happy. We were going to have a life together and a family . . . now we're so broken. He doesn't believe me.

"I was falling in love with you."

"And now you aren't?" I don't know why I asked. I really don't. Deep inside me, I know what he's going to say.

Wyatt's brown eyes shimmer with unshed tears. "No."

Just like that, the fragile pieces of my heart disintegrate into dust.

"You know?" I let my tears fall freely. "It took me thirty-six years to ever let myself love a man. I thought when I finally let myself go, it would be for someone special. Even though you just single-handedly destroyed me, I wouldn't change it." I now understand Presley's words. "I would give myself to you all over again, even knowing it would end this way."

I open the car door and head inside. I don't look back because there's no point. He's already gone.

"WYATT?" I CALL OUT IN the blackness. It's three in the morning, and he's not here. I look all around the house, but there's no sign he ever came home. After our fight, he took off. I didn't try to call him. I hadn't wanted to. He really hurt me this time, but it's strange that he's not here.

I look for his truck, but it's missing.

I call his phone, but get his voice mail.

Where the hell is he?

I don't want to worry anyone, but I can't seem to shake this feeling in my gut. Something's wrong.

"Hey, is everything okay?" Trent's sleep-filled voice comes through.

"I'm sorry to wake you, but Wyatt and I had a fight, and he left hours ago. I don't know if he's maybe with you?" I start to pace the floor. "I'm just worried."

Trent clears his throat. "He's not here, at least not that I know of. Let me check."

I stay on the phone, and he lets me know Wyatt's not there. "Can I borrow your car? I need to find him." I hate asking, but there's no way I'll go back to sleep without knowing if he's okay.

"I'll look for him. You stay put in case he shows back up."

"He's not handling this well," I inform him.

Trent releases a heavy sigh. "I know, Ang. I tried talkin' to him the other day, but he told me to fuck off. I've never seen him like this, Zach and I are at a loss on what to do. But I know him, and he'll figure himself out. He feels responsible for hurtin' you."

"It wasn't his fault!"

"I know that. You know that. It's Wyatt who doesn't."

My heart hurts for him. He has been awful, but I still can't help but only see the man who made me coffee, baked cupcakes, showed me how to fishing, and took me to the cabin. He was the man who would make me feel like I was worth everything. In a few short months, he showed me how great life could be with someone.

He's still in there. Because I won't for one second believe that this Wyatt is the real Wyatt.

"Will you find him for me, Trent?"

"I'll find him. Then you can beat his ass for wakin' me up."

I laugh. "Deal."

Thirty minutes later, Wyatt stumbles through the door. His

eyes meet mine as I stand at the door to the bedroom.

"You're still here?" he slurs.

Great. He's fucking drunk. "Where have you been?"

"What do you care?"

"What do I care?" I spit the words back at him. "I've been worried. Where have you been?"

"Out."

"Well, that's nice." I huff.

"What does it matter anyway? You're leavin', and we're done."

"So, you're going to really stand by that you never loved me? Everything we felt, everything we shared, was all a lie?"

He comes closer, and all I smell is alcohol and cheap perfume. "Nothing was a lie, until I destroyed it all." He points to my chest. "Because you're better off being where you wanted to be anyway. I'm doin' you a favor."

"By pushing me away?"

Wyatt throws his hands up and then lets them fall. "I've been tryin' to tell you, baby. I'm lettin' you go. You and I can move on now. You don't have to look at me and see the man who took it all away!"

"You don't know anything." I stare into his eyes.

He squints and purses his lips. "I know what I know."

"You're drunk."

"Yup!" He laughs. "I finally feel nothing. I can breathe and see straight."

I roll my eyes and start to walk away, but he grabs my wrist and pulls me against him. Our bodies slam together, and my heart races. It's the first time he's touched me in weeks. We stand for a moment, breathing each other in. I've missed his touch. I've craved for him to be close to me like this, but it hurts too much. I see the hurt in his eyes. I don't know how drunk he is or if he'll remember this in the morning, so I decide to lay it out.

"I love you. I know you're hurting. I know that you think all this is your fault . . ." I say as I run my hand along his jaw, feeling the scruff that covers his skin. "It's not. It was a terrible accident where we both lost something precious to us. But I would've given my life up for *you*, not because of her, but because I love you." Wyatt's eyes close and a tear leaks out. "I don't believe you're this man. This angry, hurt, foolish man who goes out and drinks himself stupid. You're the man who moves all your clothes out of the closet to give me room. The one who learns how to make my favorite drink. The guy who laid with me in bed and let me soak your shirt with my tears. The guy who took me fishing and showed me I could let go. The man I fell in love with wanted our first time as a couple to mean something. He fought through a very tough exterior to make me fall in love with him." I trail my hand from his jaw so it can rest over his heart. "The man that stands here isn't him. I'm begging you to find him. Find him before this new man finds himself alone."

Wyatt wipes the tear from my face. "You're leavin' anyway. Just like you were always going to."

I shake my head. "I'm going back for a week. It's up to you if I return."

I press my lips against his. I can't stop myself. I've missed this so much. The kiss deepens as he lets go a little more. His hands grab my cheeks as he holds me tight. I hold his face, keeping him to me as my heart aches thinking this could be it. This could be our last kiss. I try not to let my mind go there, but my emotions are at war with each other.

I love him, but he's hurting me.

I want to save him, but he won't let me.

I want to hold on to him, but he's pushing me away.

His arms begin to loosen, and I grip him tighter.

No. Hold on to me. I beg in my mind. "Let me love you, Wyatt."

Wyatt rests his forehead on mine. "Let me go before I hurt you more."

"This is what's hurting," I murmur. "If you love something, you have to fight for it. Fight for me. Fight for what we could've been."

His eyes lift as he drops his arms. "I have no fight left, and I don't love you. Go back home, Angie."

TWENTY-SIX

Wyatt

MY FUCKING HEAD IS POUNDING. How much did I drink last night? I rub the side of my head and try to recall what happened.

I remember getting to the bar, drinking a shitload of shots, and seeing Beau, the guy who didn't save Faith. He should've done something more. I remember telling him all that, and then I think my brother showed up.

My eyes open, and I look around, only vaguely realizing that something's different. I'm still too hungover to give a fuck, though.

I grab my phone to check the time. Holy shit! It's three in the afternoon, and I have four missed calls. Two from Presley, one from Trent, and one from Mama. I toss the phone back on the couch and cover my eyes with my arm. No way I want to hear from any of them. All three will tell me what a fuck up I'm being—as if I didn't already know. I can't seem to stop myself.

"Open the damn door, you asshole!" Presley yells from the other side of the front door.

Maybe she'll go away.

"Goddamn it, Wyatt Hennington!" she screams.

I sit up and drop my head into my hands. I don't need this right now.

"I know you're in there." She kicks the door.

This won't end well. I get up and open the door to find her staring at me with so much anger in her eyes it forces me to step back. "Good morning, Cowgirl."

"Don't!" Her small hands push against my chest. "Don't talk! I will beat the shit out of you with my bare hands. I can't even believe you right now. *Who are you?* Do you think you're the only man who's dealt with loss? Do you think at all? No. I don't think you do! I can't believe you said those things to her! I can't believe you just let her walk away!" Presley rants and yells as she continues to hit me.

"What the hell are you talkin' about?"

"You've got to be kidding!" She shoots straight to rage.

"Presley." I sigh. "I have no clue why you're yellin' at me."

"Look around, Wyatt. Look around your house, and let me know what you see, you stupid idiot."

I take a second and try to place what I thought was off. Everything is like I remember it, except it's not. The photo of Presley and Angie that sat on the mantle is gone. The quilt that Angie brought from home, which was draped over the back of the couch, is missing. Little things that she put out aren't there.

My feet move to the bedroom, and I throw open the closet. It's all gone. There's no clothes hanging. I rush to the bathroom to find all her girly crap is gone too. She's gone.

Then I remember what happened when I got home. It comes in chunks, but I recall the fight. The way she begged me, and how I put the final nail in the coffin. I made her think I never felt anything for her.

I lied.

And she's really gone.

In my head, I knew this was coming. It's the life she wanted, so I was trying to give her a reason to let me go. Hurting her went against everything I stand for, but keeping her here was selfish. She thought she loved me. I know she loved her life before me. When we lost Faith, there was no reason for her to stay.

I saw the goodbye as soon as she opened her eyes in that hospital room.

I just helped her get there faster.

"Yeah." Presley leans against the door with her arms crossed. "Good job."

"She was leaving anyway." I try to cover the pain in my voice.

"No, Wyatt. She wasn't."

"I saw it!" My voice rises as the self-hate flows through me. "I gave her the out she wanted."

Presley stalks into my room until she's right in front of me. "I've never seen her cry like that. Never. Not over losing her brother, not because of the hateful shit her mother says, not even over losing Faith. Not once have I seen my best friend so broken. She couldn't talk. She couldn't breathe. She was curled in a ball asking what she should do." Her green eyes shine with disgust. "After I finally got her calmed down, she told me what you said. So I told her to walk away and get on that plane. I know you, Wyatt. I know who you are, and this . . ." She huffs. "This isn't who you are. But you lost her. Good job, buddy. I hope this was what your master plan was. I really thought you loved her. I thought you were just in pain and lashing out. Turns out I was wrong."

"I do love her!" I yell. "I love her so much I let her have what she wanted. I killed myself in the process! So, fuck you, Presley! You don't know what the hell I've been going through!" I let it out and sink onto the bed and grip my head. "You have no idea!"

"No?" she asks with an edge to her voice. "I lost *everything* once! I found my husband hanging from a beam in my bathroom while my two kids were downstairs. I've dealt with losing some-one. Don't you dare tell me I don't have an idea."

It wasn't her fault. She didn't have the loss at her own hands. I did. That's the part that no one else can ever tell me how I should feel about. I watched her lose that baby. I was driving the car. I was the one who should've gotten her out sooner.

Letting her go is the least I can do for her.

"Were you responsible for that?" I push back. "Because I was."

She shakes her head. "Oh, I'm sorry. I wasn't aware that you can control what deer do? I didn't know you were the goddamn animal whisperer! All this time I thought that you were a regular guy. My bad." Presley snorts. "Or maybe you are actually related to the God of weather? It must be your fault then since you're magical. My God, must you really be this stupid?"

"It was my fucking fault!" I yell.

"No. None of that was your fault. The only thing that is your fault, is what you did after. You drove her away. You broke her heart so that you could go on actin' like a jackass! Well, good job there, you sure accomplished your goal."

My stomach drops as the truth hits me in the face. She's right. I didn't lose Angie. I made her go. I did whatever I could to make her leave me. But if she'd stayed here, would it have been what she really wanted?

She once said she didn't want to marry me out of obliga-tion. I didn't want her to stay for the same reason.

"It's for the best." I try to assure myself.

She snorts as she shakes her head. "You know what? You're right. You don't deserve her."

"I know."

Presley's jaw drops open. "You really believe that? You think because of some accident that you don't deserve happiness?"

"I believe a man does what's best for a woman he loves. I

think she loved me because she thought she had to. I would've married her, Pres. I wanted to. And then she made a few comments about when she was going back home."

She sinks onto the bed next to me, runs her hands over her face, and then slaps the back of my head. "You're so dense."

"How would I have known any different? How would we know if what we had was real? *She* didn't even know."

"The same way that you'll know what to do if you want to fix this." She pats my thigh. "And I don't even know if you can. You really screwed up. You've broken someone who's never let anyone have that ability. Getting back in . . ." Presley gets to her feet, moves toward the door, and then stops. "Listen, I've done and said stupid shit when I was in pain. I'm not judging you. I'm just going to tell you that a measure of a man is how he handles himself after he's hurt the one he loves. If you're the man that I know you to be, then you're going to have to stop your self-sacrificing bullshit and love her with no reservations. Don't hold back, Wyatt. We're not guaranteed a damn thing in life. If you find someone you love, hold on to that person, because it could be gone the next day. I think you and I know a thing or two about that."

Presley walks out the door, leaving me to think about what she said.

I didn't want to hear it. I knew—I thought I knew—what she wanted. The last thing I wanted to do was hold Angie back. Losing our daughter was the loophole she needed. So I did what I always do . . . I convinced myself that if I loved her, I had to let her go. How could I have been so blind?

Now I don't know if I can ever get her back.

I fucked up.

Bad.

chapter
TWENTY-SEVEN

Angie

"WHAT DO YOU THINK?" ERIN asks again. It's been a rough two weeks since I came back to Philly, but Erin is happy to have me back. She's been in my ear every day about looking at new properties. I figured there was no point in holding off, so today she's dragging me around to check out new locations.

"It's fine."

Erin steps in front of me. "You've said that about every single place. One of them was a dump."

"Because whatever you pick is fine, Er."

My heart isn't in anything. It's back in Bell Buckle being trampled.

When I got home, I thought it would only take a few days to get settled back into life. I had no idea it would feel like my insides have shriveled up. Nothing feels the same. Not even Starbucks tastes good. Nothing does. I miss the fresh air, rolling hills, and that hardheaded asshole. More than that, I hate that Faith is buried there, and I'm here. I can't go see her. I can't talk to her on that hill.

I'm more alone now than I was before.

My body isn't healing. I'm achy, unable to eat, and all I want to do is sleep.

"Angie, I'm worried about you." She places her hand on my arm. "I think maybe you should talk to someone?"

"I'm just sad."

"I can't say I understand, because I've never been through it, but I'll listen." She's sweet. It's why I brought her on. Not only is she smart, but she really does have a heart of gold.

"I appreciate it."

The truth is, I don't want to talk. There's nothing left to say. I fell in love with a man who didn't love me. If he had, he would've shown it. I needed him. Sure he was there physically, but he checked out every other way.

If I'd stayed, nothing would've changed. He showed me that.

It's been fourteen days and not one single word.

I've fought myself from calling or texting him, but I vowed to put my mangled heart back in my chest and hoped it would beat again. I don't think that will happen if I call him and hear his voice.

"Want to grab something to eat?" Erin asks.

"I'm not hungry."

"Angie." She sighs. "You're miserable here."

I'm miserable in general. Who knew that heartbreak could hurt so bad? I always thought people were just dramatic. I never could grasp how they couldn't move on when a relationship didn't work out. Now, I get it. I *so* get it.

"I feel like I've lost everything." I say. "I know I haven't. I mean, I have the store, you, Presley and the boys back there. I'm sure I'll snap out of it."

"Have you thought about calling him?"

Every. Fucking. Day. "I made it perfectly clear how I felt. He did the same."

I promised Presley I would definitely see her in a few

months. I don't know how the hell I'm going to do it, but I'll be at her wedding. Somehow, I'll find a way to get there and be fine when I see him.

I'm guessing copious amounts of alcohol will be consumed.

"I hate this for you." Erin's sweet voice tries to comfort me. "I don't want to push you if you're not ready."

When I lost the baby, Erin became extremely understanding. She explained that she really wanted to move forward, but as time went on, she got it. I think it had a lot to do with the guy she's falling head over heels for, but I won't point that out. She's happy, and I'm happy for her.

I look around at the empty space, thinking that it represents how I feel. I'm vacant inside. "Well, we don't have to do anything if we don't want to. It's kind of a great place to be. The store is really self-sufficient with the new manager. If we want to expand, we can, or we can keep it as is."

Erin's phone rings, and by the smile on her face, I know it's the guy she's seeing. She puts her finger up to say one minute, and I step outside and onto the sidewalk. It's a really great spot and is closer to downtown than our other store. It's also closer to my apartment. Media isn't far from me, but I'd love to have the option to walk to work if I want.

I take a step back and bump into someone. "I'm so sorry!" I start to say, but my eyes meet someone I know.

"Angie?" Nate smiles.

"Nate. Hi!"

"You're back." He steps forward and pulls me into his arms. "I've been wondering how you were doing." He glances to my stomach, which should have been very pregnant. Last time he heard from me, I was knocked up and leaving for Tennessee.

"There was an accident," I explain before he can ask.

Nate stands there with sadness in his eyes as I give him the cliff notes of what led me back here. He takes my arm and leads me over to a bench when I start to choke up. We sit, and I do my best not to lose it.

"I'm truly sorry, Ang." Nate shakes his head. "Are you and the guy . . ."

I shrug, knowing exactly what he's too hesitant to finish asking. "He was driving and took it hard."

He nods. "Guilt is a hard thing to live with. I see it with the parents a lot. They feel like it was something they did during their pregnancy or genetics. It tears apart a lot of relationships."

"I guess. Enough about me. What about you? Seeing anyone special?"

Nate chuckles. "I've yet to find that girl who can put up with my need to always work. I struggle with guilt as well. When I'm at home, I think about the patients I could be helping."

We talk a little more about what I've missed, which is nothing really. He tells me about some of the kids he's been working with and how he lost one recently. It's the truth when I make a comment that some girl is going to kick herself for not finding him sooner.

"Tell me about—" he starts to say, but his phone goes off. "Excuse me a minute."

Nate stands and speaks quickly to the person on the other line. I think about how different this conversation could've gone if I hadn't gotten pregnant. Would we be sitting and having a lunch date? Would we even still have been seeing each other? I want him to find someone and be happy, and I don't think I was ever that girl for him. Nate is a lot like I am when it comes to keeping himself safe. He "dates" girls who aren't serious and becomes more of a friend than a lover.

He's nothing like Wyatt. No, that man forced himself into my heart. He made me see what life could be like if I love someone. How things seem better. Everything feels more real. Then he showed me how much it hurts when it's taken away.

I won't cry. I won't cry.

He ends his call and walks back to me. "I hate to run, but I need to get back to the hospital."

"Of course." I smile.

"It was great seeing you." He kisses my cheek and then adds, "Maybe we can do dinner?"

The last thing I ever want to do is lead him on. "Maybe." I know he reads the wariness in my eyes.

"Not like that. But we were good friends once, Ang."

And we were. It was the thing I loved about being around him. We could never be more, but he's a good guy. "We'll always be friends." I promise. "You should get going."

"If you need anything . . ."

"I know where to find you," I finish automatically. It's what he always says to me before he leaves, and even though I won't call him, it's still sweet.

Erin comes out and hooks her arm in mine. "Let's go get some cupcakes and talk about what we want to do."

I look at Nate's back as he walks away. "Okay. Time to move in one direction."

I need to let go of what could've been. Wyatt let me go, and now I need to do the same.

It's time to move on. I don't want to love someone who doesn't want me.

∽◯

"SO YOU LOST THE BABY and didn't call me?" Mother sounds taken aback.

"Nope. I didn't think you cared."

I've had the day from hell. I figured I might as well add to it. Erin and I decided to pass on the location. They started trying to nickel and dime us. It wasn't worth the additional cost to renovate with them already trying to squeeze what they could out of us. Then, I spilled coffee down the front of my white dress. I got my shoe stuck in a grate, and I busted out in random tears when "Rhinestone Cowboy" played on the radio.

"Angelina," she chides. "Of course I care. It was my grand-child."

"No, Mom. It wasn't. You didn't know or care. You say awful things to me and treat me like I'm the shit on your shoes, and I'm over it." I'm on a roll, so I continue to spill whatever's on my mind. "Look, I'm tired of being your whipping post. I've endured this from you my entire life. I thought if maybe I took it long enough, you'd stop dishing it out, but you haven't. You don't care about me. You don't care about the baby I lost or the man who didn't love me. You don't care. So, I'm going to stop this."

"Excuse me?" She gasps.

"I'm going to stop doing this to myself."

I've learned that this isn't the kind of relationship I want. She's toxic, and I'm not going to be contaminated by her hate anymore. My life isn't hers to ruin. I've done a bang-up job of that on my own.

"You really think this way about me?" Is she really acting perplexed right now? Unbelievable.

"Mom." I'm not even going to do this. "If you truly don't know the things you've done to me, Todd, Presley, and God only knows who else, then you have issues. You've been awful to me since you had cancer. I'm sorry you were sick. I'm truly sorry that life handed you that, but I have my own problems. I lost a lit-tle girl who I loved and never knew. I held her in my hands, loved her, cried over her, and buried her. Then, because of that horrific pain, I lost Wyatt too. But the kicker is, I never even thought to call you. What do you think that means?"

I know exactly what it means. She's not someone I can count on.

"I'm going to pretend this is all just in anger and grief."

"Pretend away." I shrug. I don't care what she needs to tell herself so she can sleep at night. I'm learning pretty quickly she's never going to love me, so I'm going to stop waiting for it.

"We'll talk when you're less hostile."

I laugh. "Okay, Mom. We'll do that."

She'll never change. I'll never be okay with it. It's sad because I would've never wanted this with Faith. Not that my mom and I would have ever been like Rory and Lorelai Gilmore, but we could've at least had a friendship. I would've never treated Faith as if she were a burden. No little girl should grow up thinking she's irrelevant.

The phone disconnects, and I collapse on my couch. It's been seventeen days since I've heard his voice. I would've thought it'd be easier by now.

Instead, I'm more miserable than the day I left.

I close my eyes and try to push him out of my mind. I can't let myself get caught up in being in a world where I don't belong. There's no sense in casting wishes that'll never be granted. But I can't seem to stop myself. His brown eyes fill my thoughts. The way he'd smile when he was up to something, or how his voice sounded when he was concerned. Mostly, I think about how it felt to be in his arms. The contentment and security he commanded just by being there.

Knock, knock, knock.

Ugh. I shouldn't have been letting myself go there anyway.

I schlep over to the door and open it. "Hi. What are you doing here?"

Nate stands there in his scrubs holding a bag of takeout and a six pack in the air. "I know we said maybe, but I was hungry and I somehow ended up here."

Not wanting to be rude, I open the door wider. "Thank you." I smile. "Come in. I'm starving, and we both need to eat, right?"

"Right."

What could it hurt? Nate is one of the few friends I have here, and it's just dinner. I could use someone like him in my life, even if he's seen me naked.

chapter
TWENTY-EIGHT

"WAIT, SO THE LITTLE GIRL made it?" I ask as I open another bottle of wine. Nate and I ended up eating and then moving on to pilfering my liquor. Thankfully, the girl who watched my house while I was gone didn't drink it all.

I won't even pretend it doesn't feel great to relax. I'm curled up on the couch in a pair of shorts and a baggy sweatshirt. My hair is piled on top of my head, and I look like crap. But Nate isn't looking at me as a date, he's just a friend.

It's been good to have a little normal tonight.

"She did."

"That's crazy! You said she coded." I pour another glass of wine.

"I'm telling you, it was terrifying. But somehow we were able to get the bleeding under control." He grabs another beer from the six-pack he brought. "It's amazing what the heart is capable of doing."

"Yeah." I puff. "It's also the easiest to injure."

He grips my hand. "It is also the strongest. I've seen hearts in such bad shape that I didn't think there was any way they could come back from it. But they did."

I appreciate where he's going with this. The hope he's trying to inject into my black heart. Sometimes there's no amount of hope that can heal a shattered soul. Instead of bringing this evening to a gloomy low point, I change gears. "Good to know." I wink.

He chuckles. "I've really missed you, Ang."

I lean back, unsure of what to say. "Nate." The truth is that I didn't think of him once. Once I started to fall in love with Wyatt, I stopped missing anything about Philly. I was happy. I fell in love with more than just Wyatt. It was his world and his family. I felt like I belonged there.

"No." He puts his hand on mine. "I know what you're thinking, and I'm not trying to move in on you like that. I know you're going through something. I wasn't trying to push you."

"There's just no way I'm close to ever . . ." I press my hand against my chest. I can't even think of another man. "I didn't know that was what tonight was."

"I know, and it wasn't supposed to be. I knew you were sad, I was hungry and figured maybe you'd want some company. I didn't mean to upset you," Nate clarifies. "It's the booze. I never should've said that."

"Loose lips sink ships," I jest.

"Beauty is in the eye of the beer holder," Nate retorts.

I giggle. "There's no such thing as too much wine."

"A drunk man's words are a sober man's thoughts."

My heart plummets. I know he doesn't mean anything by it, but if that's the case . . . everything Wyatt said to me was how he truly felt. He was saying it all without the filter of sobriety. The last shred of hope I was holding on to just disintegrated.

I turn away to hide the tears building. "I remembered I have an early meeting with Erin." I lie. Once I've composed myself, I look at him. "I need to get to bed."

Nate looks at his watch and back to me. "I should get going. Rounds always come earlier than usual."

I walk Nate to the door and thank him again for dinner. I

promise to call him soon, but I think we'll need some very firm boundaries in place. After he leaves, I start to clean the mess from dinner, give up, and text Presley. Having her back in my life for those few months on a daily basis reminded me how much I love having her around.

Me: I miss you.

Presley: I miss you tons! The boys are driving me nuts about the wedding.

Logan and Cayden have found their very mischievous sides. Presley has her hands full with those two. Plus, their soon-to-be stepdad is like a giant kid. He riles them up more than anything.

Me: What did they do now?

Presley: They're crazy! They called your mother to invite her.

Oh, God no. I really hope she doesn't come. Although, I don't think she will. After Todd died my mom wrote Presley off, blaming her for what happened and saying that a "real wife" would have seen the signs. God forbid she believes that Todd lied through his teeth to everyone.

Me: Please tell me she's not coming. I don't think I can handle her and seeing him again at the same time.

Presley: No! She told me she was so sorry to decline, but since she didn't find out with enough time to make arrangements, she couldn't make it.

Me: Ha! Sounds like her. It's still over two months away. She's something else.

Presley: How are you? Did you decide on the expansion?

What she wants to say is: Are you still sobbing every night? Do you miss him? Why don't you come back?

My answers: Yes. Yes. Because I'm not a doormat.

Instead I reply.

> Me: *I'm good. Erin and I are going to hold off.*

Three solid knocks sound on my front door, and I hop up from my seat on the couch. I'm sure Nate forgot something. "Did you forget—" the question dies on my lips when I see him.

His dark brown hair, beautiful light brown eyes, face with a light layer of scruff, green shirt with his tight jeans takes my breath away. My memory has done nothing to preserve the way he looks. Everything about him was dull in comparison to real life. "Expectin' someone?" his Southern drawl is more prominent since I haven't heard it in a while.

Wyatt Hennington stands in my doorway, taking up every inch of space.

At first, I feel joy. He came here. He's in Philadelphia, clearly looking for me. I've dreamed of this night after night, and finally, he came. Then, another wave of emotion hits, this time it's confusion. Why the hell is he here? He watched me walk away almost three weeks ago. Did he get lost and end up here? I don't get it. He made it clear how he felt. Each day that he stayed away, he made a choice . . . what changed?

Finally, I settle on the most prominent feeling I have—anger. So now he shows his face? Out of nowhere and without so much as a text? After letting me feel this horrible pain for weeks? Yeah, well, fuck him. He's seventeen days too late.

"Not you." I slam the door in his face.

My back rests against the door, and I hold on to the hurt and anger. Those are emotions I can work with. My heart races as I picture him on the other side of the door.

"Angie." He knocks again. "Please, baby, open up."

I spin around and glare at the door. "I'm not your 'baby'."

"Can we talk?" he asks. "Please?"

"Nope. Go home, Wyatt. I have nothing to say to you." That's not exactly true. Actually, that's completely untrue. I rip open the door and put my hands on my hips. "You know what? I do have something to say. Screw you. Screw you so hard your dick falls off. I can't believe you have the balls to show up here like this. You promised me you'd be there for me. That you were going to fight to show me how much I should love you. Good job, jackass. You did that, and then you tossed me out like last night's trash after we'd just lost our _baby_! Our daughter died, and you couldn't man up. We're done. I'm done crying over you, waiting for you to show up at my door, and I'm fixing this gaping hole you left in my heart myself. I. Am. _Done!_"

"Good," he says and steps forward. "We're both done with the same thing."

"Yeah? What's that?"

"Waiting to show up at your door."

I move back as he comes closer. Then I hear the door shut behind him. "Just go, Wyatt. You don't belong here."

"No." His eyes hold mine. "I'm not leaving. Because I love you. I love you so much it fucking hurts. I love you with every part of my soul. I never understood why people spewed crap like that, until I met you. You're inside me, and I tried to let you go. I pushed you away because I thought this was what you wanted. I thought I was giving you the life you really missed." He takes a deep breath through his nose, "Then, I stopped caring about that."

My mind struggles to keep up. He loves me. I knew this deep inside, even though he tried to tell me different, I knew. Wyatt did more than just push me away. He was blunt force trauma to my heart. Now he says he loves me, but where was all that love three weeks ago? How could he love me and watch me fall apart?

Whether he thought he was doing the right thing or not, he still did nothing. Now he's here, saying all these things. Damn infuriating cowboy.

"You stopped caring?" I take another step back as he approaches.

"I wasn't myself, baby. I stopped caring because I broke you and me in the process of doin' what I thought was right. If it hurts being away from you this much, it ain't right. I can't sleep in that house without lookin' for you. I can't go to the stables without seein' your face. I can't go to the bakery because I wait for you to come out from behind the counter. I can't breathe without you, Angie."

He's right about one thing. He broke me. The girl who loves his boy hates seeing him in pain. We've been through so much. But the woman who had this man tear her to pieces, doesn't give a shit.

I'm not sure which side I'm teetering on, but I know I can't take him back, not when I feel like I can't trust him.

Because essentially, that's what he broke . . . my trust in him and in us.

I step off to the side and grip my neck. I don't know how, once again, I'm going to do this. "You should go home."

"You are my home."

"No." I put my hand up to stop him as he takes yet another step toward me. "You bulldozed our house that night. You set fire to our home."

"I can rebuild it. I'll build you a whole new house."

"Please, stop."

This is the Wyatt I remember. The one who says exactly the right things. It's never orchestrated—it's what's in his heart.

My anger starts to abate, and I try to hold on. I can't let him waltz in here and sweet talk me. I have to be strong. I can't go through another three weeks of what I just did. The crying, the stomach pains, and listlessness. That was hard enough. It's still hard.

"I know I hurt you." He follows me when I retreat some more. "I know I wasn't the man you needed."

"Stop."

"No. I was stupid. I was trying to save you, Angie. I was tryin' to love you enough to let you be happy."

I huff. "How did that work out? I've been miserable. You wouldn't *listen* to me. You were doing what you thought was right and didn't *hear* what I was saying."

He stands in front of me and touches my chin. "I love you."

"I don't know if that matters right now."

He lifts my head. "Before we lost Faith and you got that machine at the bakery, I kept thinkin' how you were leaving anyway. I didn't understand why you'd want that. You kept talking about needin' to go back." He shakes his head and drops his hand. "I kept waiting for you to tell me you wanted to stay."

"I asked you." I push back. "I asked you to talk to me, but you kept ignoring me and saying it was nothing. It's late, Wyatt. I'm tired and I've had a horrible day."

He glances around the apartment, seeing it's a complete pigsty. The look changes in his eyes. "You had company?"

I look at Nate's beer, which is still sitting next to my wine glass. "Yes." I know this is going to piss him off, but at the same time, it's not my problem. There would've never been a visit with Nate had Wyatt not sent me away. Maybe he should think about that. "Does that matter?"

He draws a few breaths before walking forward, grabbing me by the hips, and yanking me to his body. "It matters. Don't think for one minute that I haven't been breaking apart since you left. I've thought about you every second of every day." He grips me tighter. "You're my home. I'm not going anywhere until you're back where you belong. I don't give a shit if there's another man, because I'll win you back. I'll show you that I'm serious. I'll make you love me again."

Wyatt's lips are against mine in an instant. He kisses me hard, commanding, and completely by surprise. I don't have time to react before he pulls back. There are no words in my head. I'm a statue in front of him.

Then, he gives me a much sweeter peck before walking out the door.

Well, that didn't go how I thought.

"GOOD MORNING, BABY." WYATT LEANS against the wall outside my door.

I almost drop my purse as he scares the shit out of me. "What are you doing here?" I hoist my bag over my shoulder.

"Bringing you coffee." He extends the cup of Starbucks. I don't have to taste it to know it's the drink I love. I wonder if it'll be all that I remember now that he's touched it. As soon as that thought tumbles through my mind, I want to slap myself. I will not go there. "You look beautiful."

My hand extends as he hands me the cup of goodness. His fingers brush against mine, and I have to restrain myself from shivering.

Damn him.

Wyatt stands there in his signature jeans and Henley with the sleeves rolled. There's something insanely sexy about fore-arms, especially his. The things that stands out the most are his ridiculous belt buckle and cowboy hat. In Tennessee I get it, here . . . no.

"You should go home."

"I already told you." He grips my elbow and kisses my cheek. "My home is where you are."

"Wyatt, just go back. I know you're sorry. I'm sure you

regret whatever, but it's over. You can't come here after almost three weeks and think I'm going to run back to Bell Buckle with you." I cross my arms and stand my ground. If he did it once, there's nothing to say he won't do it again. I'm not going to be an idiot—again.

"I live here."

"Whatever."

I start down the hall. I have to get to the bakery. There's still a ton of stuff I've missed and need to get caught up on. There's also a press opportunity with the Eagles that I want to explore. If I can get my feet wet again, I know I'll be able to have some breathing room.

He walks behind me, but I ignore him. He gets on the elevator, and I still ignore him. Then he walks down the street, and I find it insanely difficult to keep ignoring him, but I manage. However, when he gets in my cab—I lose it.

"Stop! What are you doing?" I yell.

"I'm spending the day with you."

He is crazy. "Did Presley put you up to this? Is this some sort of hazing that you do in the South when you dump someone?"

Wyatt laughs and throws his arm around the back of my seat. "Baby, I'm here for you. I plan to show you how much you mean to me."

I groan. "You'll be gone in a week. This city will eat you alive."

He shrugs. "Maybe, but it'll be pretty hard since I signed a lease two days ago for the apartment next to yours."

My eyes widen, and my heart races. "You did *what*?" I screech.

"I sublet, or whatever they call it here, the apartment next to yours. I'm livin' here now. Know anyone who could use a rancher? I'll probably need to get a job at some point."

"Wyatt!" I gasp. "You can't move here! Do you see any

freaking horses or cows? No! What the hell are you going to do?"

This is crazy—completely, certifiably insane. I can't believe he moved here. Once again, he's shocked me.

"I'll be fine for a year or so, but after that, I'll need a job. I've been told I make a pretty mean cappuccino." He smirks. "If not, I'm sure I'll figure something out. I will warn you that I plan to see a lot of you."

"You—" I stop. "I can't . . . you . . ." My hands cover my face. "Why would you move here?"

He leans back and tosses his leg over his knee. "To win you back."

I sigh and shake my head. "You can't win me back."

"I will."

"You won't." I deadpan.

Wyatt leans close and brushes his finger down my cheek. "But I will."

chapter
TWENTY-NINE

EVERY MORNING STARTS THE SAME. Wyatt is outside my door with coffee and sometimes breakfast. He follows me to work, searches the newspaper for jobs, and then accompanies me back home. It's absolutely maddening and utterly adorable. I was only able to ward him off for the first two days he followed me. The other two I've failed miserably.

But each day he's back again.

I'm in the bakery, looking out the porthole door as he sits there. He signed a freaking lease. He moved all his shit here. I didn't really believe him until he showed me his apartment. There it all was, our couch, his bed, the dressers, and everything we shared in Tennessee. He wasn't joking.

What am I going to do about him?

It's really hard when I still love him. That's never changed. I just couldn't stay there and be his punching bag. I don't doubt that, in his twisted mind, he convinced himself that pushing me away was the right thing to do. But it wasn't.

He didn't understand what he was doing only caused me more anguish. It wasn't what I wanted, and I think I was pretty damn clear when I told him otherwise.

"I made a new cupcake flavor," Meghan, our baker, tells me.

"Great." I keep my gaze on him. "I'm sure it's delicious."

"I could use another opinion. Do you think our new squatter will try?"

I twist to see if I heard her correctly and find her looking at Wyatt through the window. "No, he's not really here."

"Well, I see him, and the employees can't help but to notice him." Meghan looks to me and sighs. "He's really hot, Ang."

"And an idiot."

"Most men are," she retorts. "Well, I'm going to find out what he thinks. I'm sure he's lonely sitting out there all day by himself."

He's not lonely. He has a constant flow of females attending to him, but he smiles politely and then looks for me. It's frustrating the heck out of me. Once again, I'm falling victim to his charms.

Who can blame me? Coffee each morning, food, his attention, and the man *moved* everything he owned to a freaking apartment in Philadelphia that I *know* is not cheap.

"Is it a baker thing?" I wonder aloud. "Do you all meddle for a living?"

She laughs as she walks out the door.

Meghan heads over to Wyatt and sits beside him. She giggles, and he smiles as she hands him the cupcake. Of course she's unable to resist him.

He's not even close to the man I walked away from. The man sitting at that table is the Wyatt I fell in love with.

"You're a fool," Erin says from behind me. Why is everyone sneaking up on me today? Oh, yeah. It's because I'm distracted by a cowboy I'm trying desperately to ignore, that's why.

"Seems to be the consensus."

"He doesn't seem to be leaving any time soon."

She's right. He has no intention of going away. "That's what I'm afraid of." I turn and lean against the wall.

Erin shakes her head. "I won't tell you what to do, but I will say that I've never seen a guy give up his whole life for a girl he only liked."

"Yeah," I agree. "I know that. I can't let go of some of the things he said."

"Well, I don't know all the details, but he clearly loves you. I can only imagine how badly you both were struggling in the face of unimaginable grief. I'm not saying that gives him a free pass, but maybe a little forgiveness?"

"You don't even know him!" I say with exasperation.

Sure he's here and clearly being sweet, and I'm not too foolish to see that. However, that doesn't erase the way he made me feel. Then again, he was struggling, and not just with our relationship. He was getting hit from every angle.

"I don't have to know him to see how much he loves you."

"Shut up." I grin at her.

"How long do you plan to make him suffer?"

"I think he can wait it out a bit more."

She nods. "Definitely make him feel the pain for a bit longer, just don't let it go on too long or one of your employees will scoop him up and ride off on that horse of his into the sunset."

Yeah, that's definitely not going to happen.

They continue to talk and my phone rings. "Hey, Mrs. Kannan."

"Hi, sugar. I hope I'm not bothering you."

I walk away from the window and head toward the back of the store. "Of course not. How are you?"

"Oh, I'm just fine. I got that fancy coffee maker and I can't figure out how to turn the dang thing on! It's got so many buttons and different spouts. What ever happened to a good ole cup of Folgers?"

I can't stop the smile that forms. I can picture her tossing her hands in the air as she walks around. I miss her something fierce. I miss them all.

"I'm sure it came with a manual."

"Sugar, that book was a hundred pages long. I'll be dead before I figure out how to actually make a mocha whatever it is you call it."

"Macchiato."

"Whatever," she says with exasperation, and I giggle.

"Don't you laugh at me now. I'm going to need you to get your tiny butt back here and teach me how to use this contraption."

"I wish it were that simple." It could be, but I feel as if I'd be giving in too easily. I have no doubt that she knows he's here. If his mother knows, she knows. And my intuition tells me there's more to this phone call than the machine, but I can't be sure.

Mrs. Kannan is known for her interfering. If I let my guard drop even a millimeter, she'll pounce.

A long pause goes by before she says anything. "I've been around a long time, honey. Long enough to know when two people are bein' just plain stupid. Forgiving someone isn't a surrender, it's a gift. One that not only saves the other person, but also yourself. I could sit here and lead you around in circles." She sighs. "But I won't this time. Not for something so important. Wyatt screwed up. Lord knows that. He knows that more than anyone. I don't know that I have ever seen him as devastated as I did the day you left."

"Mrs.—" I start.

"Listen, darlin'. I've been married a long time, and more than once, one of us was ready to walk out that door. It was a choice to forgive the other person for whatever hurtful things we said or did. I could've left him. Hell, I probably should've." She laughs. "I just know that no matter how bleak a situation looks, it doesn't mean that y'all can't find your way back to each other."

"And what if we're too lost? What if I'm too scared and hurt to trust him again?"

"We're not perfect people, honey. We're human and we make mistakes. He's owning that right now. He's showing you who he is and what's in his heart."

I thought I knew what was in his heart. I thought it was me. Then our life went down a very different path, and we ended up with a fissure dividing the road with him on one side and me on the other. Grief drove us apart. It didn't have to, though. We each made choices that brought us to this juncture.

"I love him," I admit. "I never stopped loving him, but he hurt me so much."

"Love is the strongest and most beautiful thing we can bestow on another person. Have mercy in your heart, Angie. Be gracious enough to see that he wasn't hurting you because he didn't love you, sugar. He was hurting himself because he didn't think he was worthy of your love. You think about that, and we'll talk soon. Take care now." She disconnects before I can say another word.

I walk to the window and look at him. Are we being stupid or do we have the ability to find a way back to what we were?

AFTER MY CALL WITH MRS. Kannan, I start seeing things in a new light. Each time Wyatt talks to me, I try to really hear him and not just listen to the words.

We have dinner together, and then he kisses me on the cheek and goes back to his apartment. I can't stop thinking about what she said. Thinking about how I can find a way to fully forgive him.

I'm getting ready for bed when my phone dings.

Wyatt: Can I borrow some salt?

I look at the text, unsure if I should respond. But I lean back against the headboard, which is against the wall that touches his apartment. He's right there on the other side. It's crazy that right now he's this close and yet he's so far.

Me: I think you're supposed to ask for sugar.

Wyatt: Then let me borrow some of that, too.

He's a mess. A very cute mess. I talked to Presley today, and she told me about their talk. I was surprised she went off, but she also said she'd never seen him like that. I feel like I'm not only resisting Wyatt, I'm resisting the entire town of Bell Buckle.

Me: It's late.

Wyatt: It is, but I really need that salt.

Me: What the hell do you need salt for at eleven o'clock at night?

Wyatt: I'm making something.

This could go on forever, but I'm actually having fun. Talking to him like this reminds me of our time together. The bickering, the back and forth, it made us who we were.

Me: I'm all out of salt.

Wyatt: Then I have to ask you something about my jackass brother and Presley's wedding. I figure since we're both going, maybe we should make arrangements.

Me: The wedding is in a few months. You'll be gone by then.

Wyatt: Not unless you're going with me.

Me: You're not going to stop this until you see me tonight, are you?

Wyatt: Not likely.

I figured as much. I have to give him credit for persistence.

Me: You're a pain in my ass.

Wyatt: Open the door, baby.

I stare at the screen for a minute. My legs don't seem to move. I can't explain it, but I feel like opening or not opening this door is a decision about something that I won't be able to undo.

I thought maybe he'd have left by now, but each day he materializes, stays all afternoon, and then finds a way to see me later. He hasn't pushed me other than by seeing me everywhere. And in the last eight days, I've been smiling. I haven't cried, and I've had a sense of calm.

Damn it.

Here goes nothing.

I open the door, and Wyatt is already standing there in a pair of basketball shorts and no shirt. My mind has trouble firing any thoughts about resisting as I stare at him. His muscles are taut, his chest broad, and now there's something even sexier on his body. Wyatt got a massive tattoo on his arm.

"You going to invite me in?" he asks after a few seconds of me just looking at him.

"Your arm." My fingers touch his skin as I trace the patterns. There are a bunch of intricate and thick tribal shapes. It wraps around his entire bicep, only breaking for Chinese lettering that cuts down the middle. "When did you—" I start to ask, but the look in his eyes stops me.

"That's the first time you've touched me like that."

My lips part. "Like what?"

"Like it wasn't a choice or a thought."

I decide not to comment on it. I'm sure I'll get back to that at some point. Instead, I continue to explore his ink. "What does this mean?" I ask, letting my fingers graze over the words.

"It means: together through thick and thin."

My eyes meet his and both our breathing quickens a bit. "Why?"

"Because when I lost you, I realized a lot about myself. I realized that no matter what, I wanted to be with you. We lost something that was so precious to us that the thick got too hard, but we're stronger than that. I know we are. I'll never hurt you like that again. I want to be with you through it all."

Tears fall as I listen to him speak.

"I don't want to make you cry." He wipes away the drops that fall. "I want to be the reason you smile again. When you were gone, I was broken, Angie. I was lost, hurt, and a fuckin' mess. It wasn't until I decided that I didn't care where I lived, so long as we were together, I would be happy. I wasn't joking when I said that you're my home."

Then, from the ashes of my previously shattered heart, the pieces come back to life. All of the hurt and anger fade away. I feel the honesty in his words, and there's not a doubt in my mind that what he says is true. I wipe my cheek, step closer to him, and cup his face. "I want you to take me home, Wyatt."

"Home?"

My heart has only ever been one man's—his. I've spent my entire life waiting for him, and I won't let him go. He's right, we've had our thick, and while we may not have navigated the fog the best way, we're here now. I have to believe that even though we faltered, we didn't fail. Loving Wyatt has shown me that it's not a weakness to love someone. It isn't always easy, but nothing worth a damn ever is. I walked away from him because it was up to him to start fighting. And he did.

He fought for me.

He loves me.

I love him.

I don't want to wait anymore to be with him. I know he's my forever love. "You're the only home I've ever known. I love you."

chapter THIRTY

Wyatt

" I LOVE YOU, ANGIE." I say it again, hoping she hears me. I should've done so many things differently, but I can't lose her again.

Angie looks up with her bright blue eyes swimming with emotions. "I love you, too."

Now it's my turn to be stunned.

"I'm pretty sure I was falling in love with you the first night we laid in bed and talked. Or maybe it was the morning we were all tangled up and you didn't try anything. It could've been when you made me my favorite coffee, which was really sweet. Maybe it was even before that when you went stupid and told me I was moving to Bell Buckle and marrying your crazy ass. I don't really know if I can pinpoint it exactly, but I know that there hasn't been a moment that I've wanted to be anywhere but where you are. When you let me walk away, I couldn't breathe, Wyatt. I fought myself from calling you or driving back there to make you see how wrong you were." I watch as her face softens. "I never loved you because we were having a baby. I love you because you're my other half."

My arms wrap around her as I hold her close. We stand in

the living room of her apartment as it hits me. "You forgive me?"

She nods.

"You want me?"

She nods again. "You would stay here if I asked you?"

"On one condition." I grin.

"What's that?"

"I move in here. No more being apart."

Angie's eyes brighten. "I missed you." Her hands glide up my arms and hook around my neck. "I missed this." Her lips press against mine, and she moves back before I can keep her there.

Since she took her mouth away from me, I brush my thumb across her lips, watching as her eyes close and a shiver travels through her body. "Are you sure? Because I can't lose you again."

"I'm sure. I tried to imagine it."

"Imagine what?"

"Watching you walk away again. I tried to picture my life without you. These last three weeks were horrific." Angie's voice trembles. "I couldn't do it again. I *can't* leave you. Not when I feel like this. Not when it *hurts*. Everything inside me hurt."

"You love me." I say the words as a statement.

"Do you love me, Wyatt? Do you really love me? Do you love me enough to never hurt me like that again? I need to know you'll be here for me."

She's so strong most of the time, but she lets me see her insecurities. Angie plays the tough girl, but I get the real her. I know her family crap and how she worries that she's not worth it. Her mother and brothers have done a real number on her, and I want to take that pain away and show her that she's worth everything I have.

I would never forsake that.

"I truly, honestly, and deeply love you." The words are straight from my heart. "I want to make you happy and prove that I'm the man you fell in love with."

The problem was I thought that guy died in that car wreck, too. She knew the real me was in there, hell, everyone but me did. I was so wrapped up in my own head, I couldn't see straight. I couldn't sleep because every time I closed my eyes, I saw her go unconscious. I couldn't go to the fishing hole because I had to walk past my baby. The one that I held. That I loved. That I lost.

It took my losing her and some very, very angry words from Presley to make me see that the only thing that was my fault was letting her walk away.

"You said once that you were going to make it hard for me to resist you." Her fingers massage the back of my head. "I just didn't know you were going to make it impossible."

I'm done talking. Now, I want to show her how much I love her.

I squat and lift her into my arms. She squeaks and holds on. "I always keep my promises, baby."

With her legs wrapped around me, I move to the bed. "It's why I love you, Wyatt Hennington."

"Yeah?" I smile as I lay her down.

"You made me love you because you're honest and loving. You give love so freely that it's infectious. I didn't want to love you. I wanted to go to Bell Buckle, bide my time, come back to Philly." She touches my cheek. "It turns out I didn't want that at all. I only wanted you."

She'll have all of that and more. I'll give her the world if she wants it. I'll buy her a damn Starbucks and run it myself if that's what it takes to make her come back with me.

I don't let her say anything else before my mouth is on hers, and I kiss her breathless. I'm a happy man right now. I have her in my arms, and she's where she belongs—with me.

Angie opens her mouth and lets me in. Every time I get a taste of her sweetness, I fall harder. Everything about her makes me crazy—sometimes in a bad way. She's not fake like some of the girls I've been around. She doesn't go crazy trying to impress me or make me want her. I don't have to question if what she's sayin' is what she means.

Angie is all mine.

My mouth moves down her neck, kissing every inch I travel. Thankfully, she's wearing one of these night dress things. It makes for very easy access. My hands roam the front of her body. She lifts her chest as I inch closer to her breasts. "You want me to touch you, baby?" I ask against her ear.

"Yes," she moans.

I love a woman who can ask for what she wants and demand what she needs. It's fucking hot.

"Tell me."

Her eyes go from soft to hard. There's my girl. "Touch me," Angie demands. "Make me remember."

I yank the strap down and my hand cups her breast, pulling it to my mouth. I know how much she loves this. Her fingers clutch the back of my head as I suck and bite down.

Her moans spur me further. I love the sounds she makes. I love knowing exactly what she likes. Men want a woman to be free in the bedroom. What we do here is ours, and Angie doesn't hold back.

"I want you," she begs. "I need you to touch me."

"I plan to, baby. I plan on lovin' you all night long."

I move down her body, kissing her stomach on the way down. I kiss the scar that she'll forever have from that night. I grip her hand and lace our fingers together as I kiss every inch of it. This will be a reminder of what we've lost, but also what we've gained.

Faith brought us together in so many ways. She'll always be a part of us.

Angie's other hand runs through my hair. "It's okay."

I look up. "It is now."

My lips descend lower against her pussy, and I let out a soft breath, which makes the muscles in her legs tense. When I use the tip of my tongue to trace her cleft, she shudders.

"Wyatt." She leans on her elbows.

She wants more. I see it in her eyes.

Without wasting anymore time, I press my tongue down and she moans. I savor her sweetness but am careful not to let her come too soon. I lick and suck on her clit. Enjoying each movement that she makes against my mouth.

"I'm gonna come!" She starts repeating. "Holy shit!"

I finally give her what she wants and suck her clit into my mouth, making her explode. I hold her hips as I continue to make different patterns with my tongue, milking every ounce of pleasure from her body. I want her to remember this time.

Then, I'm climbing up her body and pulling her nightgown with me. She lifts to remove it and then pushes me onto my back. "I love you," she says with a grin.

I reply instantly. "I love you."

"I love how you make me feel about myself." She drops kisses on my chest. "But most of all . . ." Her body moves lower, and I lift my hips so she can remove my shorts. "I love who you are. And I love that you're mine."

Angie wraps her mouth around my cock and sucks. "Fuck!" I use every bit of restraint I have to keep my hips from bucking and making her choke. She bobs up and down, taking me into the back of her throat. I have to keep my eyes closed. If I see her doing this, I'll blow my load. I try to focus on anything but the sounds she's making and the heat of her mouth.

She lets out a throaty moan, and I almost lose it.

I pull her face up, and she smiles like she knows exactly what I'm thinkin'.

Playtime is over.

I climb on my knees, and I use my body to push her back onto the bed. "Tell me you love me," I command.

"I love you."

Hearing it from her lips is like a piece of heaven in my soul.

"Tell me you're staying with me."

I line myself up, and she opens wide for me. I push myself just barely in and she groans. "I'm staying," she promises.

"Tell me, baby. Tell me why."

We never break the connection of our eyes. I'm giving her more of me with each promise she makes. "Because I want you. I need you. I love you!"

That's all I need to hear.

I bury myself all the way inside her and give her all I have.

THIRTY-ONE

Angie

~ A Month Later ~

"YOU'RE SURE?" ERIN ASKS FOR the tenth time as I hand her the papers.

"I'm sure."

I love this city. It will always be a part of me, but I miss Tennessee. I miss my family there, my best friend, and the life Wyatt and I were building. Wyatt basically moved into my apartment, and we've spent the last month finding our way again.

He's been fantastic. It's been fantastic. After the second week, though, I knew I wanted to go home.

We talked a lot, and I came to Erin with a proposal. She now is the face of For Cup's Cake in Philadelphia. I'm still an owner, but a silent one. This way, Erin will be able to move forward with whatever she wants, and I have enough money to stay afloat while I figure my shit out.

I plan to open a store in Tennessee after I talk to Mrs. Kannan. She dropped a lot of hints about wanting to retire, and Wyatt and I both agree that she is plotting for me to take her place.

"I'm sad to see you go, but I don't think I would stay either."

She gives me a hug.

"He's worth the risk, you know?" I say, looking at Wyatt standing in the bakery.

"I'm sure he is."

I say my goodbyes to everyone in the store. My apartment is all packed, as is Wyatt's. He apparently was on a month to month lease, which he failed to tell me until two weeks ago. The good thing was that since I live in a much desired area, my apartment sold very quickly. We had a contract on it the day it was listed, and the buyer pushed for a quick closing, which worked for me.

"We should do something fun before we head back," I suggest as we walk arm and arm. I bundle up close to him as the weather has definitely taken a turn. I can already smell the snow in the air.

"Like?"

"I don't know. We could take a drive to New York. I know you've never been, and I don't know when we'll be around here again."

"We could," he agrees. "Or we could go to Vegas."

"What?"

"Vegas. I've never been there either."

I have no idea how we went from New York to Vegas. It makes no damn sense. "The two aren't really alike, Wyatt."

He laughs. "I know, but it's easier to get married in Vegas."

I stop moving. Wyatt keeps going a few steps and then turns back. "Married?" I ask in disbelief.

We just got back together after a bunch of crazy shit. We've been through a whirlwind.

"Before you start making a thousand excuses. Answer this . . . do you love me?"

"Yes."

"Do you want to be with anyone else?"

"No."

"Will you marry me?" My breath hitches as he removes a ring from his pocket. "I promised Mama when I found the girl I couldn't imagine not waking up to each day that I'd marry her. I planned this big thing for how to ask you, but then we lost our baby. I've known that I wanted you to be my wife since the first time I woke with you wrapped around me. I thought we were crazy, and maybe we are, but I don't want to ever sleep without you by my side. Marry me Angie. Marry me and we'll start our life together. I'll be by your side through it all."

A tear falls down my face. "Through thick and thin."

He smiles. "Through thick and thin."

I grab his face and kiss him. I love him. It's insane and crazy, but fuck it. We only live once. If nothing else, we've learned that.

"Vegas?"

"Tonight," he demands.

"YOU GOT MARRIED?" PRESLEY SCREAMS as I show her the ring on my finger. Wyatt explained that after the festival he went and had it made for me. He really had been just waiting for the right time to propose. It's a beautiful teardrop-shaped diamond flanked by three diamonds on each side. It now sits in front of a platinum band from our wedding. "I can't believe you! I can't believe you got married without telling me! I'm _so_ happy for you but so freaking mad!"

We've been back in Bell Buckle for a whole two hours, and she's been nonstop. Felicia finally dropped the lawsuit yesterday and I figured she'd be happy and it was a good time to tell her. Apparently there wasn't going to be a good time.

"It was spur of the moment!" I explain for the hundredth time.

"Spur of the freaking moment my ass! He planned this!" she yells toward the hallway. "He knew what he was doing."

I laugh as I hear my husband's chuckle from the other room. "Seriously, Pres. I'm not the white dress and flowers girl anyway. It would've been at a courthouse. This was exactly what we wanted."

She gives me a look that says she doesn't care about my excuse. "I've known you almost twenty years and have waited for this. You deprived me." She throws her hand onto her forehead as if she's about to faint.

"And you're dramatic."

"It was my Scarlett O'Hara impression."

"You failed."

She comes back around the island and takes my hand. "It's beautiful. I'm seriously happy for you. Tell me about it!"

I sit on the chair and replay it. We got on a plane, got to Vegas, found a chapel, and that was it. We came back home after days of non-stop sex, packed our stuff, and moved here.

"This is the most unromantic wedding ever," she admonishes.

"It was perfect."

She smiles. "I can see this is exactly what you'd want. No fanfare, just him."

"Exactly!"

"I can't believe you're a Mrs. Hennington before I am."

Zach strides into the kitchen right as the last word leaves her mouth, and he stops, holding both his hands out in front of him. "I'll come back."

"Oh, no Zachary. Don't leave." Her voice is sugary sweet. "It wasn't like your evil ex-girlfriend delayed our day. I've only waited since I was like . . . ohhh . . . *thirteen* to be your wife."

I silently laugh. "Stop being hard on him," I defend him. It wasn't his fault and he honestly didn't want to push the date back. Zach would've married Presley the day she returned if he had his way.

"You're his sister-in-law for ten minutes and you're already taking his side?" she says with her hands on her hips.

Zach laughs. "I always wanted a sister."

He's crazy. I'm the last sister he'd have wanted. I was the one trying to get my brother's friends to date me just to piss them off.

Presley tucks herself against his chest. "I thought you always wanted me to be your wife."

"Darlin'," Zach squeezes her close. "You're my whole world. Makin' you my wife is the icing on the cake."

"Uh huh." She leans in for a short kiss. "Real smooth."

"You're right," he concurs. "I am."

Wyatt walks in and leans against the door. "Ready to head home, baby?"

"Yup!" I stand. "We have a lot of unpacking to do, and we need to stop by your parents' place."

Presley bursts out laughing. "Ohhh." She laughs harder. "Your mama is going to kill you! You're her first son to get married, and you go off to Vegas without tellin' her? Y'all are going to get it!"

For the first time, I start to notice that Presley doesn't sound like my city girl anymore. She hadn't said "y'all" or dropped the "g" at the end of a word once since her first year of college. Now, though, she's all country again. Looks like I'm not the only one who found my true place.

Wyatt's face falls, and he glances at me with sheer panic. "Fuck!"

Zach walks over and slaps him on the back. "You're dead, brother."

"Damn it. Maybe we can pretend we didn't get married," he suggests.

"What?"

"We won't tell anyone else." He starts to ramble. "We'll say we're engaged, you can tell her that it just happened and that you want a big ole wedding. It'll be fine. She'll never have to know."

I stand there in disbelief. "You want to lie . . . to your mother . . . about us being married?"

"You've met her. Don't act so surprised."

I'm not even sure which way to go with this. I could agree
and lie to his mom, which I'm pretty sure she's going to figure
it out at some point and that'll be worse, or I can sit back and
watch. Honestly, I've forgiven him, but it doesn't mean that a little suffering here and there is a bad thing.

"Time to man up, Little Buckaroo."

Wyatt grabs my hips and tugs me toward him. "I swear,
Angelina."

"Oh!" My eyes widen. "Going for the full name, are we?"

He mumbles something under his breath.

"Have fun y'all! Call me, and, Ang, if you record it, I'll pay
you!" Presley says loudly as Wyatt pulls me out the door.

I wave to her as we keep moving.

Wyatt is quiet in the truck on the way over, but I can't stop
smiling. It's ridiculously cute and funny how worried he is. I'm
sure it'll be fine. Macie is the most understanding person I've
ever met. Then again, this is her youngest.

We get to the front step, and the door is open before we can
knock.

"Angie!" She pulls me against her, and I hug her back. "I'm
so happy you're home, sugar!"

"Mama," Wyatt says as he's still. "Angie and I got married in
Vegas."

Not exactly the way I would've done it. I slap his arm. "Real
smooth, Wyatt."

She looks at him then back to me. "Married?"

I can't tell if she's angry or just processing.

"I promise. It was a spur-of-the-moment thing." I try to explain.

She puts her hand up.

Oh boy.

"Wyatt Earnest Hennington! You're married!" she screeches with a smile. "I'm not going to lie and say I'm happy with the fact that I didn't get to see my baby get married, but I have a daughter now!"

We both let out a huge sigh.

"Rhett!" she yells over her shoulder. "Get out here! Your son got himself hitched!"

"You're not mad?" I ask.

She shakes her head. "No! I wish I could've seen it, of course. But I'm just so happy you're here, honey. It's been a good month for us. That Felicia woman is gone, bless her heart, and now you're married to my boy, who finally got his head out of his behind." Macie gives him a bewildered glance. "I have too much to be happy about right now."

Wyatt kisses his mother's cheek. "I'm sure you'll find many chances to let us know how you feel throughout the rest of my life."

She pats his face. "Be sure of that, honey."

We head inside where, of course, there's pie.

I may be losing my bakery with all the cupcakes, but here, there's pie, and I can live with that.

EPILOGUE

"CAN YOU BELIEVE WE'RE SISTERS-IN-LAW again?" Presley asks as we sit at the table and watch her wedding guests dance.

"I think it's fate." I smile.

"I love that man." I sure hope she does. She freaking married him.

Wyatt, Trent, and Zach all stand over at the bar. They're resting their elbows against the wood, just staring out at the scene. I swear, the three of them are unfairly hot. I know two of them are my brothers-in-law, but for real, no family should be that endowed with sexiness.

Then I hone in on Wyatt. He's the most delicious of them all—at least I think so. Trent is the tallest, and the only one with sandy brown hair. But Wyatt's body is definitely the biggest of them, as is his heart.

I sometimes still can't believe I'm married and living in Tennessee. "We really hit the jackpot."

"Yes, we sure did."

"Does it feel good being married to him?" I ask.

She grins. "It does. It feels like that part of my life is over now. It's a new start."

"Well." I grab her hand. "I'm glad we still share the same last name."

Presley places her other hand on top of mine. "That's right!

We're both Henningtons! That deserves a toast!" She calls over the waiter and grabs two flutes of champagne. I don't have time to say a word before she starts. "To a lifelong friendship that has endured some of the hardest times but always comes out on top. To my sister, my best friend, and the only girl who I would share a room with in a nursing home."

I raise my glass, and we clink them together. "I can't sip this," I tell her.

"Why?"

I look at her, hoping she'll be able to deduce it.

Three.

Two.

"Oh!" Presley hops up. "Oh my God! You're . . ."

"Shh!" I pull her back to the seat. "I haven't even told him yet."

"You're pregnant?" She whispers but not very quietly.

I found out yesterday, but didn't want to tell anyone yet. I was feeling a little sluggish, and it's not as if Wyatt and I had been very careful since we were married and all.

"Yeah." I smile. "I don't want to tell him or anyone today. And I wouldn't have told you if you weren't trying to force me to drink."

"I'm so happy for you, Ang."

"I'm happy for you, my friend. You have everything you ever wanted."

She pulls me close. "We both do." Presley leans back and slaps my leg. "Now, go tell that husband of yours. I want to see his face! You can make it one of my wedding gifts."

We both stand and walk over to where the boys are.

Wyatt watches me the entire time with a predatory look in his eyes. It's the one that makes me all gooey and lets me know that I'm all he sees.

"Hey." He grins and pulls me close to him.

"Hey yourself."

Zach's arms wrap around his new wife, and Trent looks off at Grace, who is dancing with Cooper. Oh, Trent. How badly you screwed yourself.

"Can I buy you a drink?" Wyatt says playfully, already turning to the bartender.

Well, no moment like the present. "I'll take a Sprite."

"One—" He looks back at me as if I've lost my mind. "Sprite?"

I shrug. "I don't think I should be drinking."

He studies me closer. "And why not?"

I can't stop the smile. "Because it's not good for the baby."

Presley starts to squeal, but Wyatt doesn't move a muscle.

"Baby?"

"Baby."

Then his arms are around me, and he's hoisting me in the air. "We're going to have a baby?" His lips press against mine as he protects me in his embrace. I can't help thinking how different this announcement is. There's joy and celebration. No accusations or wondering what we're going to do. He pulls back from the kiss and slowly lowers me to my feet.

"We are. And there's nothing more I want than what I have right now. You give me that."

Wyatt kisses me again. "No, baby. You're who's given it to me."

I won't argue with him. Either way, we've both come out on top. I never knew that I could love so hard and so deeply, but here I am. Happy as could be.

I have everything I ever wanted.

THE END

letter to the
READER

Dear Reader,

Thank you so much for all your love and support! If you'd like to keep up with what I have going on, be sure to sign up for my newsletters. As a subscriber, you'll receive access to exclusives, lost love letters, giveaways, and lots more!

books by
CORINNE MICHAELS

THE SALVATION SERIES
Beloved
Beholden
Consolation
Conviction
Defenseless

STANDALONES
Say You'll Stay
Say You Want Me
Say I'm Yours (Trent & Grace) Coming Soon
Hyped ~ Coming Soon

ACKNOWLEDGEMENTS

I SWEAR I KNOW I'LL forget someone, so if you're that person . . . I'm sorry.

To my husband and children. You sacrifice so much for me to continue to live out my dream.

My beta readers, Michelle, Jenn, Holly, Katie, and Melissa, I love you guys. This book was a labor of love and you stuck it out with me. Thank you!

My publicist, Danielle, I love you. Thank you for dealing with my insanity and still loving me. I'm grateful for you more than you will ever know.

My readers. There's no way I can thank you enough. It still blows me away that you read my words. You guys are everything to me.

My Corinne Michaels Books group on Facebook, I wake up every single day and go there first. You're the bright spot in life. Thank you for everything.

Bloggers: You're the heart and soul of this industry. Thank you for choosing to read my books and fit me in your insane schedules. I appreciate it more than you know.

Thank you to Ashley, my editor, for dealing with my crazy voice messages and making this book everything. It is truly a blessing to work with you. Sarah Hansen, from Okay Creations, for making my covers perfect. Janice and Kara for proofreading and making sure each detail is perfect! Christine, from Perfectly

Publishable, we're on book SEVEN now and I wouldn't want to work with anyone else. (Probably they'd beat me by now, but you just send me kisses). Your support is invaluable. I truly love your beautiful heart.

My agent, Amy Tannenbaum . . . thank you for believing in my work and all of your support.

Squad, BBFT, & Holiday Reads Authors—Thank you for your friendship, love, and the way you push me to step outside of the box. I love you guys!

Christy Peckham, I'm running out of things to say, but the one thing that stays is: THANK YOU! I love you. You're the best author keeper around. HA!

Melissa Erickson, you're amazing. I love your face.

Kristi, your friendship means everything to me. I value our friendship more than anything. Books may have brought us together, but so much more keeps us together.

Vi, Claire, Mandi, Amy, Syreeta, Kristy, Kyla, Mia, Tijan, Alessandra, Meghan, Jessica, Christine, Michelle, Laurelin, Kennedy, and Lauren—Thank you for keeping me striving to be better and listening to my crazy.

ABOUT THE AUTHOR

CORINNE MICHAELS IS THE NEW York Times, USA Today, and Wall Street Journal Bestselling Author. She's an emotional, witty, sarcastic, and fun loving mom of two beautiful children. Corinne is happily married to the man of her dreams and is a former Navy wife. After spending months away from her husband while he was deployed, reading and writing was her escape from the loneliness.

Both her maternal and paternal grandmothers were librarians, which only intensified her love of reading. After years of writing short stories, she couldn't ignore the call to finish her debut novel, Beloved. Her alpha men are broken, beautiful, and will steal your heart.

www.corinnemichaels.com

CPSIA information can be obtained at www.ICGtesting.com
Printed in the USA
BVOW06s2357121016

464801BV00002B/1/P

9 781682 307540